MW01611067

YOU ROCK MY WORLD

THE BLACKWELLS OF CRYSTAL LAKE

JULIANA STONE

JULIANA STONE PUBLISHING

Copyright © 2017 by Juliana Stone

All rights reserved.

No part of this book may be reproduced in any form or by any electronic or mechanical means, including information storage and retrieval systems, without written permission from the author, except for the use of brief quotations in a book review.

Cover designed exclusively by Sara Eirew www.saraeirew.com

Editor Linda Ingmanson

CHAPTER 1

*T*ravis Blackwell didn't do babies—at least not if he could help it. Sure, they were cute in a red-face, squirmy kind of way. But they were small. And delicate. And their damn necks were noodle soft. They made him nervous as hell, and even though his brand-new nephew clearly fell into the cute category (he was a Blackwell, after all), Travis had no interest in cradling the little guy.

At least not until the kid was old enough to hold a hockey stick in his hand.

Content to watch his brother Hudson and wife, Becca, from across the hospital room, Travis leaned against the wall near the door and crossed his arms over his chest. He was trying to decide if he could duck out without causing a scene. His father and Darlene were on one side of the bed, while his other brother, Wyatt, and his lady, Regan, were opposite. Even Liam, Becca's son from her first marriage, was sprawled across his mother's feet, seemingly enamoured of his new brother.

All the adults were kicking up a fuss, and Travis supposed he couldn't blame them. Up until a year or so ago, he was pretty sure most folks around these parts thought none of the Blackwell men would settle down and have babies. Hudson had been AWOL for years, living and working in DC, while Wyatt had become the darling of the NASCAR circuit. Neither one had seen the love train heading their way, and in a short period of time, both men had fallen hard for the women in their lives. They'd settled down. Become respectable. Had babies. Technically, *baby*, but considering the goofy look on Wyatt's and Regan's faces, they might not be too far from the state of baby bliss currently enjoyed by the eldest Blackwell.

As for Travis? He had no interest in a baby or a wife, or any of that respectable stuff his brothers were into. He'd been there once and learned hard and fast that it wasn't his gig. He'd been young and dumb, but hell, at least he'd been smart enough to know he wasn't cut out for that kind of life. Smart enough to know that love didn't always make things right. In fact, when the love was raw and fragile and wrapped up in hurt, it made things unbearable.

Wasn't everyone's story, but it sure as hell was his.

Thoughts dark with ghosts from his past, he straightened, restless. With one last glance at his family, he slipped out the door. The corridor was empty, and he managed to make his way out of the hospital without having to make unwanted, polite conversation, and for that, he was grateful. He wasn't in the mood for pretend—nothing harder than acting interested in what someone was saying when you didn't give a damn.

Travis paused on the steps of the hospital and took a moment to enjoy the warmth that hit him and to breathe it all in. Water. Fresh-cut grass. Peonies. It smelled like home.

It was late June. After a nasty winter and a wet, cool spring, Crystal Lake was finally heating up. The air was fresh, the sky robin's-egg blue, and the few clouds that dotted the atmosphere looked like small puffs of cotton candy.

The sunshine was blinding, and he yanked on the brim of his tired and frayed ball cap, pulling it lower over his forehead as he stepped down. A Yankees fan, his agent had given him the signed cap the night they'd won the World Series back in 2009, and even though it was falling apart, he couldn't toss it. Not a chance in hell. He'd get one more season out of it and then retire it to his memorabilia case. He was that guy. The kind that liked familiar. The kind that liked his boat gentle, not rocked.

The kind of guy who stuck to routine.

Which was why he hated feeling out of sorts and on edge. He glanced around and scowled. It was this place. Crystal Lake. It wasn't the same. Sure, there were remnants of the hometown he remembered—the high school, the old mill, the dam where he nearly drowned when he was five, Pottahawk Island. But there was a hell of a lot more change. New developments across the lake, condos, and housing, and a thirty-six-hole golf course sitting smack dab in the middle of a fancy new clubhouse. Members only, he'd been told. What the hell was wrong with the old eighteen-hole executive by quarry?

"Not a damn thing," he muttered, spying his truck.

Hell, even the city limit sign was all spiffy and new. Gone was the faded blue sign showcasing a guy fishing. Now it was slick, shiny, and way too generic.

The development had brought a ton of new people to the area. His scowl deepened. He didn't like it one bit. Some could argue he had no right to have an opinion either way. He hadn't called Crystal Lake home in nearly ten years. Not since he'd signed his first NHL contract. Not since that last night. But still...

Travis shook off the memories and headed for the parking lot, not really sure where his head was at. He told Hudson he'd be home for a few days and had taken one of the cabins at the resort his brother owned and ran with Becca. They'd delayed the grand opening because of the baby, and he pretty much had the place to himself. He could take out the boat, sit back with a cooler of beer, and contemplate life. He could head to the gym and work out until he was fatigued. Or, hell, he could sit on the dock, do nothing, and enjoy the last Cohiba that Marcel, one of the French-Canadian guys on his team, had given him.

He reached into the pockets of his faded khaki shorts to retrieve his keys and aimed the fob at the shiny new Dodge Ram. It was then that he spied a woman a few rows over, talking animatedly with someone. From where he stood, he could only see shoulders and the back of a head—a blonde head full of thick wavy hair that snaked out in the breeze. The long tendrils mesmerized Travis, and his vision blurred because he watched them for so long. The woman nodded to whoever she was talking to, and she bent forward slightly.

Something tugged at him. He wasn't exactly sure what it was, but it brought him to a halt and kept those keys frozen in his hands. His heart rate sped up. His palms became cold and clammy. And damn if he didn't feel a bit light-headed. Him. Travis Blackwell. The guy his teammates called "ice between the pipes." Nothing cracked his exterior or made him falter. Nothing.

Except Ruby.

He shook his head and took a step back, eyes never leaving the woman. Was it her? Travis angled his head a bit, just as two male hands reached up and she bent even lower. She was kissing someone.

A stab of something hot and fierce shot through him, and he had to look away because his composure was crumbling faster than a landslide. What the hell? First off, the chances that the woman less than twenty feet from him was Ruby Montgomery were slim. And secondly, even if it was Ruby, why the hell was he all tied up over it? He hadn't seen or talked to her in more years than he cared to remember, not since he'd signed their divorce papers. As far as each of them was concerned, they were done. Their foolish, young, hot romance had gone nowhere fast. Just as his father had warned him it would. At the time, he wasn't sure what pissed him off more, the state of his marriage or the fact that John Blackwell had been right.

Travis had moved on, and the last he'd heard, she'd done the same. Taken the proceeds from her divorce settlement and disappeared.

He couldn't help himself and glanced back in time to see the woman straighten and wave to whoever it was she'd been locking lips with. She tucked a long strand of hair behind her ear and turned toward the right wing of the hospital. It was in the opposite direction from where Travis stood, and, like an idiot, he watched as she made her way through the parking lot. Long limbs draped in an elegant navy skirt that came to just above her knee, an understated, classy cream blouse, and a small sweater loose on her shoulders.

When she reached the steps leading up into the Deacon Memorial Wing, she paused and turned around as a gust of wind sent her hair flying once more. She rummaged through a large camel-colored leather bag and shook her head, tugging on the loose waves that drifted across her face. They did nothing to hide the creamy complexion, delicate eyebrows, and pillow-soft lips. She turned back and waved to a nurse who'd exited the building.

That was all it took for Travis to know. It was her. His Ruby. He swallowed hard, unable to tear his gaze away.

Ruby Montgomery chatted for a few seconds with the nurse and then disappeared inside the hospital.

He wasn't sure how long he stood in the parking lot, clutching his key fob so tightly, his knuckles were white, but it was long enough for the nurse to cross the parking lot and give him a strange look as she passed by. Travis tugged on the brim of his ball cap and unlocked his truck.

He sat in it for a long time, drumming his hands on the steering wheel and ignoring the text messages from his brother Hudson, wondering where in hell he'd disappeared to. His heart was still beating a mile a minute and his scowl deepened. Not once had it crossed his mind he'd run into her. Not once.

His phone beeped again, and a quick glance down told him

one of his childhood pals, Jason Marsdale, was stopping by the Coach House for some beer and wings. He didn't hesitate. He pulled out of the parking lot and headed for the south side of town. Travis was pretty sure booze wasn't a good idea at the moment, but hell, spending the afternoon at the lake with his thoughts wasn't either. When in doubt, a cold one would always suffice. Besides, maybe he could pump Jason for some info on life in Crystal Lake and all the things he'd missed. Namely, what had Ruby been up to? And why the hell was she back?

The Coach House was quiet when he arrived—his watch told him he had nearly an hour to go until Jason got off work. Travis slid onto the nearest barstool, happy to note this place hadn't changed at all. Even the massive moose antlers still hung behind the bar. He grinned. He and Jason and a few of his hockey pals had stolen the damn thing the night he'd been drafted to the minors. Of course, Salvatore, the owner of the Coach House, found out who the culprits were, and within hours, Sheriff McVeen had been knocking down the Blackwell door.

Travis's smile slowly faded. Sal was gone, taken by cancer the year before, and Ruby...well, maybe that was a ghost he should just forget about.

"What can I get you?"

He glanced up and frowned, not recognizing the mountain of flesh behind the bar. The guy was easily six foot four, broad, and built like a Mack truck. The top of his bald head shone beneath the lights, and his long beard was impressive.

"Is Nash around?"

Mountain Man looked annoyed. "He's interviewing in the back."

"Oh. Do you know when he'll be done?"

Mountain Man's eyebrow rose half an inch. "If you figure out what you want, princess, let me know."

Before Travis had a chance to order a beer, the guy headed to the far end of the bar and took his time wiping the damn thing down.

"He's friendly. Once you get to know him."

A man sat a few stools away from Travis, nursing a brew. He looked a little too polished for these parts—his clothes were expensive and his hair had more product in it than a guy's should, but hey, Travis wasn't about to judge. He offered a half smile. "Thanks. I'm not used to all the new faces in town."

The man chuckled. "Tiny has been here longer than I have."

Travis's eyebrow darted up, and he chuckled. "That guy's name is Tiny?"

"It's what everyone around here calls him."

The man in question came back with an ice-cold draft and set it down in front of Travis. "Do you want a menu?"

"Nope. I'm good."

Travis took a long gulp of beer and settled back in his chair. He struck up a conversation with his neighbour, a guy named Chance McDougal. Now, in Travis's books, that was one hell of a moniker, but again, the no-judging thing came into play. The guy was from Texas and had played division one college golf, so he couldn't be all that bad. He'd hoped for a future in the PGA until a car accident had taken away some of the mobility of his left hand.

Luckily, he still had skills and was now settled in at the new golf and country club across the lake. As their new pro, McDougal was looking to set down roots. He'd met a girl, fallen in love, and his path was set. Good for him.

Travis let him talk and was nearly done with his beer. He was okay keeping his business to himself, and was content to listen to the man.

"So, you're from town, I take it?" Chance asked, checking his watch and reaching into his back pocket for his wallet.

Travis nodded. "I am."

"I didn't catch your name."

Travis hadn't offered it up. McDougal obviously didn't follow hockey, and that was okay by him.

"Blackwell." He glanced up as Tiny scooped up his empty mug and moved to fill it.

"Blackwell." Chance got up from his seat and tossed a few bills onto the bar. His phone buzzed, most likely a text message, and he glanced toward the door. "I know that name."

Travis wasn't surprised. His family had deep roots in Crystal Lake.

Travis shrugged and accepted another mug from Tiny. He didn't get a chance to answer the man because the door to the bar opened and a woman stepped inside. She was on her phone, but her voice cut through Travis like a knife through butter. He turned around fully, mouth catching flies, eyes wide in disbelief. Was the universe trying to tell him something? Did he need to be hit over the head twice in one day?

Ruby walked toward the bar, forehead furrowed in concentration, white teeth biting the edge of her lip. She wasn't happy about something, Travis could see it, and she was unaware of his presence. She walked toward Chance and pecked his cheek, nodding at whatever was being said on the other end of the phone and murmuring, "Hey, baby," to Dougal.

Chance was looking at Travis.

Travis was looking at Ruby.

And Nash walked in at that exact moment. He settled in to watch the event unfold, and would later be overheard telling more than a few guys that Travis hadn't seen it coming.

"I knew I recognized the name," Chance said. "You're Ruby's ex-husband."

Ruby's head shot up, and she froze, her hazel eyes wide with surprise. *Trav?* she mouthed, sliding her cellphone back into her purse.

Chance moved closer to Ruby, as if protecting her from someone. That really got Travis's goat, because first off, she didn't need protecting from anybody. If he knew her at all, he'd at least know that. And secondly, Travis could break McDougal. Easily.

Like a twig.

Travis shook his head, his brain now focusing on what his eyes had already seen. Her hand was on Chance's forearm, and the guy was all up in her business. He snorted. Seriously? The guy was plaid shorts and fucking pink collared shirts. Christ, he probably got regular pedicures and facials. Instant, red-hot dislike coursed through Travis, and he got off his stool. This punk-ass golf softie was in love with his Ruby?

"You're banging my wife?"

The fist came from nowhere and sent him reeling. When he gave his head a shake and cleared the stars from his eyes, Ruby stood inches from him, chest heaving, cheeks flushed, and looking hotter than anything he'd ever seen before. The air literally cracked with electricity. Friction. It was sexual. Primal. Full-on anger. He would take all of it and more, because truth be told, he hadn't felt this alive since...well, since Ruby.

"Who I *bang* is none of your business," she spat, eyes flashing. "And the name is Ruby, in case you've forgotten. Don't ever call me your wife again. Don't even call me your ex."

She turned on a dime and headed for the door, while Travis rubbed his sore chin and watched Chance follow her outside like the good little puppy dog he was.

"You sure as hell know how to stir things up, Blackwell." Nash shook his head from the other side of the bar. "I'll get you some ice. You're gonna need it."

"No shit," Travis muttered, sitting his ass back down on the stool. Ruby Montgomery was still as volatile as he remembered. Still as infuriating and quick to anger. She still rubbed him the wrong way, and apparently, he did the same. Fights were second nature to them. It was how they communicated. But the making up had always been hot as hell.

9

He accepted the ice from Nash.

"You were a dick," Nash said.

"Yeah."

"She's pissed." Again, Travis had to agree.

A slow grin swept across his face. It seemed as if some things hadn't changed after all.

CHAPTER 2

"*Y*ou *punched him?*"

Ruby stared across the table at her best friend, Sid, and nodded. "I did." It wasn't as if she could lie. Hell, it was probably all over town by now, and she was surprised Sid hadn't already heard about it.

"And Chance saw this?" Sidney's mouth fell open.

"He had a front-row seat."

"What did he say?"

Ruby's gaze slid away, and she shrugged. "Nothing. We didn't really talk about it." That was a bit of a white lie, but hell, it was one she was going to take. Chance had wanted to talk, but she shut him down. In fact, their evening had ended in a fight, and she had no one to blame but herself. She made a face. And Travis Blackwell.

She was a bad girlfriend. With bad impulses. Oh, and there was the whole control-issue thing. All it took was one encounter with Travis and she'd lost it. It was if the last ten years hadn't happened. As if the smart, sophisticated woman she'd become had never happened. As if the life she'd built for herself *had never happened.* How the heck had Travis Blackwell managed to destroy all that in less than a minute?

That had to be some kind of record.

"I can't believe you punched Travis." Sidney slowly shook her head.

"He just……" She groaned and blew out a long breath, still out of sorts and annoyed that she was. "He made me angry, and I probably overreacted."

"Probably?" A hint of a smile curled around Sidney's bright pink lips, and she leaned forward. "Did you hit him hard?"

"Hard enough to hurt my hand." Which still felt tight and bruised.

"Where?"

"The Coach House."

"That's not what I meant." Sidney's sleek, short, blonde hair swished around her face, and Ruby could tell she was trying not to laugh.

"It's not funny."

"No, it's not." Sid cleared her throat. "Where did you hit him?"

"I don't know." Inwardly, Ruby winced. "His face, I guess."

"You guess?" Sidney's tone was incredulous, and then she giggled. "Did you break his nose? Please tell me you broke his nose."

Ruby crumpled her napkins and tossed them into the garbage bin before flopping back onto the bench. They were in the park, down near the water, and she'd made quick work of the greasy fries and burgers offered up by The Caboose.

"No, Sid. I didn't break his nose."

"Too bad."

Ruby didn't say anything for several moments. She knew Sidney had her back, and even though there was no love lost between her best friend and Travis Blackwell, it seemed somehow wrong to take delight in the notion of breaking the man's nose.

Even if he deserved it.

"I guess he's back visiting his brother," Sidney murmured, watching Ruby closely.

Ruby arched an eyebrow. "Hudson?"

Sidney nodded. "When I was grabbing my coffee downtown, Melissa told me him and Becca had their baby yesterday. A boy."

Right. Their baby. A stupid lump formed in her throat, and Ruby had to work hard to clear it. "I didn't realize." Of course, she knew Hudson and Rebecca Draper had hooked up again the previous year. In a town this small, it wasn't surprising their pregnancy had made the gossip rounds, considering it had happened so quickly. Ruby had heard they were expecting and pretty much put it out of her mind.

It wasn't as if she socialized with any of the Blackwells. They were one family she avoided at all costs, and it wasn't hard to do. The boys had been away for years (until recently), while the elder Blackwell, John, kept to his immediate friends and family. Ruby had never been part of that circle—not even when she'd been married to Travis. His brothers hadn't been around, and the last time she'd spoken to John had been a blur. She'd been back in Crystal Lake for nearly five years, and not once had she run into her former father-in-law. She'd seen him from afar a few times, at various functions and charity events, but managed to keep out of sight.

The fact he hadn't bothered to get in touch with her was telling.

"Hey," Sidney said quietly. "Are you okay?"

She nodded. "I'm good." She leaned back on the bench with a small smile. She *was* good. Kind of. She sighed. Not really.

Damn, Travis Blackwell. She'd been living in a bubble and hadn't seen that one coming. She should have been prepared. Should have had her armor in place. Instead, she'd let him press every button she had going. God, she couldn't even remember what he'd said, other than *banging* and *wife*. As if he had the right to think such things.

She made a sound of disgust. Ruby decided the best thing to do was forget about it. Travis wasn't here to stay. This was just a quick visit to see the new baby (what a joke that was), that was all. Heck, he'd probably already left for LA and the fancy home he owned on the coast.

Her cheeks got hot at the thought. She would die if anyone knew that on occasion she grabbed a tub of chocolate ice cream, sat her butt in front of the computer, and Googled her ex. Why in hell he'd purchased a home in Los Angeles when he played hockey in Detroit didn't make sense to most. Ruby got it. Detroit was too close to home. She'd done the same thing. Left town without any intention of returning.

But life, such as it was, had decided to give her more than one cross to bear, and less than two years after she'd left, she found herself back in the one place she didn't want to be. A lesser woman would have crumbled or taken the easy way out and not come back. But Ruby wasn't that girl. Besides, Ryder needed her.

"Ruby?"

She jumped up from the bench and glanced at her watch. "I've got to go, Sid. I'm already late."

Her friend brushed crumbs from her pale pink skirt and joined her. "Ryder?"

Even though Ruby didn't have to pretend with Sidney, she pasted a smile on her face—one that said everything was fine—and nodded.

"How is he?" There was more than just concern in Sidney's voice. Considering the history between her bestie and her brother, Ruby wasn't surprised.

"Well, he didn't show up for work today, and he's not answering his phone. That's never a good sign. I guess I'll find out when I get to the house."

"Let me know, okay?" Sidney said quietly. "We still on for dinner?"

"Can I get back to you about that?" At the moment, Ruby had no idea what she was walking into. On top of the crap week she'd already had, she wasn't sure she'd be good company for anyone. Even for someone as understanding as her girlfriend.

Sidney hugged her and pressed a kiss to her cheek. "For sure. Let me know."

Ten minutes later, Ruby was headed across the bridge, her expensive Mercedes pointed in the direction of The Rails. Her roots were dug in deep here, but it wasn't nostalgia that pumped through her veins as she drove along streets that needed to be paved, lined with older homes. Some sported overgrown lawns or weed-filled flower gardens, while others were long abandoned, their boarded-up windows now sad, dark, unseeing eyes that stared silently into the street.

She didn't really have a name for what filled her as she turned onto First Avenue, mostly because it was a culmination of a lot of different things. Sadness. Pain. Anger. Hurt. Shame.

It was dumb, really. She was a grown ass woman who'd made something of her life. She'd done what others hadn't—made it out of The Rails. She'd taken a chance, gambled all her money, and invested in the new development across the lake. She was the sole owner of The Pines Spa and Wellness resort, and in only five short years, it had become one of the premier spas in the country, catering to those with deep pockets and a need for seclusion.

She'd given one hundred and fifty percent of herself to make sure it was a success, and with a waiting list up to six months, she'd reached a level that made her feel as if she could finally live a little. She'd accomplished a lot for a woman of twenty-eight, and yet this place still made her feel like that twelve-year-old girl in used clothes from the thrift shop. The girl who felt as if she didn't deserve to belong. The girl whose mother had taken off for something better when Ruby was five, leaving her with a cold, distant father and a twin brother to share the misery. There'd never been enough money. Or food. Or love.

She was the cliché. The classic "girl from the wrong side of the tracks," full of false bravado and attitude. A girl who kept her heart hidden beneath invisible scars. That girl was never far away, because there was no running from the past.

Ruby pulled up to a small bungalow, the last one on First Ave, and the closest to the railway line. The paint was new—she'd managed to get that done the last time Ryder was in treatment. But the shutters needed repair, and the front step was sagging. The flowers in the garden were overgrown with weeds, the purple and pink impatiens barely alive, and she pursed her lips as her gaze ran over the knee-high grass.

"Jesus, Ryder." He must have done something to piss off the landscape company she'd hired.

Ruby slipped from the car and gave a quick wave to old Mrs. Davis. The woman sat on the front porch of her equally small and nondescript bungalow. Her place was tidy and well kept, and Ruby felt that old familiar sting of embarrassment. She made a mental note to contact another company to look after the place. Mrs. Davis nodded back at Ruby, her frizzy gray hair bobbing around her chin, and drank her tea as she settled back on her rocker with a book. There were no words exchanged, but then Mrs. Davis had never been much of a talker.

Ruby stepped gingerly onto the step and scooped up a pile of flyers that littered the front door. Balancing what had to be at least a few weeks' worth of adverts, she tried the door handle, and it swung open easily. Ruby hesitated for a moment and then walked into the house she'd grown up in.

It was dark and quiet. She wrinkled her nose and tossed the flyers on the small table near the entrance before heading to the kitchen. Dishes were left on the table and countertop and in the sink. The milk carton was expired, and she made a face as she grabbed it and emptied the sour contents down the sink before turning around and gazing about in disgust. The place was a pigsty.

It looked as if Stella, the cleaning lady, hadn't been in days. She spied moldy food on the floor beside the garbage bin. Hell, Stella probably hadn't been in weeks.

A slow burn began in the pit of her stomach, and she headed down the small hall that led to the three modest bedrooms located at the back of the house. All the doors were closed, though her focus was on the last one. It used to be her father's, but when he went to the home, Ryder had taken over.

She didn't hesitate and reached for the door, not flinching when the damn thing swung open and banged into the wall. It took a few seconds for her eyes to adjust, and with a grimace, she took a few steps toward the bed.

"What the hell?" A woman sat on the edge, half dressed with a cigarette dangling from the corner of her mouth. Dark, tangled hair snaked down her bare back, and she looked over her shoulder at Ruby. Her makeup was smudged badly, her mouth exaggerated and her raccoon eyes hollow. She was thin, her shoulder blades sharp, but then again, weren't all addicts?

"Oh, it's you." The voice was rough, hoarse from cigarettes, and the tone dismissive. More than just annoyed, Ruby moved an inch closer, eyes now fully adjusted to the dim lighting, and frowned. Fiona Winters.

Ruby's gaze moved to the other side of the bed, where the top of her brother's head poked out from underneath the covers. Jesus. Some things never changed. Ruby cleared her throat, eyebrows raised. "I'm guessing Dan is away?" Fiona's husband was a good guy. Too bad he was married to an addict and—again her eyes rested on her brother—an adulteress.

Fiona shrugged, though there was a wary look in the recesses of those dark, racoon eyes. "I don't know." She took another puff from her cigarette and slowly blew it out. "I haven't been home in a few days." She reached for her cell phone and held it in her hand. "He stopped calling me yesterday morning." Her voice now hushed, a slight tremble rode beneath her words.

Before Ruby could respond, Fiona yanked up her dress and shimmied until it settled properly over her hips. She scooped up her purse, smokes, and a jacket from off the floor, and, with a pair of fire-engine-red, four-inch spikes in her free hand, walked past Ruby.

"He's probably out cold for at least a couple of hours. We tied one on last night." Fiona disappeared down the hall, and a few moments later, Ruby heard the front door slam shut.

She wasn't sure how long she stood there in the dim light, eyes on the sleeping form of her brother. But it was long enough for those old emotions to take hold. The ones that clawed at her. Kept her up at night. Would her brother ever defeat the demons that haunted him? Would he ever be healthy again?

Throat tight, Ruby quietly left the room and shut his door. She walked back to the kitchen and stared at the mess before her. It was midafternoon, and she had a ton of work waiting for her back at the spa. Reports to go over, emails to return, and a conference call at four. She glanced down at her expensive shoes, at the cream Gucci skirt wrapped around her hips. The sleeveless pink blouse she'd never worn before. Her manicured nails a matching shade.

It was a study in contrast, to be dressed like this, standing in this kitchen. She glanced at her watch once more and, after a slight hesitation, kicked off her shoes. The cupboard by the front closet still held her old slippers, and Stella's cleaning products were stored neatly on the shelf. She carried a bucket, mop, and all the other stuff she needed back to the kitchen, then tied her hair up into a loose knot.

Ruby tucked away all those feelings that clogged her chest and made it hard to breathe. She tucked them away fiercely, because there was no time to dwell on things that couldn't be changed.

She grabbed a pair of rubber gloves and got to work.

CHAPTER 3

"*S*o, what's your plan?"

It was Sunday, and the first rays of sunlight had just broken open the night sky. Outside, the birds greeted the coming morning with an enthusiastic burst of song, and, with a yawn, Travis reached into the cupboard for a coffee mug. He looked back at his brother with a frown.

"Christ, Hudson, it's not even six yet. What the hell are you doing here?" His brother's loud knocking had dragged him out of bed less than ten minutes earlier.

"Couldn't sleep and didn't want to wake Becca or the baby."

Travis held up a second mug and, at Hudson's nod, poured two black coffees. The men didn't say a word and headed outside to the dock. Travis grabbed a small towel on the way out, and once he dried off the Muskoka chairs, they settled in to watch the sunrise.

Travis glanced at his brother. "How's the kid?"

"Hank's doing great."

Travis paused, mug halfway to his mouth. "I thought his name is Jameson?"

Hudson nodded. "It is."

"But you call him Hank."

"Yep."

Travis took a sip of coffee. He wasn't going to ask.

Silence fell between the two of them, and Travis's thoughts moved to Ruby. No matter what he did, he couldn't seem to shake them. Hell, he'd even dreamt about her the night before. He'd woken up hot and sweaty and horny as hell. And she was the number one reason for his current grumpy mood. Though Hudson was coming up a close second.

"Travis!"

Startled, he glanced at his brother. "What was that?"

Hudson set down his mug. "I was wondering what your plans were. Would you consider sticking around Crystal Lake for the summer? I could use a hand out here. Someone to keep an eye on things, at least for a month or so until Rebecca's back on her feet. With all the construction, we've decided to stay in town."

The resort was in the midst of a major renovation. Travis had been lucky enough to score one of the newly updated cottages, but there were still several in various stages of work. He sat up a little straighter, eyes once more on the water. He forgot how much he missed this place. This lake. This resort. How many summers had he spent here with his family? Too many to count. Back then, things had been good. Back then, his mother had still been alive, and his father hadn't been eaten up by bitterness and guilt.

"I hadn't really thought about it," he admitted, slowly turning the idea around his head. There'd been talk of deep-sea fishing with some of the guys on his team, and a golfing trip to Scotland, but he hadn't committed.

Hudson set down his mug and swore. "Jesus, Trav, I didn't…" He paused and turned in his chair. "I guess it would be hard with Ruby back here and all."

Travis shook his head. "No worries there. She wants nothing to do with me, so we're good."

"Have you seen her?" Hudson asked quietly.

Staring straight ahead at the lake, he nodded. "Sure have."

"And?"

He waited a bit and then shrugged. "She pretty much hates my guts, and if I walked in front of a bus, I don't think she'd care."

"That's a little harsh."

"Accurate, though."

Silence fell between the two men as the gray morning brightened. Hudson finished his coffee in one last gulp and got to his feet. "So will you think about it?"

"Yeah." Travis nodded. "I will." He frowned. "You leaving already?"

Hudson stretched and ran his hands along the whiskers at his chin. A wry grin slashed across his face as he nodded. "Hank is due to wake up soon, and I like to be there when he feeds."

Travis watched his brother until he disappeared from sight, and as the low rumble of Hudson's truck cut through the silence, he settled back in his chair, eyes falling on the lake. The water was like glass, not a ripple to break the glossy surface In the distance, fog slowly rolled away from the shore, and he spied a Loon near a piece of driftwood.

A feeling of melancholy washed over him. A strong tug that had him clearing his throat and sitting a little straighter. Could he handle an entire summer in Crystal Lake?

Could I handle seeing Ruby all the time? He rubbed his jaw, which was still sore. Could *she* handle seeing *him*? More importantly, was it fair to put her through that?

The thought slid through his mind, and it was one he still pondered an hour later as he laced up his shoes, grabbed his iPod, and hit the road for a run. It didn't take long for Travis to find his rhythm, to find that sweet spot of quiet and contentment running gave him. Without conscious thought, he took River Road and eventually ended up in town. It was quite the hike, and by this time, the sun was fully up and the sleepy folks of Crystal

Lake were buzzing around like bees after honey. Some were on their way to church, others getting ready for a day of family, sun, and fun.

He headed to the main square downtown and grabbed a coffee. Said hello to several of the regulars he recognized, and talked about the coming season with those who cared. Ralph Benedict was concerned about their draft picks, while Mason Smith thought the Red Wings were paying too much for most of their roster, including Travis. "You tell them bigshots in the front office to free up some money and get some young talent onboard. You're not getting any younger."

Travis just smiled and said nothing. Old? Hell, he was barely thirty and in the best shape of his life. No way was some rookie taking his position. Not for a good long while.

By midmorning he found himself at the edge of town, near the park that bordered the lake. He took a breather and doffed his T-shirt, hot and more than a little sweaty. He sat down on a bench and leaned back, enjoying the sounds and smells of summer in Crystal Lake.

He closed his eyes and relaxed, and he might have dozed off except a small dog came ripping out of nowhere and barked up a storm. With one eye now open, Travis spotted the little fur ball running madly after a blown dandelion that dipped and turned in the breeze. The fluffy white stems teased the little thing until the dog managed to grab it and destroy it.

Amused, Travis chuckled as the dog turned wildly, barking up at the now-freed stems as they rose higher and higher out of his reach. Judging from the bright pink collar and—he winced—pink bows set behind its ears, the little critter was obviously a female.

The dog spied Travis and ran over, her little tail wagging crazily.

"Hey." Travis bent over and ran his hands over the top of the dog's head. "You gonna stop yapping or what?"

The dog sat back on her haunches and cocked her head to the

side as if she knew what he was saying. She barked and then glanced over her shoulder, and that was when Travis spied a woman, slowly making her way to him. The sunlight danced around her head, making a halo of blonde hair.

Long. Lean. Curves in all the right places. *Ruby.*

Travis's heart sped up on sight, and he sat a little straighter.

She was dressed in running gear. Slim black leggings. Black tank top. All that wavy hair pulled back into a ponytail. Dark sunglasses covered her eyes so he couldn't get a good read on her, but she held a pink dog leash in her hand as she came to a stop a few feet from him.

Was she annoyed? Her lips pursed slightly, and he recognized the meaning. She was definitely annoyed. Two guesses as to why.

"Tasha, come." Her voice always got to him. The whiskey-soaked undertone. The way she took her time and rolled her words. Even when they were angry words, they were still sexy as hell.

The dog looked from Travis to Ruby but didn't move. Ruby inched closer, the dangling leash trailing along the ground. There was color in her cheeks, and she'd gone from annoyed to a level of pissed off that the dog should take seriously. Travis knew this. He'd been on the receiving end of that look many times. She shook her head and tapped her toe.

"I mean it, Tash. Get over here."

Tasha barked and jumped to her feet. She ran towards Ruby but then ducked and did a few loops around the both of them. Travis wasn't one for small dogs. He liked them big, a German shepherd or retriever. But there was something about the crazy little terrier. The dog's infectious joy was hard to dismiss. Once the dog settled, Ruby turned her attention back to Travis.

"You're still here." Gone was the whiskey-soaked undertone. Her voice was flat, her words a statement, not a question.

He ignored her comment and got to his feet. "I didn't think you liked dogs."

An eyebrow shot up, and she folded her arms over her chest. "Why would you say that?"

He shrugged. "I've known you pretty much your entire life, and you've never had a dog."

"My dad could barely keep enough food in the house to feed Ryder and me." She looked at him as if he were an idiot. Which, now that he thought about it, he was. "We didn't have a dog because we couldn't afford one." She took off her sunglasses, and he saw the old bitterness there. The chasm he'd never been able to bridge.

"I'm sorry, Ruby. I was just trying to make conversation."

Her mouth dropped open and then was snapped shut just as fast. Her fingers closed over the leash in her hand, and she bent forward, grabbing Tasha and tethering the animal before she could run away again.

When she straightened, all emotion was gone from her face. She slowly put her sunglasses back in place. "We don't do that anymore, Travis." She enunciated her words slowly. "Make conversation."

He clenched his hands into fists. "We could." He said the words and suddenly realized how much he wanted that back. The friend thing—something they'd been way before they'd been lovers.

"No." Ruby shook her head and stepped back, tugging on the leash. "We can't."

"Why not?" He wasn't giving up. It wasn't in his nature, and besides, there was a tug on his heartstrings so strong, it nearly took his breath away.

She glanced over her shoulder, and he followed her gaze, his gut tightening as a sliver of cold grew in the pit of his stomach. When she turned back to him, her blue eyes were clear, that beautiful mouth curved into a bitter smile.

"The list is too long for me to recite right now, Travis, and honestly, I have better things to do with my time." A small frown touched her forehead. "Do you *remember* our last conversation?"

"I…" He searched her face and slowly shook his head. The past was something he'd tried hard to forget, and a lot of the bad stuff, he'd buried. He didn't want to go back there any more than she did. And he sure as hell didn't want to talk about it.

"Didn't think so." She paused as if gathering her thoughts and organizing the right words. "You don't remember because we never had a last conversation. There was just paperwork and lawyers and cold offices. There were no conversations about anything that mattered." Her voice dropped. "You walked out the door, and I never saw you again. Not even when…"

Silence followed her words as she regarded him with eyes like chips of ice. When she spoke again, her voice was soft, but there was still an edge there. A sliver of steel that cut to the bone. "You told me you would never leave me. Do you remember that?"

She didn't wait for him to answer, though he remembered. Hell, it was a night he would never forget.

"It was a Wednesday. The night of the big bonfire, after you were drafted to the juniors. You told me you loved me and that you would never leave me. You said we would always be together." She paused, her voice lowered. "No matter what." She yanked on Tasha's leash and turned away. "You lied."

She left and didn't look back.

Stone-faced, Travis pulled his T-shirt back on and watched Ruby as she jogged out of the park and disappeared down the street. He stood there for a good long while, because it took some time for his heart to slow down. For the anger and frustration inside him to abate. It didn't go away, but it was manageable.

Mouth grim, he set off at a slow jog, heading in the opposite direction. It didn't take long to reach the entrance to the old cemetery that climbed up the hill overlooking the lake. He'd only been to this place twice. Once when they'd buried his mother, and the second? Well, that had been last fall, when he'd been home for a few days. He knew where he was going.

The old oak tree still stood, though by the looks of it, some branches were missing. Its greenery shaded a large area, and Travis walked to the south side, where the large Blackwell mausoleum stood, filled with many of his ancestors. His mom, however, was buried outside, a large angel marking her final resting place. It had caused a bit of controversy, he remembered that, but she'd never liked the mausoleum, and his father had, at least, honored her last wishes.

He paused as a fresh wave of pain rolled through him. God, he missed her. What would she think of the mess he'd made of things?

Beside her angel, a small gray slate stone was set in the earth. Fresh blue hydrangeas had been laid next to an old, battered blue teddy bear. A knot formed in his throat, and for a moment, Travis looked away. The guilt and pain made it hard to breathe. When his eyes eventually found their way back, he scrubbed at them and read the simple inscription.

Nathan Montgomery Blackwell
God needed an angel, and you answered the call. Though your time here
was short, you will never be forgotten.
May 1, 2009

THE DATE STUNG. It was the date of his birth, the date of his death. Little Nathan. His son.

Chest tight, Travis stood there for a long time. Long enough for his legs to cramp and for the pain in his chest to subside. Long enough for him to remember things he didn't want to. Long enough to face some hard truths. Among them? His past with the only woman he'd loved. He'd always blamed his youth and immaturity for what had happened between him and Ruby. Hell, he'd grabbed at the sad dynamics of his family and used them as an excuse too. He'd acted like a selfish bastard who decided to run from his problems instead of dealing with them. He'd taken the easy way and left Ruby behind, convincing himself it was for the best. He told himself they weren't good for each other. That they wanted different things. It was all bullshit.

He hadn't wanted to deal with any of it, and he'd used hockey as a way out.

There was no doubt that he and Ruby should have waited to marry. They were kids, and growing up would have helped a lot. But that didn't negate how he'd behaved. How he'd embraced a new life without her and left her here to deal with the pain of losing a child. Alone.

He swore and shook his head.

Conversation? He remembered their last conversation vividly. It had been over the phone when she'd called to tell him their son had been born and then died within hours. She'd calmly told him the name and that she would look after all the details of the burial. She'd asked him not to come home. Not to call. Ruby told him she didn't need anything from him.

He'd sent flowers.

"Fuck," he muttered, turning away. It had been years since he'd felt like this. Thoughts muddled and confused, he didn't feel his cell vibrate, and when he did, he absently pulled it from his shorts. It was his pal Marcel, wanting to confirm the deep-sea diving trip.

Travis ran his hand through his sweaty hair, his gaze drawn to the blue slate stone. Drawn to little Nathan.

"Trav? You in? Dave's got everything looked after. House. Booze. Women."

"I think I'm gonna pass," he murmured.

"Pass?" He heard the disbelief in Marcel's voice. "You sure? Dave and the guys will be disappointed."

Travis slowly shook his head. Maybe it was time he dealt with his past. Maybe it was time he put some old ghosts to rest. Made things right. Or as right as they could be.

"Yeah. I'm sure."

He stood there under the glaring hot sun until he noticed a couple watching him a few rows over. Travis pocketed his cell, slipped his earbuds back in, and headed for home.

CHAPTER 4

"*J*'m heading down for lunch, Jaylene. Don't forward any calls unless someone is dying."

Ruby scooped up her cellphone (just in case some∂ne *was* dying) and walked past her assistant's desk. She eyed the private elevator but headed for the stairs instead. She'd slept in—missed her five a.m. workout—and could use the exercise.

Her office suite was bright and airy. It overlooked the lake and let in an incredible amount of sunshine. Today, the soft hues of blue and cream swam in a swath of light, a perfect foil for the simple and elegant furnishings and décor. Normally, these things calmed her, but today? Well, today, nothing seemed right.

"Not even if it's Ryder?"

Ruby paused at the top of the stairs and scowled. "Especially if it's Ryder." She was still annoyed with her brother and didn't feel like caving so early. And she would cave eventually. When it came to Ryder, she always did.

Less than five minutes later, she walked into the Blue Elephant, the upscale restaurant located in a huge pavilion near the water. She'd partnered with an Indian chef she'd met in London, and the result was a renowned eatery featuring a lush tropical décor with an international cuisine hard to come by in these parts. Raj was an award-winning godsend whose culinary skills were as legendary as his temper. Somehow, he and Ruby clicked, and she counted him among her closest friends.

Raj greeted her at the door, his small, delicate frame dressed impeccably in white Gucci. His thick black hair was slicked back, and a mischievous glint lit his dark eyes. He winked and grabbed her hands warmly into his, lips grazing her cheek as he murmured into her ear.

"You're having dinner with Mr. MacDougal, no?" His crisp British accent resonated softly as she pulled away with a nod.

"Yes." Puzzled, she glanced over Raj's shoulder. "Is he late?" She scanned the restaurant, which, at half-past twelve, was nearly full.

"No. The bloke has been here for nearly twenty minutes," Raj replied with a smile. "He's already seated at your private table." Raj's smile widened. "I was curious, though, as to who the gentleman is over there. I heard him asking after you."

Ruby followed Raj's gaze, and her heart stopped. Literally stopped. She had to take a moment because she couldn't speak. Her ex-husband was chatting with another man, someone she didn't recognize, but he was definitely an athlete. She knew the type. Tall. Broad shouldered. Long arms. Muscular thighs. The guy was either into hockey or football.

"He's got a really nice ass."

"Which one?" she quipped lightly, though her stomach had fallen like a stone. She angled for a better look. The other guy definitely had a hockey butt.

"The fellow who was asking after you."

"That's Travis," she replied with a scowl. What was he doing here? Why was he still in Crystal Lake?

Raj's smile vanished in an instant. "Oh. Well." He shrugged. "His butt's not *that* nice."

"Yes," Ruby said, tearing her gaze from Travis and settling it on Raj with a frown. "It is." She paused. "You said he was asking after me?" That surprised her, considering their run-in at the park.

Raj slowly nodded. "He asked Mira if you had your lunch in the restaurant, and she told him no, not usually, but today you were lunching in. We haven't seated them and can certainly turn them away."

"No." Ruby cleared her throat and attempted a smile even though the thought was tempting. But that would be rude. And childish. She had no idea why Travis had decided to come out to the spa for lunch, but she certainly didn't care. "Tell Mira not to seat him anywhere near my table." She cocked her head to the side. Her chef had Mondays off, and in fact was on holidays until the weekend. "What are you doing here anyway? I thought you took off with..." She frowned and thought hard. "Johnny?"

"Frankie."

"Oh. What happened?"

Raj sighed. "He's much too much of a drama queen for me. Second day in and all he did was whine and complain. The thread count on the bedsheets didn't meet his standards. The food was too heavy. The wine too continental. The bloody bloke is a gym rat. What the hell does he know about wine?" Raj swore under his breath and smiled at a customer as she walked by. When she passed, he shrugged. "I decided to catch up on some paperwork and try a few new recipes once the lunch crowd is finished."

She kissed him once more, aware that Travis's eyes were fixed on her. She didn't have to turn around to know this—she felt his gaze like a hand against her cheek. She hated that he still pulled a reaction from her. Hated that her weekend had been filled with thoughts of him, of their past and all the pain and heartache that went along with it.

He didn't belong in her life anymore—he'd walked away. She had to focus on that. She had to remember that. She had to not care.

And she didn't. *Not one bit.* She was going to forget he was here and have a nice lunch with her perfectly lovely boyfriend.

Ruby headed for the alcove near the back of the restaurant and spied Chance perusing the lunch menu. He'd already ordered calamari, and she kept a smile in place even though she wanted to scream. She hated calamari. The taste. The texture. *The smell.* Even now, her stomach rolled.

Chance glanced up from the menu as she settled in across from him. They hadn't talked since their argument over Travis, and he seemed a bit quiet. Fine. She got that. Her gaze dropped. She knew she should relax and work to smooth things over. But calamari?

His eyes followed hers, and he swore. "Damn. I forgot."

"It's okay." She pasted a smile on her face. She could do this. She was a big girl. A grown-up. She could ignore the plate in front of her.

"I'll ask the waitress to take it away."

"No. I'm fine." She reached for the glass of pinot grigio. At least he'd gotten that right. Inwardly, she winced. What the hell was wrong with her? Since when was she so damn petty? Chance was a great guy. Everyone said so. Sharon at the bakery gushed over him. Janelle at the dry cleaner asked Ruby every week to let her know when and if he was available. Heck, even her brother didn't mind him, and he minded most people.

But she knew the reason, didn't she? With some effort, she pushed all six feet four inches of Travis Blackwell from her mind. "So," she said brightly, gazing across the table. "What are you having for lunch?"

The two of them enjoyed a spectacular meal. Chance had the beef short rib with avocado salad, while Ruby, a creature of habit, asked for a bowl of tomato soup and a grilled cheese, ham, and onion sandwich. It was comfort food, but today, she needed it.

They talked about nothing important, the weather (hot and sunny for the week), the latest Hollywood blockbuster (how many superheroes were there?), and local construction (was the damn bridge ever going to be finished?). Ruby had just begun to relax when Chance set aside his plate and tossed his napkin. His gaze settled on Ruby, his eyes holding hers for a long time. Long enough for their waitress to clear the plates and bring coffee. To set down the dessert menu. Long enough for the silence to scream louder than words.

"Should I be worried?" Chance finally asked.

Ruby automatically shook her head. She knew what he was talking about. "No." Because it was true. Chance didn't have to worry about a thing. Travis might still get under her skin, but then, he always had. There was nothing more to it than that.

"You sure?"

Ruby sighed and leaned forward. She grabbed his hand and gently squeezed it. "I'm sure. Travis was a part of my life a long time ago, and, yes, there's history there. Some good. Some bad." Her throat tightened. "Some really bad. But it's over."

She sat back in her chair and brushed away crumbs from her lap. "I feel nothing for him."

Chance nodded behind her. "He's headed this way."

Ruby's smile faltered, but she quickly recovered. "That's fine." She reached for her glass of water and realized it was empty. Her hand was still hovering over the empty glass when Travis stopped by their table. Dressed casually, his handsome dark looks complemented the beige trousers and plain white T-shirt.

A few seconds of awkward silence passed, and then Travis spoke. "This place is amazing, Ruby. The spa, the food. I've been to a lot of similar type establishments, and this is right up there with the best. I didn't want to leave without letting you know that."

Her gaze was averted, and slowly, she looked up at him. He stood there, hands shoved into the pockets of his pants, his dark eyes sincere, his voice subdued. There was a time when a look like that would have been everything to her. But right now, she didn't know how to react. So Ruby did what she always did when she was cornered. She reverted to sarcasm.

"Well, thank you, Mr. NHL, for your worldly view on things. I can go on with my day now that I know you think this place is up to your standards."

Travis didn't take the bait, which was something he would have done in the past. Something that would have led to an argument. Which, if she was being honest with herself, she enjoyed. She loved fighting almost as much as she liked making up.

He just smiled and nodded to Chance before glancing back to Ruby. "I want to apologize for my behavior the other day. I don't really have an excuse other than I was surprised to see you two together. It's none of my business."

"You're right about that." Ruby glared at him, but again, he ignored her.

Travis offered his hand to Chance. "I've heard you're a good guy and well..." He glanced back to Ruby. "She deserves one, so...we good?"

Chance stood and accepted the handshake, which pissed off Ruby, but she managed to hold her tongue this time. What the hell was Travis up to? The two men talked for a few moments, but Ruby didn't hear a word they said on account of the fact she was seething inside. She didn't want Travis anywhere near her, and she sure as hell didn't want Chance chatting him up like they were old buddies. She looked everywhere but at them. The table. The window. Raj, who was gesturing madly, probably wanting to know if she needed help.

After a few more moments, Travis stood back, and with a small nod, he turned, and she watched as he headed for the exit. She noticed every single woman in the Blue Elephant did the same, and her irritation knew no bounds. His pal was there waiting, and she didn't stop looking until they disappeared from view.

"What was that all about?" she asked as Chance sat back

down. She made sure to keep her voice neutral. No need for him to know she was all fired up, because that would lead to questions she didn't want to answer.

Chance finished his beer and sat back in his chair. "Your ex is sticking around this summer. Did you know that?"

She didn't speak. She just shook her head as that seething pit of anger expanded to the point she could barely breathe.

"Apparently ,his brother needs him," Chance replied. "He was asking about the tournament this weekend."

Her eyebrows shot up as alarm bells rang in her head. "Tournament?"

Chance was watching her closely, and she got the feeling that maybe he was testing her. That was something she didn't like, but considering the way she'd been acting, she kind of got it. He needed some reassurance.

"The Fourth of July charity golf tournament at the club. It's this Saturday. His brother Wyatt and some other NASCAR drivers are playing. We've got Cain Black and his bandmates as well. A top-tier NHL goalie and some of his friends would only add to the draw, don't you think? Especially since he's a hometown boy."

"You asked him to play in the tournament?" How she got the words out without sounding like a complete shrew, Ruby had no idea.

Chance waited a beat. "I haven't yet, but I'm thinking about it. How would you feel if I did?"

Oh yeah. This was a test.

Ruby smiled. It was a practiced smile. One she'd perfected over many years of pretending she didn't care. Like when she was a kid and the only one in her class with no lunch. Or when she was six and had no clean underwear to wear to school and a hole in the crotch of her lime-green pants. Like when she was teased endlessly about a mother who'd taken off with another man.

It was Travis who'd stopped that particular piece of nastiness.

He'd punched Liam McGregor, a kid two grades ahead with about thirty pounds on him, in the face and broke his nose. He'd been sent to the principal's office over it and hadn't been allowed out to recess for an entire month.

Liam never teased Ruby again, and at the tender age of eleven, she'd fallen in love with Travis Blackwell.

"Ruby?" Chance prompted.

She slowly exhaled. "I think Travis playing in the charity tournament would make a lot of folks happy. If he's willing to do it, it's a win-win."

Chance leaned back in his chair and smiled. "Okay. Good. I think so too."

Ruby's face felt like the oldest, thinnest china on the planet. It felt as if she would break into a million pieces if she didn't do or say something. She pasted that damn smile on her face again and said brightly, "Did you decide on dessert?"

CHAPTER 5

"*Y*our ex is hot."

Travis glanced at his buddy Zach and frowned. His fellow Redwing and one of his closest friends sat on the edge of the dock, long legs dangling in the cool water, a wide grin on his face. Zach's dirty-blond hair was on the long side, and he hadn't shaved in days—he looked more surfer dude than hockey player. But it was off-season and the guy was in relax mode.

"Like seriously hot."

And he was a pain in the ass half the time.

"Yeah. I know."

Travis continued to clean his fishing gear while Zach watched him. The big defenseman had decided to head to Crystal Lake when Travis pulled out of the fishing trip. Said he couldn't handle the crew without Travis and that some much needed R&R was more what he was looking for.

Travis chuckled at that. The truth was, the guy was chomping at the bit to do something, and hanging here on the dock all day wasn't gonna cut it.

"So what happened?"

Travis set down his pole and stretched. The new reel worked like a charm and was pretty much ready to go the next morning. The plan was to head out early and catch as much as they could before the heat rolled in. He got to his feet, looked down at his friend, and saw the curiosity there. He knew Zach well enough to know he wouldn't give up until he had some sort of answer—they'd never talked about Travis's past or his short-lived marriage. In fact, Zach hadn't known about Ruby until a few days earlier when he'd shown up.

"It's a long story." Travis gathered up his gear.

"The good ones always are."

"Yeah, well. This isn't a good story. I was an asshole, and she deserved better. That's pretty much it."

Zach got to his feet and joined Travis as he headed back to the small cottage.

"You still got a thing for her?" he asked.

"Nope."

"Really?"

Irritated, he shot a look to Zach as he stowed his gear inside the deck box. "Why do you sound so surprised? Ruby and I haven't been a thing for years. Besides, even if I thought I stood a chance in hell with her, she's with someone else now."

"That's never stopped you before." The not so subtle dig brought a scowl to Travis's face. Was he ever going to live down Clarisse Hall? Hell, he hadn't known the woman was married (he thought maybe a boyfriend) until her husband showed up and surprised them in bed. That had to count for something.

"Yeah, well. This time, there's no chance of that happening. She can barely look my way without wanting to throat punch the hell out of me."

Zach followed him inside the cottage. "Then why are you here?" At Travis's scowl, he laughed. "Hey, not that I'm complaining or anything. But seriously, the fishing trip was your idea."

"It was Dave's."

"No, it was yours and he ran with it."

"Whatever," Travis muttered. "My brother needed me to look after this place, and I told him I would. There's nothing stopping you from joining the guys."

Zach grabbed a towel from the cabinet and headed to the shower. "Nah. I think I'm going to have more fun around here." His grin was wicked. "Just sayin'."

Zach disappeared before Travis could respond, which was fine, because his pal was absolutely full of crap. Travis didn't have a thing for Ruby; he just wanted to make things right. Hell, it was normal for a man to feel a little jealousy over the new guy. He looked at his reflection in the window above the kitchen sink.

Totally normal. *Right?*

AN HOUR LATER, they rolled in to the Coach House. He spied his brother Wyatt and some pals sitting in the far corner but took a moment to look around before heading over. The place was hopping, filled to near capacity, and a country/blues band had just taken the stage. So many memories here. So many good people he'd left behind.

"Regan let you out of the house tonight?" Travis said with a chuckle as he approached the table. He slapped his brother on the shoulder.

Wyatt grinned. "Hey, I'd rather be home with Regan than sitting here with these ugly mutts, but she's out of town for a conference." He held up an empty beer mug. "You buying?"

"It's worth the trip to the bar, my friend." Adam Thorne grinned. "The new waitress is damn easy on the eyes."

"Yeah?" Travis raised an eyebrow. "And how does Violet feel about that?"

Adam chuckled. "My wife would probably agree."

"Mine too." The big man beside Wyatt smiled and shook Travis's hand.

Travis took the hand, but moved closer and gave him a hug. "How's Patrick?" His words were quiet as he studied Brad Bergen. He'd met his son the previous year when he'd come back to Crystal Lake. Little Patrick was sick. Damn sick, and his throat tightened as he studied the father.

"He's a fighter. Doing better than anyone expected." Brad took a moment. "We take each day as it comes, and thank the Lord we're still together at the end of it."

"That sounds good," Travis replied with a small smile. He knew the outlook was grim for the boy. "I'll grab that round."

Zach slid onto one of the stools, and after introductions were made, Travis headed for the bar to grab a couple of jugs of whatever was on tap. He spied Tiny and veered to the left, deciding he'd rather check out the new bartender than deal with Grizzly Adams. The band was good, the bar area three deep, and by the time he said hello to all the people he knew, which was a lot, and talked hockey to those who cared—it took some time for him to sidle up to the bar.

Adam was right. The new bartender was a looker—a tattooed, edgy woman with a killer smile. She looked at home in torn jeans and white midriff top that did nothing to hide taut abs and—he angled his head for a look—another tattoo that snaked around her right side. Long dark hair was pulled up into a loose bun, with tendrils that fell to her shoulders, and the lady had guns. Her arms were solid.

She must work out more than I do, he thought, clearing his throat and glancing up into dark eyes that regarded him silently.

"What can I get you?" He couldn't place the accent, but Travis was thinking she was from the South. Maybe.

"A couple jugs of the honey blond."

"Are you being funny?" Her eyebrow shot up so fast, he was surprised it was still attached to her head. He wasn't sure what the hell had just happened, so Travis smiled and shook his head.

"No?" She frowned. "Is that the right answer?"

She said nothing, but grabbed two jugs from under the counter and then moved to the taps.

"You're new in town." Travis wasn't used to being shut down so quick, and thought he'd try again.

"Yep." She didn't bother looking up.

"I'm Travis."

"I know who you are."

Okay. Now they were making progress. He grinned as she set aside the first jug. "Hockey fan."

"Not at all." The way she said those three little words, you'd think hockey was the devil's sport. Huh. He didn't feel he had to try so hard anymore.

"You got a name?"

"Don't we all?" She pushed both jugs his way and met his gaze full-on. There was a challenge there, though for the life of him, Travis couldn't decide for what. And something else. Something that didn't belong in this place of beer and wings.

"Yeah. I was nice enough to introduce myself, which is what we do here in Crystal Lake, so..."

She was silent for a few seconds, and a strange feeling washed over Travis. He tossed a twenty on the bar and reached for the jugs. He didn't have time to play games with some strange woman in a bar.

"Honey, you got an order of wings you waiting for?" Nash walked up behind her, and she visibly jerked. She motioned to Travis's left. The guy who sat there was leaning half off his stool. "He's cut off." She grabbed the wings from Nash, and both men watched her head to the other end of the bar.

"Not that I give a damn, but what's her name?"

"Honey."

"What?"

Nash shrugged. "Her name is Honey."

"What kind of person names a kid Honey?"

At the look on Travis's face, he chuckled. "Hell if I know. I asked her the same thing, and she nearly bit my head off. Told me she was from the South, like that should explain it."

"Where'd you find her?" Travis asked, curious to know where she'd come from.

"She just showed up last week."

"She's not exactly a people person."

"No." Nash shook his head. "She's not."

"Then why'd you hire her?"

Nash frowned and shook his head. "I have no idea."

"Well, good luck with that." Travis took a step back and swore as his hip butted the edge of a barstool. "Hey, sorry," he said, turning to the guy sitting there. It took a moment for his brain to catch up to his eyes, and when they did, he wasn't sure how to feel. Holy. Hell.

"Ryder?"

The man looked up from his empty glass, eyes glassy, a scowl touching his handsome face. The glass indicated he'd been drinking, but there was something else there, and Travis remembered all too well Ryder Montgomery's dark side—his need to dance with the devil. From the looks of it, it seemed Ruby's brother was on the wrong side of this particular dance. Again.

"So, it's true, then." Ryder pushed back his glass and got to his feet. He stumbled a bit, and Travis nearly lost one of the jugs of beer he held. "You're back."

Travis nodded but kept silent. He and Ryder had been close once, but blood is blood, and the last time they'd seen each other, the two of them had gotten into it and things hadn't ended well. Both of them had taken a trip to the ER, and that was pretty much it for Ruby and Travis.

"Sorry, Ry." Nash grabbed the empty glass. "But the lady says your cut off."

Ryder didn't acknowledge Nash. He shoved past Travis and headed for the exit. "Should we…" Travis cleared his throat. "How's he getting home?"

Nash shrugged. "I can't babysit every drunk in the place. Ryder Montgomery can figure it out. I've got his keys, and he won't be getting behind the wheel. That's all I'm concerned about."

Travis headed back to table, but by the time he got there, he knew what he was going to do. It just didn't seem right letting Ruby's brother head off on his own. Hell, depending which way he went home, he could lose his balance and end up in the damn lake. He set down the jugs and told the guys to start without him. At Wyatt's raised eyebrow, he shrugged and said, "Ryder needs a lift home."

His brother nodded—he got it—and Zach was already occupied chatting up a pretty girl at the next table. He scooped his keys out of his pocket and headed for the parking lot. Ryder was already on the main road and didn't stop or look his way when Travis pulled up alongside. Rain was just starting to fall, the drops light and probably refreshing. But the dark clouds over the lake coupled with the high humidity meant something mean was rolling in.

"Get in, Ry."

"Fuck you, Blackwell."

He kept pace with Ryder. "You really want to get caught in this storm?"

Ryder stopped and laughed. "Why the hell do you care?"

He put the truck in park. "I don't. But Ruby does."

"You don't care about anyone but yourself, Blackwell."

"Kind of like you?"

Ryder's face darkened. "You don't know shit."

Lightning arced across the sky, and an ominous roll of thunder followed. Ryder stumbled again, and Travis gritted his teeth. He should just head back to the Coach House and forget he'd run into Ryder Montgomery. Some guys would. Hell, a few years ago, he would have been one of them.

Except Ryder looked like hell and the sky looked even worse. Regardless of what Ryder claimed, Ruby loved her brother more than anything, and she *would* kick Travis's ass if she found out Travis let him wander the streets in the state he was in. The ass kicking, he could take (hell, he would enjoy it), but the disappointment he'd rather not face. He'd been responsible for too much of that in her life, and with the new leaf turning and all, it wasn't an option.

"I'll follow you anyway, so why don't you save us both the time and effort and get the hell in."

Another roll of thunder sounded, and with a curse, Ryder yanked open the door and slid inside the truck. He sank back in the seat and rested his head.

"Where you living these days?" Travis asked, heading back down the road.

"Where do you think?" he mumbled.

"First Ave?"

Ryder mumbled something else, and Travis took it for a yes.

His passenger was silent as Travis headed down familiar streets that hadn't changed for years. A heaviness he was becoming familiar with settled in his chest, and it was more than just a case of nostalgia. He pulled into the driveway of the Montgomery bungalow, put the truck in Park, and glanced over to Ryder. The guy was out cold.

By now, the rain was pounding the windshield, small cannons of water exploding against the glass. He stared through it, eyes resting on the house...the simple white boards and faded blue trim. The gray stone planter to the left of the porch. The missing trellis from the side fence.

He rubbed his hand across his temple and frowned, remembering things. Things he hadn't thought of in years.

Ruby asleep on her red-and-white quilt. Long hair snaked around her.

Sneaking in the back door late at night.

The squeaky last step on the deck.

The smell of lilac bushes in the summer.

This house, God, it had been a refuge for him. Back then, his father had been in a dark place and his older brothers had taken off, leaving him to deal with all of it alone. Ruby had gotten him through, and he'd spent more time here than he had at his own place. If he wasn't on the ice, he was here with Ruby. Hell, if it wasn't for Ruby, maybe he wouldn't have made it to the big league.

Jesus, when had things gone so wrong?

He glanced at Ryder with a sigh and slid from the truck. By the time he reached the passenger side, he was soaked, but Travis didn't feel the rain. Hell, he didn't feel anything but regret and something that hit harder. Something that twisted his insides up so damn tight, he could barely breathe.

He managed to get Ryder out of the truck and half carried the man up the stairs. The front door was unlocked, and walking through the entrance was like falling into the past. Creaking floorboards, and the smell of pine. The painting of a sailing ship caught adrift in storm that hung in the hall, still crooked and leaning to the left.

He didn't stop. Didn't bother to take off his wet shoes either. Travis headed to the back, and Ryder pretty much toppled onto bed on his own. He groaned and rolled onto his back, eyes sliding open as he did so.

The two men stared at each other for a few long moments, and then Ryder broke the silence.

"Why are you really here?" he asked gruffly, wincing as if in pain. Which, considering the man was on his way to a massive hangover, didn't surprise Travis.

"I've got a lot to make up for," he replied, surprised as the words rolled off his tongue. Ryder grunted, called Travis a bastard, and then rolled onto his side. Seconds later, he was out cold.

Carefully, Travis stepped back and closed the door behind him. He stood in the darkened hallway, the sound of rain on the roof a melody that fit his mood. After a while, he glanced at the closed door across the hall, and before he could stop himself, Travis reached for the knob.

It slowly swept backward, and he leaned against the doorframe—unwilling to step inside, but unable to look away. Faded pink-and-white wallpaper, torn in some corners and looking just as worn as he remembered. Red-and-white comforter. Small bureau to his left and an antique mirror hung on the wall above it.

He used to position Ruby on the bed, just so, and they'd watch each other in the mirror. Naked. Straining. Sweat-slicked limbs grabbing at each other frantically.

Travis exhaled and looked to his right, to the desk propped against the wall, and he spied a small frame turned over so the picture was hidden. Without thinking, he took a hesitant step inside, and then another. He reached for the simple white frame and scooped up the picture, turning it over quickly before he chickened out.

He stared at the damn thing for so long, his eyes blurred. Lightning streaked across the sky and lit up Ruby's old bedroom, washing the worn and shabby furniture in a ball of light. The rain still pounded against the house, and there was no doubt the storm had settled in for the evening.

Travis backed out of the room, his mood just as dark and dangerous as the storm. He looked down at the picture in his hand and then closed the door, heading out into the elements and wishing like hell the rain could wash away his hurt and guilt.

He slid into his truck, set the picture down on the seat beside him, and gritted his teeth so hard, his jaw ached. He didn't deserve forgiveness. He knew that. But he couldn't seem to help himself. He'd come back to Crystal Lake and somehow managed to set himself on a path that was either going to screw him over, which he deserved, or finally set things right.

It wasn't lost on him—the complete one-eighty. The old Travis would have cut and run. That guy would have disappeared, using the excuse of not hurting Ruby again. And yet he couldn't. He couldn't leave. So what had changed?

He glanced out the window, up at the house once mcre, and frowned. Did it matter? The pull was just as strong as it had ever been, and right or wrong, he was staying put. He'd deal with the consequences, whatever they might be.

A heartbeat passed. And then another. Eventually, Travis dragged his gaze from the house, reversed out of the Montgomery driveway, and headed back the way he'd come.

CHAPTER 6

*S*aturday morning crept across Crystal Lake. Lazy beams of sunlight spilled over the horizon and lit up the town, awakening the heady scents of lilac and honeysuckle. The warmth was tempered by a fresh breeze off the lake, one that made things bearable. Because there was nothing worse than thick humidity on a day when most everyone was outdoors.

And Crystal Lake was crowded. Red, white, and blue greeted the eye as far as you could see. Flags. Banners. Homemade signs. It was patriotism at its best, and the town did it up right. Even old Mr. Ainsworth had been down at the parade, dressed from head to toe in America's colors, and he was on the wrong end of ninety.

A lump formed in Ruby's throat. "Get a grip," she muttered, quickly clearing it. There was no time for nostalgia or sentiment. Not today, anyway.

She scooped up Tasha and glanced at her watch, brow furrowed as she turned in a circle, looking for Ryder. He'd promised to meet her in the main square by the clock tower at ten o'clock and take the dog for the day. That was fifteen minutes ago.

"Don't do this to me, Ry," she muttered, pulling her cell from her back pocket. He hadn't called to say he'd be late. Typical.

She had maybe another fifteen minutes to spare before she had to leave for the golf course. Sighing heavily, she trudged into the coffee shop, deciding a shot of caffeine would make things better. The place was busy with patrons who'd just watched the parade, and by the time Ruby made her way back outside, her fifteen minutes were nearly up.

Her phone pinged, and she grabbed it again, shifting Tasha to her other hip as she answered. It was Chance. She stared at his name and then, feeling silly, hit the button.

"Hey," Ruby said. She could hear voices in the background.

"You on your way?"

"Yes. Just getting organized," she replied, a little breathless as she balanced her coffee and Tasha. "Well, in five minutes or so."

"No worries. I just wanted to touch base since we didn't see each other last night." There was no hint of accusation. No subtle knock on the door. And for whatever reason, that made Ruby feel guiltier than she already did.

"I'm sorry. I just...I had such a bad headache." Truth. "And I worked late." Lie. "I would have been awful company." Truth.

There was a pause.

"I'm just glad you're feeling better today. I saw Sidney a few minutes ago, and she's wearing bright pink. You won't be able to miss her."

A smile crept over Ruby's face. "She does love pink."

"I gotta run, but have a good game. Not sure if I'll see you until after the tournament."

Wait. What? "I thought we were golfing together?" She spied Ryder on the sidewalk just across from her and waved, nearly dropping Tasha and her phone. She swore, and by the time she had her phone back to her ear and the dog under control, Chance was saying goodbye and telling her he'd see her at dinner.

Click. The end.

49

Annoyed, she pocketed her cell and glared at Ryder. Dressed casually in faded jean cuttoffs, sandals, and a plain white T-shirt, he looked good. His hair was on the long side, the scruffy beard on his jaw all the rage, and his handsome face always turned heads. It wasn't until he got closer that the signs of his addiction became more apparent. He was too thin. His classic features too pronounced. And the dark circles under his eyes dulled the vibrant blue. But today, for some reason, shades of his past were present, and he looked better than he had in a long time.

His smile was wide, but it faded as he reached his sister, replaced by a look that pissed her off even more. He was looking at her as if *she* were the one with the problem.

"You're late," she managed to say coolly.

"You're pissed." He reached over and scratched Tasha under the chin, eliciting a soft bark in return.

"You could have texted me. I would have met you at the house."

"My phone was dead."

Unbelievable. "And you're how old?"

"Same as you," he quipped, a hint of a smile touching his face once more. "Only three minutes older."

"Are you high?"

His smile immediately vanished. "No." He took a step back and shoved his hands into his front pockets. "Jesus, Ruby lighten up. I was late because Mrs. Davis's air-conditioning unit stopped working, and it's gonna be hot as hell. She asked me to look at it." His eyes narrowed. "Why are you so grouchy anyway?"

"I'm not grouchy."

"Yeah, you are. Grouchy is actually too a nice word." He reached for Tasha again, and this time took the dog. "I'm guessing Blackwell has something to do with your mood."

Ruby handed her brother the leash and took a moment to consider her answer. "Travis Blackwell is old news, Ry. He's in the past."

"Uh-huh."

"He is." She stuck her chin out, aware that her voice had risen and several people were now staring at the two of them. Awesome. The Montgomery twins at their finest.

"If you say so."

Annoyed, she had to stop herself from thumping her brother in the chest. "I'm not discussing Travis with you." She looked at him quizzically. "Who told you he's back?"

He gave her a look that said, *Really?* "It's Crystal Lake."

"I just never thought you were one for gossip, is all." She smiled at Amelia Danforth and her pack of girlfriends as the women walked by. They all said hello, but Amelia's eyes lingered on Ryder a lot longer than they should have. Her brother ignored the woman completely, and that got Ruby's mind turning so fast, she saw red.

Jesus. Mary. And Joseph. Would her brother ever learn?

"She's married," Ruby said carefully.

"What?" His eyebrows shot up, his blue eyes wary. That was enough for her to know.

"What the hell, Ryder? It's one thing for you to screw Fiona Winters. I mean, it's pathetic and wrong. But Amelia? Her husband is nasty, and he's built like a tank. The biggest tank within one hundred square miles. He'll run you the hell over if he finds out."

"Don't worry about me, kid."

Ruby clenched her teeth together. She hated when he called her that. Kid. That was something she hadn't been in a very long time.

"Fine," she snapped. "Just don't call me when you're lying in the hospital, broken to pieces. Because, trust me, Kyle Danforth will hurt you."

"Don't worry. I won't bother you. I can always call Travis."

She inhaled sharply at her brother's words. "What the hell does that mean?"

A muscle worked its way across Ryder's jaw, and he swore beneath his breath. "Nothing. Never mind." He sighed and ran a hand through his hair. "It's too early in the morning for this shit, Ruby. I just came to get your dog."

Her cell pinged again. It was Sidney.

Where the hell are you?

She pocketed the damn thing. It wasn't even eleven in the morning, and she felt as if she were out of gas. Completely drained.

"Go play in your tournament. I'll see you later." Ryder turned, and with Tasha at his side, the two of them took off down the street. She watched until they disappeared from sight, and, with her heart heavy, she headed for her car. She needed to shake this cloud of darkness that had settled over her. And she needed to do it fast. Thanks to her boyfriend, Travis Blackwell would be on the course today. No way was she facing him feeling like this. Off-kilter. Weak. Not in control.

If she didn't get it together, she'd go and do something stupid. With a quick mental shake and a new mindset to go with it, Ruby sped toward the golf course. By the time she parked and ran to the clubhouse to get her clubs, she had barely five minutes to spare before they were to head to their respective holes to tee off.

The carts were lined up and ready to go, and she said hello to several participants, her eyes scanning groups of people as she looked for Sidney. A flash of Pepto-Bismol pink caught her attention, and, with a smile, she spied Sidney talking to a tall, athletic-looking guy. Wide shoulders. Long legs. Ruby angled her head for a better look. Definitely a hockey butt.

It was Travis's friend.

As she approached them, Sidney turned, and the panicked look on her face made Ruby falter. That was about the same moment she spied Travis, securing his clubs to the cart beside theirs. Her heart sank so low, it felt like the bottom of her stomach fell out. This could not be happening.

On what planet would anyone pair her with Travis in a golf tournament?

The headache that had been threatening all morning erupted in a shot of pain that nearly took her breath away. She was hot. And cold. And dammit, her hands were shaking. Hell, even the corners of her eyes started to sting, and she had to take a moment. She fiddled with her brand-new golf watch, pretended to make sure the GPS was working, and then, with a deep breath, glanced up.

Travis stood beside his friend and Sidney, his dark eyes regarded her in silence.

She froze. Her heart took off like a rocket, and it felt as if the world was closing in around her.

There were moments like this one, when it didn't matter what her mind thought or what her heart felt. This moment right here was about her body responding on a level she didn't quite understand. It had always been this way. No matter how mad or how hurt she'd been in the past, there would always be these quiet moments of realization. Moments of him and her. Moments when nothing mattered, save for the way he cocked his head to the side when he was thinking hard. Or the way his bottom lip curled when he laughed. That male smell that was all him. The thick wave to his hair. The color of his eyes, the taste of his mouth. The way her nipples hardened. The sweet ache between her legs.

All these things slid through her mind as she studied him. Dressed in black shorts and a pale green golf shirt, he looked like he could grace the pages of GQ magazine. His dark eyes were intense, and that pulse to the right of his mouth told her he wasn't as relaxed as he wanted to be.

She approached them slowly, and for a few seconds, there was awkward silence, and then Travis stepped forward.

"Hey," he said quietly. "I ah...guess we're a foursome today."

"Looks like it," she replied coolly, gaze swinging to the man beside him. She offered her hand. "Hi. I'm Ruby."

"Zach Rogers." The big man's voice was warm, and his large hand enveloped hers. He smiled widely and openly, and in spite of herself, she did the same.

"You're a hockey player."

He chuckled. "My meathead persona give it away?"

"No." Ruby shook her head. "Your butt."

He looked surprised, and it took a few seconds for him to recover. "My butt?"

"Yes." She glanced at Sidney. "That right there is a hockey butt, no?"

Sidney hummed and hawed, then slowly nodded. "I'm going to say......" She bit her lip. "Defense?"

Zach laughed so hard, several heads turned their way. "You girls are good."

The warning horn blew, and Ruby started to walk past Travis, but he reached for her forearm before she could sidestep him, and when his warmth closed over her skin, her breath caught at the back of her throat.

"This wasn't me," he said quietly. "I want you to know that."

She stared down at his hand on her arm, and the world fell away. Her vision blurred; her heart skipped a beat.

"We can ask to change foursomes." His voice penetrated the fog, and she blinked as he came into focus.

"What?" Her tone was sharp as she yanked her arm from his grasp.

"I don't want you to be uncomfortable."

Now he cared about how she felt? "Me being uncomfortable would indicate that I still have feelings for you." She looked him right in the eye. "I don't."

He slowly nodded. But wait...was that a hint of a smile hovering around his mouth? Seriously? Heat flushed her cheeks, and she gritted her teeth.

"If you'd rather golf with friends, let me know," he said.

No way was she going to let him get off being the bigger person. No way in hell.

"I'm golfing with Sidney. I'm good."

A shot of adrenaline punched through Ruby. She reached for her sunglasses and plopped them on her nose, waiting a few seconds for her heart to slow down. Then she turned and headed for her cart, looking over her shoulder before climbing into the driver's seat.

"You and I don't have to be friends to golf together, Travis. You just need to keep up." She secured her clubs and climbed inside.

The horn blew a second time, and she placed both hands on the wheel, gripping it tightly as she waited for the cart in front of her to move forward. Her heart was still beating a mile a minute, and she was pretty sure a sheen of sweat coated every inch of her skin.

"You okay?" Sidney asked, watching her intently.

"I'm not sure."

The cart in front of them took off, and Ruby headed toward their first hole. The tournament would last about five hours tops. She could do this without getting into a nasty altercation with him. Right?

"Just don't kill him," Sidney whispered as they approached the first hole. God, her best friend knew her better than anyone.

"I can't promise that."

"And definitely don't punch him unless he asks for it."

"Got it. Only if he asks for it."

Sidney climbed out of the cart and leaned against the back end as the men prepared to tee off first. "If you do take a swing, just make sure your aim is good. I'd hate for you to miss and take out his buddy Zach."

She arched a questioning eyebrow at her friend.

Sidney shrugged. "He's kind of cute."

"Seriously?" Ruby tried to keep a straight face.

"Seriously."

"Okay," Ruby responded, reaching for her glove. "I won't take out Zach." She glanced up and caught Travis looking right at her. And she was glad her sunglasses were still firmly in place. No need for him to know he affected more than she wanted…more than he should.

Considering she didn't care if the earth opened up and swallowed him whole.

She settled back in the cart and sighed. It was going to be a hell of a long day.

CHAPTER 7

"*S*he really doesn't like you."

Travis flung his four iron in frustration, having just hit from the rough. The scowl on his face would make most people take a step back, but not his buddy Zach. The guy was looking at him and shaking his head, a half smile gracing his face. "Seriously, doesn't like you."

They were bearing down on the last hole, and Travis was more than happy to put this particular round of golf behind him. Ruby had played the entire day cool and aloof, and he was just about done. He'd take her anger over this. At least when she was angry with him, she acknowledged his existence. But today? They hadn't exchanged more than a dozen words over the entire eighteen holes, and every single one of them had been indifferent or reserved.

"I don't think I've ever met a woman who didn't like you."

"Jesus, Zach. Can you shut the hell up?" Travis scooped up his club and returned to their cart. Up ahead, the girls were approaching the green. Zach followed him and slipped onto his seat. For a few moments, the men watched as Ruby lined up her ball and chipped onto the green with a perfect shot. She turned to Sidney, the smile on her face natural, wide, and open.

Something inside him loosened, and he had to look away. That smile used to belong to him.

His gut tightened, thoughts churnings as fast and furious as his heart beat inside his chest. How the hell was he ever going to make things right with Ruby when she had no desire to even talk to him?

"What are you doing here anyway?" Zach asked quietly. "Are you trying to win her back?"

"No, I......" The denial came fast and sharp. "I..." He swore. "I hate that she hates me. I hate that I did this. I ruined everything."

"Did you cheat on her?"

Travis shook his head, slowly pressing down on the accelerator. As the cart moved forward, Ruby and Sidney watched them from the green.

"Nah. I did something worse."

Zach looked at him and frowned. "What's worse than cheating?"

Travis looked at his friend. "It's complicated."

"You know what the problem with a word like complicated is?"

"Not really, but I'm guessing you're going to tell me."

"It's too broad. It's like when I'm defending the blue zone, I use my stick, my body, anything I got to create a smokescreen so their guy doesn't get a chance to shoot at your ass."

"Doesn't always work."

"Screw you, Blackwell. I'm trying to have a moment here. I'm just saying complicated is a cop-out. It means there's shit you need to face."

"Trust me. I'm trying."

"Try harder."

"Thanks, Coach." He shot an irritated look at Zach.

"No problem."

A crowd was gathered around the eighteenth hole, and he put on his game face as he reached for his putter. These people had paid a lot of money to watch him and a bunch of other so-called celebrities golf, and they didn't deserve a sourpuss asshole.

He heard his name shouted several times, along with Zach's, and the two men nodded and waved before lining up for their final shots. It wasn't long before the game wrapped, and he made his way over to the crowd, posing for selfies and signing autographs. Ruby had disappeared—probably because of him. But, there were a lot of folks gathered around, many he knew, including his peewee coach, Mr. Hoder. This particular man had meant a lot to Travis, and he hadn't seen him in years. Hoder was definitely older, with thinning hair and a paunch, but the kind brown eyes and big smile were the same.

"Mr. H," Travis said with a wide grin. He bypassed the man's offer of a handshake and pulled him in for a hug. "Why the hell are you standing here? I could have got you a VIP pass."

"I bet you could," Mr. Hoder said with a chuckle. "But, son, the day I ask for special treatment is the day they roll me down the fairway in a wheelchair."

"We both know that day won't ever come." Travis stood back, genuinely happy to see the man. "You look real good, Mr. H."

"Travis, you're a grown-ass man in the NHL. You can call me Carl."

"Sure." That wasn't happening. The man would always be Mr. H to Travis. "You still coaching?"

"No. The wife came up sick a few years back, and I had to refocus my priorities. She passed in the spring."

Travis offered his condolences. Hoder's wife had been a small, fiery little thing with a love of hockey and a big laugh.

"So, now I get out to the grandkids' games in the winter and keep busy with landscaping in the summer."

That surprised Travis. "You still working?"

"My son, Ollie, took over Green Thumb, but I still like to get my hands dirty. Nothing worse than too much time and nothing to do. What about you?"

Travis was embarrassed to say he couldn't remember the last time he'd sunk his hands in dirt and planted something real and alive. He'd worked at Green Thumb all through high school. It was something he loved, and as he stood there, he realized there were a lot of things he'd let fall away from him.

"Bah," his coach said gruffly. "You're a busy man."

Not that busy.

"I'm here for the summer," he found himself saying. "If you need help with anything, let me know."

Mr. Hoder smiled. "I just might take you up on that, Travis. Now go on. There's a lot of folks who want a piece of you right now."

"I'm serious." He wiggled his thumb and pinky fingers in a phone salute. "Call me." He gave his old coach one last pat on the back and turned, hearing his named called loudly. A young kid came barreling through the crowd, dressed in Red Wings gear, which was saying something on account of how warm it was. He recognized the shirt. The sight made Travis grin widely, and he welcomed the young boy with open arms.

"Hey, I was wondering when I'd see you. I've been home for almost two weeks." Travis put the boy down, but as he got a good look at Patrick Bergen, his heart sank. His complexion was pale, the eyes a little too bright, and the puffiness of his features attested to the medications he was taking. Travis knew from experience it was a lot.

"I had to stay in my room because my mom doesn't want me to get sick again," Patrick said with a shrug. "But I'm out now. I got to ride on the golf cart with Wyatt, and he even let me drive it." Patrick looked over his shoulder and yelled, "Mom. Dad! It's Travis, from the Red Wings."

Travis spied Patrick's parents, Brad and Gwen, and walked

over to them. He shook Brad's hand warmly and gave Gwen a big hug.

"Good to see you guys," he murmured, dropping a kiss to Gwen's cheek before stepping back. He knew Gwen from his childhood. She'd babysat him and Wyatt at one point when he'd been a kid. And Brad had been a familiar face from the past he'd had no real connection to—he was older, more his brother Hudson's age—until the previous year.

Through his brother Wyatt's efforts, he'd gotten to know the Bergens, but more importantly little Patrick. The kid was special. Travis's throat tightened. He was damn special.

"I hear you're staying for the summer," Gwen said softly, hand on her young son's shoulder.

"You are?" Patrick's head shot up.

"I am."

"Sweet! Maybe we could go summer skating. That would be like…" Patrick's face glowed, and his enthusiasm was heartwarming. "That would be awesome."

"Sign me up."

"Really?" Patrick's eyes nearly popped out of his head.

"Sure. I need to keep the old muscles working and ready to go in the off-season. What do you say, Zach?" He turned around, but Zach wasn't there. He spied him a few feet away chatting with Ruby. She was listening attentively to whatever bull crap Zach was saying, and kind of smiling at him in a way Travis didn't like.

He frowned and took a step forward.

"Woah, is that Zach Rogers?" Patrick tugged on Travis's arm.

"Yeah."

"Do you think he'll remember me from last year?"

The kid's earnest voice tore his gaze away, and Travis nodded. "I don't think anyone can forget you, kid." Travis had brought several of his teammates back to town for a hockey game as a favor to his brother Wyatt. But in the end, Patrick had made it so much more. The boy was seriously ill, and yet his ability to live, *really live*, touched everyone.

"Let's go."

Patrick reached for his hand, and a knot formed in Travis's throat as he took it. He cleared the damn thing, nodded to Brad and Gwen—"I'll bring him inside"—and they headed over to Zach.

"Hey," he said as he approached, eyes on Ruby.

"Zach, do you remember me?" Patrick blurted, a huge grin on his face.

Zach gave him a high five. "Sure do, kiddo."

"Are you staying the whole summer too?"

"I'm not sure," Zach replied with a grin. "Guess that depends."

"Travis is taking me summer skating. My mom said I could go." Patrick paused, his body melted into Travis's side, his hand still engulfed in Travis's large one. "Who are you?" he asked, voice curious as he looked up at Ruby.

"Oh." Travis straightened a bit. "This is......" His voice died at the look in her eyes. It was there for only a moment, but it was enough. She was still in pain. After all this time.

She bent down, that sweet scent that was all hers infiltrating the air as she leaned toward Patrick. "I'm Ruby. Nice to meet you."

"My name is Patrick Bergen."

"Gwen's son?" Ruby shook his hand. "Nice to meet you Patrick."

"Are you Zach's girlfriend?" It was a question only a kid could ask.

"No," Ruby replied softly.

"Oh." Patrick looked up at Travis. "Do you have a girlfriend?"

Okay, this had to be the most awkward conversation Travis had had in ages. He looked at Zach for help, but his buddy was grinning and was obviously enjoying the show.

"Nope. I don't...have...one of those."

Patrick nodded. "I don't either. But I'm only eight."

"Right," Travis replied. "You've got lots of time for that stuff."

Patrick made a face. "Well, I don't even like girls. And my dad told me that they're a lot of trouble."

"That they are, my friend." Zach chuckled and looked at Ruby. "No offense."

"None taken." She took a step back. "It was nice meeting you, Patrick, but I have to run." She didn't meet Travis's eyes, and didn't offer a goodbye to him either. She nodded to Zach and headed for the clubhouse.

"She's pretty," Patrick said.

"Yeah," Travis murmured, eyes on her as she made her way through the crowd. No doubt on her way to see Chance.

"You should ask her to be your girlfriend. I bet she would say yes."

He looked down at the kid. "I doubt it."

"You could try," Patrick said, yanking on his hand and grinning widely.

"Listen to the boy," Zach said, slapping him on the shoulder. "What does Coach say?" He leaned closer and mouthed the words. *Try harder.*

If Travis didn't have Patrick's small hand in his, he would have hauled off and used his fist to wipe that silly-ass grin off Zach's face. As it was, he had to settle for a mental *fuck you.*

"Who's ready to eat?" he asked, looking down at Patrick.

"Me!"

"I'll grab our clubs," Zach said. "And meet you inside."

Travis led the way toward the clubhouse, and once he found Gwen and Brad, deposited Patrick at their table before heading to the bar. He could use a stiff drink before dinner. He rested his hands on top of the bar, eyes sweeping the room. Chance and Ruby were huddled close together on the other side, having a "conversation."

"Bet they have lots of those," he muttered to himself. His

mood was dark, and he probably should leave. He wasn't sure he could handle seeing Chance and Ruby together for the next few hours.

"What was that?"

He jerked his head away from his ex, his gaze landing on dark eyes that were more than a little unsettling. It was the new bartender from Nash's place.

"What are you doing here?" he asked, the words spilling out more rudely than he meant.

"I'm serving drinks," she replied without missing a beat. "What's it look like?"

"Honey, right?"

"Yep."

"I need a drink."

She raised an eyebrow as if to say *no shit*, and held up a beer mug. Travis shook his head.

"You need something stronger. That means one of two things." Her voice was naturally husky, as if she should be serving in some blues club in the bayou instead of an upscale clubhouse in Michigan. She reached for a bottle of Glen Fiddich. Travis nodded and waited.

He accepted the tumbler and tossed back the entire thing back in one gulp. "What's it mean?" he asked, waiting for another.

Honey poured him a second, neat, and then stood back as he held the glass in his hand.

She shrugged. "It means you either lost something or you're trying to get something back." She watched him closely. "Which one is it?"

Travis couldn't help himself. His gaze found its way back to Ruby and Chance. "What if I said it was both?"

"Well then." Honey set the bottle of Glen Fiddich on the bar and stepped back. "You might as well drink the whole damn thing, because you're screwed." She paused. "A word of advice?"

"Isn't that what bartenders are for?"

"Some people aren't meant to be together. No matter how much you want it. Lovers. Families. Friends. Just people in general. The hard part is figuring that shit out before you get hurt or worse."

"What's worse than that?"

She held his gaze steadily. "Before you hurt them."

"How do I do that?"

"That's the million-dollar question, isn't it?" Honey grabbed up a cloth from the bar. She turned away but paused, looking at him over her shoulder. "Good luck."

Travis sighed and tossed back the second scotch. It burned going down, and he wiped his mouth before setting the tumbler back onto the bar. He eyed the bottle of Glen Fiddich but turned away. Booze didn't help any situation. That was something he'd learned a long time ago.

Feeling more disjointed and out of synch than ever, he leaned against the bar, listening to the buzz of voices around him. A quick look told him Ruby was no longer with Chance. He had a hard time calling him boyfriend. He needed to find her. Needed to say some things. And now was as good a time as any.

Travis put on his game face and decided to follow Coach Zach's advice.

He would try harder.

CHAPTER 8

*R*uby was livid. And upset. And a whole bunch of things she couldn't even name.

She blew out a long, hot breath and gripped the edge of the railing. She needed to get it together, because no way could she lose it here. The old Ruby wouldn't have cared. She would have caused a scene and said to hell with the consequence. But the new, improved version? She thought before she acted, especially when her first thought was to strangle someone.

She didn't have time to go to jail.

She was outside on the patio that overlooked the award-winning golf course, but she didn't see any of the beauty. She was too damn mad to see anything. Ugh. Sweat pooled between her breasts, and her clothes clung to her body. It was still hot and muggy, even though the dinner hour was well underway, and she swatted at a fly that got too close. The voices inside, a dull buzz out here, should have soothed her mind, but not tonight.

The charity golf tournament had been a huge success, with hundreds, if not a couple of thousand, willing to pay to watch a bunch of celebrities hit the links. The silent auction had run throughout the day, with the live auction still to go. The recipient of the funds raised was to be announced just before the live auction—a tradition for the now yearly event. However, Chance had told her just a few minutes earlier where the money was going.

Green Thumbs for the Soul. It was cause near and dear to her heart, and she was pissed right off that Chance had ruined what should have been an absolute thrill.

Chance. Her teeth ground together so hard, her jaw ached. She tried to relax, but it was no use. Her cellphone rang, and she pulled it from the front pocket of her shorts. It was Sidney. Ruby wasn't in the mood to talk to anyone at the moment, but she knew her girlfriend would keep calling, or worse...come and find her.

"Hey," Ruby answered, trying hard to keep her voice neutral.

"Where are you? Dinner has started."

"I'm on my way. I just had something to take care of."

A pause.

"You sound weird."

Ruby could picture the wheels turning inside her friend's brain. "I'm good."

"Good at lying."

"Sid...I just need a moment."

"Hey," Sidney's voice softened. "Travis isn't at our table so you don't have to worry about, you know, having to see him."

At least that was something.

"Though he seemed sort of nice today. I mean..." Sidney stumbled over her words. "He kind of surprised me."

"I don't want to talk about Travis. I don't..." She swore and blinked rapidly as tears threatened.

"I knew you sounded weird." There was a muffled noise as if Sidney moved her phone. "What happened? What did Travis do?"

The anger inside Ruby boiled fast and hard. She so didn't want to get into it, but she couldn't seem to help herself. "Travis didn't do anything. For once. This is all on Chance. *He* put us with Travis and Zach because he..." She still couldn't believe it. "Because he was testing me." She made a strangled sound. "*Testing me.* He said he wanted to make sure there were no feelings between me and Trav. Who the hell does something like that?" She rolled her head back and spied a hawk flying low over the trees. The large bird arced high and then floated on the breeze. Its solitary flight pulled at her, making her heart heavy.

"Son-of-a......" Ruby could hear the surprise in her friend's voice. "He's obviously insecure."

"Ya think? God. I don't even know what to say. I just feel so..."

"Upset?"

"Yep."

"Pissed off?"

"Yes."

"Betrayed?"

She nodded. "Exactly."

There was a pause and her head filled with the sound of her own labored breathing. If anyone was in the immediate area they'd think she'd just run the Boston marathon.

"Do you think that maybe, even though he was totally wrong, I mean seriously wrong...But do you think that he kind of has a point?"

"What the hell does that mean?" Was everyone in her life lining up to kick her when she was feeling so damn vulnerable?

"Maybe there is unfinished business between you two."

"I can't believe you just said that." She tried to keep the hurt from her voice. Sidney was her person. She should know better.

"Do you want me to be honest?"

"Of course I do but—"

"There's something there between you guys. I don't know what it is. Vibes maybe?"

"Vibes?" The word exploded like a shot and echoed over the course. "Are we talking singular or were there more than one?" Her sarcasm was scathing. "I barely talked to Travis."

"It wasn't the talking, Ruby. It was the way you looked at him. And the way he looked at you while you were busy ignoring him."

Okay. Sidney was her best friend. And while Sidney wasn't a huge fan of Chance (he wore too many pastels and carried a toothpick everywhere) she hated Travis.

Ruby swore under her breath. Maybe hate was a strong word, but Sid disliked him just as much as she disliked canned peas, and that was a lot. She was on Ruby's side. But her last comment sure as hell sounded as if she was standing on the other side of the fence.

"Ruby?"

"I can't do this right now."

"I didn't mean to upset you."

"Well you did."

There was a pause.

"I'm sorry."

"Look, don't worry about me, Sid. I'll be there in a bit." Ruby pocketed her cell and headed for the bar. She needed to calm her nerves before she opened her mouth and said something she was going to regret. Right now, the only person she wouldn't piss off was Mister Jack Daniels.

Thankfully, there were several bars in the large banquet room, and she made her way to the smallest one in the corner, not far from where she'd walked in off the terrace. Large green tropical plants gave some kind of cover, and she felt free of prying eyes. A young woman with dark hair and eyes was busy cutting lemons and limes as she approached. She wore a crisp conservative white blouse, which only managed to emphasize the colorful tattoos adorning her right arm. Creamy skin, large luminous eyes, and bright red lips gave the woman an exotic look.

"What can I get you?" Her voice held a rasp that Ruby liked, the words cradled in a soft Southern lilt.

"Jack and coke."

Her perfectly arched eyebrow shot up. "Not diet?"

"Hell no," Ruby said. "I want the real deal."

"Okay." The woman got busy with the drink, and after garnishing it with a lime, she handed over the glass.

"Do I know you?" Ruby asked, curious. The woman looked familiar, but she couldn't place her. She definitely wasn't a townie.

She didn't answer right away, and Ruby got the impression she was mulling over her words, deciding how much information she was going to give. And that made Ruby wonder.

"Honey," she said after a while, her voice even.

"What?" Ruby was confused.

"My name is Honey."

"For real?" Ruby blushed as the words fell out of her mouth. "Sorry. That sounded rude. My filter seems to have been lost on the golf course."

"Don't worry about it," Honey replied. "I realized about ten minutes after I arrived in this lovely town that my name was going to confuse you folks."

"I'm Ruby." She took a sip from her glass, grateful to have something to take her mind off Travis. "Do you have relatives in town?"

Honey's head jerked up. "Why do you ask that?"

Ruby swirled the amber liquid in her tumbler. "I guess I was just wondering why you would move here from down South is all. I didn't mean anything by it."

"I don't have any relatives. I pretty much hopped in my car and ended up here by accident."

"Oh?"

"My car died."

"Oh. That sucks." Ruby studied the woman as she got busy cleaning the bar. There was something about her. Her eyes? The voice? "Do you work for the golf club?"

Honey shook her head. "No. I heard some of the organizers

talking about this event a few weeks back, and they needed volunteers. When I found out what they were doing with the money raised, I said I'd help out."

"That's big of you," Ruby replied, truly touched by the woman's actions.

"Not really. My mother was an addict, so…" She shrugged and moved a few paces away to serve an elderly gentleman holding two empty glasses of wine. When Honey had served the customer, she nodded to Ruby's near-empty glass.

"No." Ruby downed the last bit and set the tumbler on the bar. "I have to be good."

"Being good is overrated." Honey half smiled as she reached for Ruby's glass.

It hit Ruby then. She had seen this woman before. "You work at the Coach House."

Honey nodded. "I do."

"I used to go there a lot when I was younger." An image flashed through her mind. Soft summer rain. Dark parking lot. Travis. Skin on skin. Steel against her back. Lips on her neck. Hands between her legs. Music from inside the Coach House drifting on the air.

"When you were younger." Honey made a face. "When was that, five years ago?"

"More like ten," Ruby said slowly, eyes moving over the crowd, searching for the one person she shouldn't be searching for. She found Travis almost immediately. He was sitting with the Bergens and their little boy. Patrick's head rested against Travis's chest, and her breath caught when Travis turned his head, a smile meant for the boy, still on his face. Their eyes caught and held until she looked away, throat tight, heart aching.

"So you work for Nash," she found herself saying as she turned away from the past, half listening to Honey's response.

"What was that?" Honey had spoken, but for the life of her, she had no idea what the woman had said. *Pay attention.* Easier

71

said than done with the image of Travis and Patrick burned into her brain.

"Nash. He's an arrogant prick sometimes."

"Right," she murmured. "Aren't they all?" Her answer was automatic, and with some effort, she focused on the bartender.

Honey nodded. "Most of 'em." She tossed her rag. "Nash is also way too opinionated for his own good. And most of the time, his opinions are the exact opposite of mine. So…" Honey scooped up the rag she'd just tossed. "It makes it hard to work sometimes." She paused, eyebrows raised exaggeratedly. "All the time."

"Why don't you quit?"

"I needed a job, and he was hiring. Right now, I'm where I'm supposed to be, even though sometimes I don't like it."

"I hear ya there," Ruby murmured, eyes drawn to Travis once more.

"Do you know the Blackwells?"

That question turned Ruby's head right back around. "Everyone does."

"I met the hockey player earlier, Travis. I just wondered if you knew the family well."

Something unpleasant bloomed inside Ruby's chest. It flushed her skin and made her breath quicken. Was Honey interested in Travis? Her eyes fell away. Why did that bother her?

"I'm sorry. I didn't mean to pry."

Ruby found herself shaking her head and stepping back. "No. It's fine. The Blackwells are pretty much royalty around here. Their roots are deep. Generations deep. The boys are…" She stumbled over her words. "Hudson's a great guy, and Wyatt is too."

"And the hockey player?"

"I used to be married to him."

She saw the surprise in Honey's eyes but didn't wait for a response. No way could she eat, but she could drink. Honey was right. Being good was overrated. She grabbed a bottle of white wine and a glass from one of the tables and headed back outside. The sun was setting, the corners were in shadow, and she could disappear for a while.

Which was exactly what she did until the reason for her bad mood walked his ass onto the terrace and didn't stop walking until he stood a couple of inches from her chair. She leaned back and gazed up at him. Like always, her body reacted. Her breathing quickened. Her palms sweated. Her heart ached.

Even now. After all this time and all the pain between them. It was both unfair and inconvenient.

"Why are you here?" The words slipped from her lips, the tone aggressive and hard.

Travis didn't answer right away. He ran a hand through the mess of hair on top of his head and then shoved his fists into the front pockets of his shorts. His handsome face was somber, those dark eyes of his intent.

"I wanted you to know it wasn't me who picked our four-some. I wouldn't do that to you."

"You already told me that."

She sat straighter, wanting to lash out because all that pain she insisted on remembering, well, it was there nestled between her heart and her mind. It was big and ugly, and thank God, its shadow concealed everything else. The want. The yearning. *The need* for all those things she could never have.

"Why are you here?" she repeated, spitting out the words like venom.

Travis opened his mouth to answer but then closed it for several moments as he watched her. "I came to apologize."

"For what?" She got to her feet and nearly upended the small table holding the half-empty bottle of wine.

"For everything."

"What makes you think I care to hear it? Or accept it for that matter?"

"I'm not the same guy I was, Ruby."

"And I'm not the same woman. Guess we're even on that score."

"I want to make things right between us."

"To ease your conscience?" She took a step closer, her body now shaking.

The anger in her was like a category five hurricane. It was strong and swift and all-consuming. She moved to him, her hands at her sides, small fists that wanted nothing more than to hurt him. *Hurt something.* Anything to deflect what she was feeling.

"No." He swore. "Maybe? I just want the chance to make up for all the things I ruined. For ruining us."

She laughed in his face, but it wasn't anything to do with joy. "Us? Do you mean you and me? Or You, me, and Nathan."

His eyes widened, and something flickered in their depths. Was it shame? Sadness? Pain? Did she care?

Ruby spoke slowly so that there was no way he could misunderstand the meaning of her words.

"You gave up on us. On me. You were the one who went away."

"Ruby, I was young and stupid and selfish. I'm not those things anymore. Let me prove it to you. Let me show you."

"There's no point, Trav."

"I think there is."

"You're still so damn sure of yourself."

He was slowly nodding, and something about the way he was looking at her made her heart squeeze harder. "Because I'm right."

"Not this time, cowboy. No way in hell would I ever consider letting you back into my life." She had to take a moment. "You gave up that right when you walked out. When you went about your life like nothing happened." Her voice broke. "Like Nathan never happened."

His nostrils flared, and his eyes narrowed. If Ruby had been on her game, she would have noticed those things. She would have known that she'd finally pressed a button that maybe she shouldn't have pressed. At least, not here on the terrace of the Crystal Lake Golf and Country Club.

"That's low."

Her chin jutted out. "It's true."

"Your truth needs a little tweaking. I'm willing to take my fair share of hits for the crap that went down. But I'm not a hundred percent to blame for the shit marriage we had. I know about the pills, Ruby. I know you stopped taking them. You got pregnant on purpose."

His words sliced through her like a knife through butter. Shocked, she could only stare at him like an idiot. She was going to cry and make a complete ass of herself, and right now, breaking down in front of Travis wasn't something she could handle. She needed to get away from him. Needed to make the memories stop. Make his words go away.

If only for a moment. *She just needed a moment.*

Ruby took a step, hoping to move past him without another word spoken between them.

His hand reached for her, but she sidestepped.

He made a strangled sound. "I think about Nathan. I need you to know that. I just didn't know how to handle things back then. How to handle us. You were so…broken. But that doesn't mean I didn't love you. Jesus, you were my world. The only thing that kept me going when my own life was shit." He was close now. So close. His warm breath fell on her cheek. His scent filled her nostrils. His pain fed her own.

"Don't touch me." She barely got the words out. The anger was long gone; instead, she was filled with panic. Filled with dark thoughts of a past she wanted to remain buried. *Because he was right.* She'd done things. Things she wasn't proud of.

"Why? Because you're afraid of what you'll feel?"

God, she was cold. And confused. And tired. Her heart ached because of the pain, but also because of the guilt. She looked Travis in the eye, as clarity hit her square in the gut.

"I'm not afraid, Travis. I'm terrified." Her voice broke, and Ruby shoved past Travis, disappearing into the darkness.

CHAPTER 9

"*A*bout time you showed up." Darlene Atwell stared over the top of her trendy leopard glasses and continued to stir the contents of a large pot. The Blackwell home smelled like heaven, though the only person in sight was the woman who'd helped raise the Blackwell boys after their mother died, and the woman who'd fallen in love with their father.

"Is that goulash?" Travis sniffed the air, eyes warming as he watched Darlene.

"It is."

"Man, I haven't had that in ages."

"I know."

He walked into the kitchen and dropped a kiss to her cheek. It was his dad's birthday, and along with the goulash, he couldn't remember the last time he'd been present. Not surprising on account of their history. But he was trying. "Sorry I'm late. Where is everybody?"

"Wyatt took Regan out on the boat, but Hudson and Becca are down at the boathouse with your father. He hasn't let that baby out of his sight." She set the ladle down on the counter and turned to him, her face beaming. "I'm just so damn glad all you boys are here. And so is John."

I bet.

The sarcastic response filled his head, but Travis pushed it away as quickly as it had come. It wasn't the time to hash out old hurts, and maybe that time would never come. Maybe it didn't need to. Maybe they were better off forgetting all the crap that had gone down in this house. Maybe it was time to move on.

"Where's your friend?" Darlene tucked her silver hair behind her ear and set her glasses on the counter. She put a lid on the pot and reduced the heat, tossing aside an oven mitt as she did so.

"Friend?"

"The hockey player. I heard you were hosting a visitor."

"Zach decided to golf."

Darlene nodded. "Nice day for it."

"Sure is." He hid a grin. Travis wasn't exactly sure how much golf Zach was going to get in. He'd taken a shine to Honey, the bartender, and the two were hitting the links.

"What's that?" Darlene's eyebrow rose quizzically as she stared at the bag in his hand.

"Something for Dad."

"You should give it to him." Her soft eyes filled with tears, and Travis looked away. He didn't know how to react to Darlene's feelings for his father. Mostly because his own were so damn complicated. "He's outside."

"Yeah." He moved toward the patio doors. "I'll see you out there."

Travis headed outside and took a few steps before pausing on the sweeping deck to take in the scenery. God, he loved this house. Loved the land and the lake. As a kid, he hadn't appreciated all that he'd been given. He was literally the kid with the silver spoon and hadn't wanted for any kind of material thing. It was the other, the emotional stuff, that had disintegrated when his mother died. The father he'd known had left for work one day, and come home a different kind of animal. At first anguished, then angry and distant. If not for Darlene, the household would have fallen apart.

Travis gazed out at the midnight-blue water, a half smile on his face as he took in the familiar sight. Crystal Lake was bordered on both sides by a thick forest of evergreens, maple, and birch. They rose from the shoreline like soldiers, standing tall, hiding the many expensive cottages and homes behind their branches—the only evidence of their existence the boathouses and docks. Motorboats dotted the lake, zipping across the surface pulling water-skiers and kids on tubes, while Ski-Doos raced along, charting their own course. Laughter and shouts echoed on the water, jumping the waves and landing on the shore. In the distance, right smack dab in the middle of the lake, he spied Pottahawk Island. And directly across from that, Byron Campground.

Byron Campground.

He sighed and closed his eyes, head raised to the sun as a wave of memories washed over him. He thought back to the summer he'd turned sixteen. The summer he and his pals had swum from Pottahawk island over to the only public beach on the lake, the one in front of Camp Byron. He was one of the Blackwells, an anointed prince of Crystal Lake, and Ruby was unlike any girl he'd ever known. Up until that day, she'd been the scrawny kid with the big sad eyes. The girl whose biting tongue could cut a guy in two. The girl most guys didn't mess with.

But something sure as hell had changed, and his young self wasn't exactly prepared to handle it.

"Holy shit." Jason Marsdale poked Travis in the arm. "Check out Ruby Montgomery." The two of them, along with a couple of pals from the hockey team, had just dragged their asses out of the water. Travis shook drops from his eyes, his gaze wandering the beach. Ruby Montgomery?

He hadn't seen her in a couple of years and from what he remembered, she was a small little thing with a big mouth. But Shelli Gouthro sure as hell caught his attention. She was old, at least twenty-three or -four, and filled out a bikini like nobody's business. At the moment, her ample assets were barely kept together by a black-and-pink zebra-print bikini.

Who said the public beach wasn't fun? This was way better than at the resort or his father's private club up the way.

"You're kidding, right?" Jason shook his head and laughed following his gaze. "Seriously. You're not in her league. She won't give you the time of day."

"Watch me," he retorted.

At sixteen, Travis was already pushing six-three, his body hard and muscled from years of hockey. He didn't look or sound his age. And ever since he'd had sex the summer before, it was pretty much all he thought about. Well, after hockey, of course, but still, getting laid was almost as important.

"Melanie isn't going to like this."

He shot an irritated look at Jason. "Melanie doesn't own me."

"You're crazy. She's going to shoot you down."

Travis wasn't so sure. His brother Wyatt had bragged about having sex with Shelli the summer before, and he was younger than her. Obviously, she didn't give a crap about that stuff. Travis puffed up his bare chest and started across the sand. He was feeling lucky, and he darted a knowing smile at his pals, turning away with a grin when they all hooted and hollered.

He stopped in front of Shelli, a killer smile in place as his shadow fell across her. She lifted her head. Pulled down her sunglasses and looked him up and down.

"Travis, isn't it?"

"Yep." Cool. She knew who he was.

"You're Wyatt's little brother."

Feeling cocky, he grinned wider. "I'm not so little."

Shelli slowly rose, resting back on her elbows. "No," she said, licking her lips. "I guess you're not."

His mind was working fast, thinking of the next thing he should say, when a flash of blue caught his eye. He looked over Shelli's head, and his world kind of tilted.

Long tanned legs. Jean cutoffs. Crisp white T-shirt and hair that reached down to the nicest butt he'd ever seen. He stared at the girl, willing her to turn around and look his way, but all he caught was a glimpse as she chatted animatedly with the young kids in matching blue shirts. Camp Byron kids.

Something inside him shifted, and he rubbed the back of his neck as his heat-infused skin began to sweat. The girl bent close to listen to what one of the little kids was saying, and Travis couldn't take his eyes off her. She turned slightly, and he caught her profile. It hit him then. Like a punch to the gut.

Ruby Montgomery. When the hell had she changed from a scrawny kid to the knockout in front of him? He was sure he'd taken classes with her freshman year. Hadn't he?

Shelli kicked sand up at him and frowned. "Hello? I'm still here."

But Travis was already moving away, unable to process how his body could move without him actually telling it to. He halted a few feet from Ruby, unsure what to do. What the hell was he going to say to her anyway? How's life? Everyone knew her old man was a screwup. A boozer and the biggest pot supplier in the county.

Travis was about to make a hasty exit when she abruptly turned, the smile on her face fading away as quick as the tide. Her blue eyes widened, and she pulled on her T-shirt.

"What are you staring at?" Her chin jutted up.

"You," he said slowly. He wanted to smile and do something to smash open that wariness in her eyes. But he was pretty much frozen in place, staring at a goddess who made his young body react in a way that wasn't exactly appropriate. His mind was going places it shouldn't be, and he was damn glad his bathing suit was still wet and cold, and baggy, because at the moment, he needed some extra room down there.

"Why are you looking at me?" Her chin shot up another inch, and she let go of her T-shirt. The wariness in her eyes was replaced with something else. Fire. It touched something in him, and his heart took off like rocket. Never had a girl made him feel like this. Just from looking at each other.

He kind of liked it. A lot.

A slow grin spread across his face. It widened when he noticed her cheeks flush a deep red.

"There's a bonfire on Pottahawk island tonight."

"So?" She shrugged, but her eyes didn't leave his.

"Come with me."

She opened her mouth, but it was a few seconds before she actually spoke. "Why would I do that? We haven't spoken since sixth grade."

"Sorry, but you're wrong about that."

"I am not," she retorted quickly.

"I made you laugh at middle school graduation. You were pissed at Ryder for something, and I made you laugh."

She didn't say anything, and Travis waited a beat, that cocky side of him oozing out of every pore. "I'll pick you up at eight."

Her eyes narrowed a bit. "I thought you were with Melanie Smith?"

"Nope." He didn't skip a beat. "So, eight o'clock."

"I never said I'd go with you."

"You will." Travis wasn't sure how he knew that, but his gut told him he'd just won some sort of battle, and he was feeling mighty good about it.

"You don't know where I live."

He paused at that. Shit. "What's your address?"

The two of them stared at each other for a long time. Long enough for the little kids standing beside her to get antsy and for one of them to pull on her arm. The little guy had to pee and was gonna let it happen on the beach if she didn't walk them back to camp.

She took his hand and turned away.

"Ruby."

She was silent for a few more seconds and then turned slightly, offering him her profile again. His palms were sweaty; his blood roared in his ears. Shit, he felt like he did when a game was decided by a *shootout and his team was up by one with a sharp shooter heading his way.*

"First Ave. Last house on the right.

It was the beginning of the summer that changed his life.

"Son?"

Travis shook the memories from his mind and glanced to his right. God, when had his father gotten so old?

"You're looking good," he said, taking a few steps and offering John his hand. His father took it, but his grip was definitely shaky. He was pale, and though he'd been near death a while back and had made one hell of a recovery, his heart was still weak, and they all knew he was on borrowed time.

"I look like shit, and you know it." John Blackwell had never been one to beat around the bush. "What's this I hear about a young pup coming up through the ranks? There's talk this O'Connor kid is after your position."

Travis offered a tight smile. He didn't feel like talking hockey with a father who'd barely made any of his junior games and had been to exactly three NHL ones. *Three* over a ten-year period.

"There's always someone coming up. It's good for the team. It's what keeps us on our toes. Everyone is expendable. The smart ones realize that, and they work harder."

"That why we haven't seen you?" John asked. "You been working harder?"

This had to be some kind of record. Ten seconds in and he was already getting under Travis's skin.

John sighed and shoved his hands into his pockets. "Never mind," he said gruffly. "Don't mind an old man. We're not always polite. We think age gives us the right to say things we probably shouldn't."

An awkward silence fell between them, and Travis finally

broke it by offering up the bag in his hand. "I, ah... This is for your birthday."

John accepted the bag and carefully pulled out a slim black box. He shuffled over to the patio table and sat down before setting the box on his thighs. He stared down at the thing for a couple of seconds before opening it.

A lump formed in Travis's throat and made it hard to swallow. His father's hands were shaking, and damn but it was hard to hold on to all the bad things when the man responsible for most of it was so frail and old. He cleared his throat, or at least tried to, but the lump only got bigger at the smile that broke open on John's face when he took out one of the cigars in the case and ran it under his nose.

"They're Romeo & Julieta."

His father nodded. "I see that."

"I remembered you liked them."

John looked up at Travis, and Travis was shocked to see tears in his father's eyes. The last time he'd seen his father cry was the day they'd buried his mother.

"Thank you," John said haltingly. He set the case down on the table and motioned to the empty chair across from him. "You feel like a cigar? Maybe we can catch up?"

His father's words were full of emotion. His eyes misty and beseeching. John Blackwell was asking for so much more than sharing a cigar. The old Travis would have made an excuse and headed for the beach. He would have helped himself to a cold beer and sat with his brothers on the dock. They would have talked about anything other than what really mattered. The past. Their family. The screwed-up couple of decades they'd survived.

"Bah. Never mind." John offered a sad smile. "Go see your brothers. Darlene would kill me anyway."

Travis looked out to the lake and spied Wyatt and Regan heading in on the boat. Hudson and Rebecca were set up on the beach, comfortable underneath the shaded gazebo, and some little three-legged dog ran crazily along the edge of the water. This scene before him, a picture of domestic happiness, wasn't something he thought would ever happen here. A new wind was blowing, and change was headed his way. It was time for him to embrace it.

Travis slid into the empty chair. "Darlene is busy in the kitchen. We won't tell her."

He lit his father's cigar, grabbed one for himself, and the two men smoked their Romeos in silence. They caught up without catching up, as men do sometimes. Travis knew his father was unwell and that he was seeking forgiveness. He was pretty sure his father knew exactly what was going on his life—hockey and not much else.

"I saw Ruby this weekend," Travis found himself saying.

John looked at him, blowing a slow swirl of smoke in the air. He slowly nodded. "I heard." At Travis's look, John shrugged. "Wyatt." He sat back in his chair. "She's done real well for herself."

"She has." Travis cleared his throat and glanced away. "That must surprise you."

His father was silent for a few moments as if considering his words. Which in and of itself was something—the man never took the time to think about how his words affected people.

"I wasn't happy about your marriage because you were both too young. Not because I didn't like her. This world is hard enough without taking on marriage at such a young age, and I knew it wouldn't work. But that girl always had spunk, and it's that spirit that got her through the baby dying. Lord knows she got no support from us."

Ashamed, Travis bowed his head.

"She reminds me of your mother." John held the cigar and studied the red embers, turning the cigar slowly. "I've done a lot of things I'm not proud of, and I've hurt a lot of people. Sometimes I think if I'd been a better man, a better husband, things would have been different. My Angel would still be here. She wouldn't have been on the road that day. She wouldn't..." His voice drifted off, and Travis was silent, watching the pain spread across his father's face. He had no idea what the hell his father was talking about, but he would listen.

"I loved her." John looked up then, his eyes glittering. "And she loved me more than I deserved. When your mother died, things between us weren't great. I was selfish. I was too proud and too weak to face my problems. Too distracted to fight for my family. I took your mom for granted and lost everything, including you boys." He sat back in the chair and swiped at his eyes. "That's my biggest sorrow. But you can do better, Travis."

Travis had nothing. He just stared at his father in silence. Or maybe it was shock. This had to be the longest conversation he'd had with the man in years.

John Blackwell looked him in the eye. "Do you still love that girl?"

"I..." He stumbled over his reply and gave up. First of all, he didn't want to talk about Ruby with his father. And secondly, how could he answer that question when he didn't know? Was it love or guilt that crowded his mind when he thought of Ruby?

"Your inability to answer the question tells me all I need to know. You need to fight for what you lost, Travis, or you'll end up like me. Sitting in this chair looking back on a whole lotta life lived with regret and the inability to deal with that regret. You need to fight for Ruby."

Travis might have been embracing change, but some of the old resentment was still there. This man had never been there for him when it counted. "I guess this is supposed to be our moment? You're going to have to try harder than that, John. Since when are you the guy to dole out advice?"

His father looked away. He butted his cigar and slowly got to his feet. He stared out across the water, his hand trembling slightly as he pulled his sweater tight. "Dying can be gift because it's inescapable. It makes even the most stubborn men take pause.

Look back. See the good and the bad he's done. Mostly the bad. If a man is smart, he'll use what time he's got left to make amends. Heal old wounds. Or just say he's sorry."

A pause.

"I'm sorry, son." John looked at Travis and made no effort to hide the pain and sorrow that lived inside him.

Travis watched his father shuffle toward the patio doors and then disappear inside. He sat back in his chair, the cigar still in his hand. What the hell had just happened?

The patio door slid open again, and his father poked his head out.

"You know Coach Hoder's organization has the contract for the new park and condominiums your brother is building? The ones for people in need down by the old mill."

"No." Travis cleared his throat and replied, "I didn't."

John offered a crooked grin. "Ruby's on the board, and she's very involved."

"That right?" He wasn't surprised. Ruby had always had a penchant for those in need.

"You still like digging in the dirt?"

"I haven't really had time."

"Maybe you should make some." His dad reached for the sliding doors, pausing as he stared at his son. "I hear they're looking for volunteers."

Travis had no response. He sat back in his chair and finished his cigar, turning his father's words over in his mind as he watched his brother Hudson rocking his newborn son. For the first time in forever, he was going to have to agree with his old man. He reached into his pocket, retrieved his cell phone, and called Coach Hoder.

CHAPTER 10

*T*he spa was closed Monday, on account of July fourth falling over the weekend, and for that, Ruby was grateful. Saturday was still fresh in her memory even though she'd spent considerable effort trying to erase it. Sunday had been a day of licking wounds, eating copious amounts of chocolate ice cream, and stuffing macaroons in her mouth as she watched *Steel Magnolias* for the fifth time. Not exactly the movie to lift your spirits, but then Ruby was, if anything, unconventional.

She winced as she pulled on sunglasses and got out of her car. The wine hadn't helped either. Tasha hopped out and took off at a run, ignoring Ruby, who shouted at the little animal to stop.

"That's it," she muttered to herself, reaching into the back for a large canvas tote. "No treats tonight." She smoothed out her old T-shirt, pulled up her jean shorts, and yanked on the brim of her ball cap, before locking her car and heading in the direction Tasha had run. She knew where the dog was, so she wasn't concerned, only miffed that after nearly a year, the little thing didn't know what the word "no" meant. Or stop. Or stay, for that matter.

She spied the little fur ball's tail wagging crazily as the dog jumped up and down near a bunch of guys working near the new playground. A shock of white hair told her Carl Hoder was already there, and she was happy to see so many volunteers out early on this Monday morning. Several trailers were parked nearby, filled with trees, shrubs, and flowers. Rain the night before had cut the humidity, and the early morning temperatures were in the mid-seventies. It was the perfect combination of sunshine, fresh air, and spirit. The conditions were perfect to plant things and make them grow. But more importantly, at least for Ruby, she could forget how in less than a month her life had spiraled (and not in the right direction), and she'd taken two steps backward.

No. More like ten. The thought was depressing, and maybe it was childish, but she was going to pull a Scarlett O'Hara and think about it tomorrow. Or the day after that. Or maybe never.

"Ruubeee!"

Ruby smiled and spied a little girl running toward her. Her gait was uneven and she couldn't run fast, but Miley Wellington's enthusiasm was hard to miss. Her little arms waved crazily, and she nearly toppled herself at one point, but her giggles had wings and seemed to pick her up. She didn't stop running until she collided with Ruby.

Thin arms wrapped themselves around her waist, and Ruby dropped her tote so that she could scoop the girl into her arms.

"Hey you," she said warmly, hugging Miley close. "You smell like sunshine."

"You look like sunshine and rainbows and unicorns."

Ruby laughed. "You've been watching the princess video again."

"Uh-huh," the little girl said with a wide smile. "It's my favorite."

Ruby dropped a kiss to Miley's cheek and shifted her so that she rested on her hip. The girl was six years old, but small for her age. She sometimes had trouble talking because it took a while for her brain to figure out what it was she wanted to say, and her coordination wasn't great, but the love in her heart was bigger than all of it. And that was a tribute to her mother, Thena. The woman had been an alcoholic most of her teen years and well into her twenties, which meant that Miley had been born suffering from the effects of fetal alcohol syndrome.

They say every addict has a trigger. A button that once pushed, plunges them further into addiction or the reverse. For Thena, holding her newborn, an innocent suffering because of her alcoholism, a disease that had seen her drinking a fifth of vodka per day, as well as six to twelve beers while pregnant, well, that had been her trigger.

She forged a new path, took responsibility for her life—the past that had shaped her—and hadn't had a drink since delivering her daughter. Green Thumb for the Soul had been involved in helping out the young family, and it made Ruby feel blessed to have been able to play a part, however small.

"I miss you too." She squeezed Miley one more time and then set her down, smiling as the little girl instantly shoved her hand into Ruby's. "Where's your mom?"

"She's over there." Miley pointed toward one of the trailers filled with plants, and with an eye on Tasha (who was now chasing her tail) Ruby headed over. She took a few minutes to catch up with Thena and then left Miley with Tasha. She headed over to Carl. The man was dressed in long pants, long sleeves, and a wide brim hat that had seen better days. Ruby shook her head.

"Carl. You must be baking in those clothes."

He offered a wry smile. "Better that then a sunburn."

"You have heard of something called sunscreen, right?" She chuckled and set down her tote. "I've got extra."

He made a face. "They all smell like coconut."

"Carl," she chuckled. "You need to broaden your horizons. I

brought a new product we've been selling at the spa. It's called Ocean Breeze."

"No offense, Ruby, but that sounds like the fancy spray my wife," he looked toward the sky, "God rest her soul, used to keep in the bathroom."

Ruby knew she couldn't win, so she gave up and looked around. "So what's the plan for the day?" She glanced back to Carl and caught him staring at her with an expression that was off. He looked...weird. "Something wrong?"

"I didn't think you'd come today."

That left her puzzled. "Why wouldn't I? We talked about this at our board meeting last week. You know how important this project is to me." A thought hit, and her stomach clenched. "Is it Ryder? What's he done now?"

"I haven't heard from Ryder. I just..." He grimaced and scratched his chin. "Did you listen to my voice mail?"

"No." She frowned. "My cell phone died last night, and I forgot to charge it this morning. What's going on, Carl?"

She watched the man as a growing sense of unease settled in her gut.

"It's Travis," Carl admitted, eyes still on her.

"What about him?" But she knew. Somehow, she knew, and her gaze scanned the area behind them.

"He's volunteered to help out, and I, well, I didn't think. I know you two aren't exactly friends."

"Carl," she said gently. The man's discomfort was obvious. "Don't be silly. We need all the help we can get. I'm fine." She pasted what she hoped was a normal-looking smile on her face. "Really. I'm good."

Carl wasn't fooled. Not one bit. He cleared his throat. "He's working with the crew planting trees on the other side of the park. I don't expect you'll see much of him if you stick with me. We're working on the perennials."

She kept that smile in place even though her emotions were all over the place. She felt nauseous and light-headed, and her muscles tightened in protest. Stress had never been her strong suit.

"Put me to work where you need me."

"You're sure?"

"Carl, I'm not a pussy." The fact that she felt like bolting wasn't something she was proud of. "I'm positive."

"Okay." Carl pointed to the large trailer full of grasses, hydrangeas, and lilies. "You're with me. Let's get started."

They worked together for several hours, and eventually, the tension in Ruby's shoulders dissipated as the fresh air, the earth and flowers, worked their magic. For a brief moment, she almost forgot that the only man on the planet who could throw her off balance was several hundred feet away. She should be mourning the fact she and Chance were done. She should be pissed that he'd betrayed her. Tricked her. But all she could think about was Travis.

Ruby sank back onto her haunches and wiped sweat from her brow. Her gaze found its way back to the other side of the park, and she watched as Travis and Zach propped up the last ornamental pear tree and readied it for planting. Travis's face was hidden behind by his old ball cap and aviators. Dressed in old work boots, beige khaki shorts, and nothing else, he attracted more than just her gaze. In fact she noticed at least five women who kept glancing his way. Why wouldn't they? His wide shoulders and impressive pecs glistened in the sun, and his killer smile was in full force as he chatted with his buddy.

Did he even know she was there? Honey, the bartender from the Coach House, was with them, and Ruby looked away, patting the dirt around the hydrangea bush. Something dark coursed through her. It was hot and sharp, and she might have attacked the dirt a little too aggressively, but hell, she needed to release whatever it was before she said or did something she'd regret.

No way was she jealous. She didn't care that the attractive

brunette was practically leaning against him as they planted the tree. Or that she'd been with him the entire day. Travis could do whatever he wanted with whomever. He meant nothing to her.

She closed her eyes. That wasn't true. God, she wished it was, but after the other night, she couldn't deny there was still something there. Was it a need to find closure? A need to confess her sins? The acknowledgment that he wasn't entirely to blame?

Was it guilt and nothing more?

She didn't know what it was, but Ruby was about done with it. At least for today. She'd finish up and head home.

She reached for the watering can and nearly knocked the damn thing over, cursing under her breath as she stood and bent over, making sure the plant got enough water to survive its first few days after transplant. She was so focused on ignoring Travis Blackwell that she had no idea anyone was behind her until she straightened and backed up, stopping cold when a hard, male body stopped her progress.

A hand on her hip. The other on her shoulder. She didn't have to turn around to know who it was. Travis.

"Hey." His voice was low. "I didn't want you to fall."

It took a lot of effort to keep her shit together, and Ruby carefully extricated herself from his touch, turning slowly so that she faced him. She had to tip her head up to see him properly, and he dragged off his aviators, his warm brown eyes serious as he looked down at her.

She didn't know what to say. Or do. She was very aware that a lot of folks were suddenly interested in what was going down in the hydrangea garden. Some of them were discreet. Others, like Lou Anne Simmons, not so much. She was bent over her wheelbarrow so far that if she wasn't careful, she'd topple the damn thing.

"These look great," Travis said, eyeing the bushes she'd just planted.

"They do."

His eyes were searching as if waiting for her to say something. But then he surprised her. "I met a woman—Thena. She said she's a friend of yours."

Ruby nodded. She couldn't get any words out. Her throat was too tight. The damn lump too big.

"She told me what you did for her and her little girl." He motioned behind him. "What you do for most of these folks." A slow smile crawled across his face. "You always had a thing for those in need. People with real problems or those who were just plain dumb. Remember Mason Winkworth?"

"Mason?" The lump cleared, the muscles relaxed. "Oh my God. I haven't thought of him in years." She nodded and looked away, hiding her face and feeling vulnerable.

"It was the harvest dance, right?"

She nodded. "Grade five."

"Nope. Middle school grade six. I remember because our teacher was Mr. Buckburn and, man, the lecture we got."

Before the dance, there'd been a celebration of harvest in the gymnasium, not unlike a typical fall fair. Artwork dotted the walls, music filtered through the speakers, and there were several competitions on the go. One of them was a throwback to the strength of the many lumberjacks who'd settled in the area hundreds of years earlier. Now, with the event taking place inside the school and for safety concerns, there were no saws or axes. There were heavy pieces of wood and a bunch of boys full of bravado and bragging rights.

Mason Winkworth was a kid who'd matured early for a boy, and in grade six, he was already head and shoulders above the rest of his class. He wasn't known for his mental prowess or his athletic ability, but the kid was brawny and determined to win the last competition. It was a test of strength and endurance.

He'd lined up at the chin-up bar, a young Travis Blackwell at his side, among others, and when the whistle blew, the boys hauled themselves up and held their bodies in place for as long as they could.

Slowly they dropped, until there were only four boys left. And that was when…

"Wasn't it My Little Pony?" Travis asked chuckling.

"No." Ruby shook her head. "SpongeBob."

"Right."

Mason Winkworth's track pants had slowly fallen down around his ankles, and his choice in undergarments had left the entire gym in giggles, with more than a few hecklers in the bunch. Not only that, the boxers were on the small side and he… well, he wasn't.

"His face got so red, and he was so embarrassed," Ruby said slowly. "I knew he wouldn't give up until he won, and I knew you wouldn't give up because you were having too much fun."

She'd jumped from her seat in the bleachers and run to the boy who was now grunting with the effort to hold himself up, while using his feet, rubbing them along his calves to somehow get his pants back up. Which wasn't happening. She yanked them back into place and held them so they couldn't fall back down.

And she stood behind him for at least another five minutes until Mason Winkworth was the last man standing. Or rather, hanging.

"I asked you to dance." Travis's voice took on a husky tinge that had all sorts of alarm bells ringing inside Ruby. "Do you remember?"

"I said no." She swallowed thickly. He was so close, she could count the individual lashes that framed his eyes so beautifully. She could see the gold flecks that lit the depths of his dark eyes.

Travis cracked another smile. "You said I was a jerk. Told me I should have dropped as soon as Mason's pants had."

"You should have," she replied, licking her lips, a nervous gesture she wished she could take back. His eyes had followed her movement, and now they rested on her mouth, their depths dark and intense.

"I like to win."

"But you didn't." Ruby watched him closely.

"Not that time," Travis replied, his expression changing. Were they even talking about the same thing anymore? He took a step back. "We're heading to the Tappery, next county over, for burgers. My treat. You coming?"

Ruby stared up at Travis for several moments, not sure what to say or how to act. In the end, she took the coward's way out. She shook her head. "I've got Tasha here." She turned in a circle. "Somewhere. I don't think she'd be allowed in a restaurant."

"You could take her home and then come."

"Why?" The question fell out of her mouth before she could take it back.

Travis sighed and ran his hand over the back of his neck. He yanked on the brim of his hat and nailed her with a look she knew all too well.

"We need to talk, Ruby. Can we do that?" His tone was cajoling, his eyes warm and inviting. And Jesus H Christ. The man had spent the entire day working outside in the hot sun. Did he have to smell this good?

"I can't." She backed away before she could change her mind. "I promised Ryder I'd swing by and we'd do dinner. It's like our Monday-night thing." She'd promised no such thing, but it was the only excuse she could come up with.

Travis was silent for a few seconds. "Okay. Another time?"

"Travis." She had to take a moment. "You've moved on and so have I. And as you pointed out the other night, you're not the only one to blame. I did things too. And maybe it's time for me to let go of the anger. There's nothing else to say or do. Let's just leave things alone."

"I can't do that." Those alarm bells that had fallen silent were now clanging again, heavy against her chest, making it difficult for Ruby to breathe or think or speak. The air was rife with an invisible force that was drawing her to him. It scared the crap out of her.

"Why not?" she managed to squeak out.

"Because I like to win."

"This isn't a game, Travis." She took a step back, anger making her hot and fidgety.

"It is, though." He got up in her business again. "It's the most important game of my life." Travis reached for Ruby, and God help her but she couldn't move. It was as if her feet were encased in cement. Her heart fluttered, and she felt dizzy.

Or maybe quicksand.

His hands settled on either side of her face, and he held her gently, bending even lower so that when he spoke, his breath caressed her mouth like a kiss. She tried to move as panic set in, but he held her firm, his voice throaty. "Let me do this, Ruby. So that we know. *So that I know.*"

He held her gaze a second longer and then swept his mouth across hers, a gentle caress that lit fires and rang those bells and made her knees weak. It made her want to close her eyes and go back in time. Back to before the marriage and the baby. Back to that first summer. It wasn't a kiss so much as promise, and she barely managed to hold herself together. When he stepped back, she finally exhaled, a long, slow, ragged breath.

"What do you know?" Did she speak the words out loud?

"This thing between us, it's not going anywhere. It's part of us. Like DNA." He was dead serious. "So why are we fighting it?"

"Why are we *fighting* it?" Unbelievable. Ruby had to take a moment to try to process what he was saying. "I can think of a million reasons why, Travis, starting with the fact that we're divorced. We didn't do so well the first time around."

He looked away for a moment, and Ruby was able to catch her breath. She waited, like a fool, she waited, and when he turned

97

back, her heart squeezed so damn tight, it brought tears to her eyes.

"Maybe this could be different."

She was confused. And angry. Strangely exhilarated. And scattered. She tried to make sense of the jumbled thoughts rambling around inside her head. She tried again. "Too much has happened between us, and too much time has passed."

"Doesn't matter."

"It *does* matter." He wasn't going to make this easy. "Our history is complicated, Trav. And aside from that, I live in Crystal Lake now, which I'm sure has surprised the hell out of you, but I've made a life for myself. One that I'm proud of and one that fulfills me." Okay, the proud thing was true. The fulfilled? Not so much. "You don't live here anymore. You live in Detroit. You live in LA. You have a house in the Hamptons for God's sake."

His eyebrow shot up. "Been stalking me online?" He grinned. "I'm cool with that."

Embarrassed, she was silent for a few moments, because, yeah, she'd stalked him online. "I'm just saying we could never work from a logistics point of view."

"If that's your only reason, then I'm feeling pretty confident considering a few days ago, you hated my guts."

He was always so damn cocky and sure of himself. "What is it you think we're going to do? Pick up where we left off? Because that's never going to happen."

"No," he said. "But that doesn't mean we can't start a new chapter. I'm not going anywhere anytime soon."

A lightbulb went off. "This is about sex. You want to have sex with me."

He looked confused at first and then shrugged, offering a smile that would make most women melt. Except Ruby wasn't most women, and she was an expert when it came to Travis Blackwell's charm.

"We never had a problem with sex," he replied, that damn smile still intact.

"No. It was the other stuff that kicked our asses."

"Maybe we need to forget about the other stuff."

The air was electric. Practically sizzling. "And just have sex?"

"Is that what you want?"

"I don't want anything," she replied.

He stepped close, and she held her breath, afraid to breathe. "You're lying. You want me as much as I want you."

Ruby Montgomery had taken leave of her senses, because she was actually considering his words. Sex with no strings? Could she do that with Travis and survive?

Travis held her gaze a heartbeat longer. He gave her a smile that told her he didn't give a damn about anything she'd just said. It was a quick, wicked smile that spoke volumes. It was a warning. Travis Blackwell was playing to win.

"I'll see you around."

"I don't think so, Travis." It was an attempt to make things clear, but even to Ruby, her voice sounded unsure.

"It's a small town. Won't be a problem."

"True, but there's lots of hiding places. I can disappear if I want to. Make myself scarce." She thrust up her chin, praying her knees didn't give out.

"Good," he murmured. "It'll make finding you a lot more interesting."

He winked at her, slipped his aviators back in place, and walked away.

CHAPTER 11

*T*hree days earlier, Travis had had his come-to-Jesus moment. He knew what he needed to do. Where he needed to go. But damned if he was stuck on which way to get there.

He tossed his hammer and stood back, wiping sweat from his brow as he gazed across the water at a fast-approaching boat. It was Thursday evening, and he'd spent the entirety of the afternoon fixing the dock at his dad's place, along with Wyatt and Zach. The boys had decided the day before to tackle the project when Wyatt found out their father had hired a company to come out and do it. His brother was taking some time off from the NASCAR circuit and cooling his heels at Regan's place, and Travis, well, he was fed up trying to nail down Ruby. She'd been good on her word. He hadn't set eyes on her since Monday, and that wasn't from lack of trying.

"It's Nash," Wyatt said with a grin as the boat slowed.

"I think that's Hudsy with him." Their older brother had gone to the city with his wife and newborn for a doctor's appointment earlier in the day. Travis was glad to see him.

"Thought Nash would be busy at the bar." Travis stretched

sore muscles. It had been a while since he'd worked with his hands, and he glanced down at the blisters forming along his palm and fingers and smiled. It felt good.

"Hudson was looking for an excuse to get away, so I ordered us up some food."

Travis's stomach rumbled at the thought, but he nodded toward the house. "You don't think Darlene is gonna have a problem with that?"

The woman lived for cooking and liked nothing more than to have all "her boys" gathered around a table laden with food she'd prepared.

"Nope. She and Dad are going to the Little House Theatre to see a play."

Surprised, Travis yanked his head back. Since when was their father well enough to sit through a play?

"I know." Wyatt shrugged. "He makes an effort for her, but I won't be surprised if they come home early." He rubbed his hands together. "In any case, I thought Nash could look after us and save firing up the barbecue."

"Since firing up the barbecue is such a chore."

Wyatt shoved Travis. "It's not the barbecue so much as Darlene's pristine patio. That new set they bought is worth more than this damn deck. All we'd need is one of you ding-dongs to get crap all over it. I just didn't want to deal. You know how Dad gets. Remember when we had the party, that time he and Darlene went away for the weekend? That girl Hudson was seeing spilled red wine all over the white sofa in the family room. Jesus, I thought the old man's head was going to pop off. He made us work the whole summer to pay him back what it cost to replace the damn thing. And I'm pretty sure we could have had it cleaned."

Travis nodded but didn't respond. John Blackwell had always been a hard-ass. It had just gotten worse after their mother passed. Nothing seemed to please him, and he'd taken every opportunity to point it out.

After a while, Travis offered, "He's changed."

"Most men do when they're dying." His brother's words were eerily similar to what his father had said only a few days earlier.

"Sometimes it's too late, and sometimes it isn't." Wyatt looked back at Travis. "And sometimes it just doesn't matter anymore."

As his brother walked away from him, Travis realized just how fractured his family still was.

Nash and Hudson hopped onto the dock and handed over two extra-large pizzas, a basket of dry Cajun chicken wings, and three boxes of piping-hot fries. Wyatt disappeared into the boathouse and returned holding a large bucket filled to the brim with beer and ice.

"This is more like it." Travis grinned, slapping the oldest Blackwell on the shoulder. "Rebecca let you out to play?"

"More like I ran when she gave me the opportunity."

"What's that mean?" Travis asked, reaching down for a beer and tossing a cold one to Hudson.

"There are at least thirty women in my house, six babies, four toddlers, and two dogs."

"I thought you liked women and babies," Travis said with a chuckle.

"I do. Especially mine." Hudson cracked open his can and took a long pull. He wiped foam from the corner of his mouth. "But a guy can only take so much. I bolted when they all started in with their war stories."

"War stories?" Travis repeated.

"Labor. Delivery. Contractions." He winced. "Stitches."

"Stitches?" That one had Travis scratching his head. Man, giving birth was a hell of a lot more complicated than he imagined. He frowned. Stitches?

Hudson shook his head, the look in his eyes dead serious. "You don't want to know."

Travis decided to take his brother's word for it and turned to Nash. "Since when does the Coach House deliver on the lake?"

Nash handed him a slab of pizza. "Since I took the night off to kick back."

Zach sidled in for a slab and scooped out a beer for himself. "Honey working tonight?"

Nash practically growled. "Sure is. Thought you'd be polishing a barstool at my place instead of out here."

Zach was too busy shoving pizza down the hatch to notice the particular undertone to Nash's words. "I might head up there later."

"You do that."

Zach caught it that time and gave Nash a look, but the man had turned away to secure the boat properly.

Travis chewed off a piece of double cheese and looked at his brothers. Hudson shrugged, and they all sat back, content to listen to the waves rush up against the shore, eat their pizza and wings, and listen to some vintage Zeppelin.

The boys sat on the dock for a good hour or so. They polished off both boxes of pizza, all the wings, and not one fry was left behind. Travis gathered the empty containers and trudged into the boathouse, looking for the recycling bins. Hudson followed him and they got it all squared away. They made their way back outside just as the motor on Nash's boat revved, and watched Wyatt and Zach head out.

"Where they going?" Hudson asked.

"Your hockey pal wanted to see Pottahawk island. I told them to take my boat instead of hauling yours out of the boathouse." Nash got to his feet, and the three of them headed down the beach. Hudson grabbed the cooler while Nash and Travis gathered some kindling for a fire.

The sun was low in the sky as vibrant reds and oranges lit up the horizon. Twilight would be setting in soon. Already, Travis heard an owl hoot in the distance. The air was still heavy from the heat, but a breeze made its way across the lake, teasing white-caps that disappeared as soon as the waves hit the shore. Boats still zipped along the water; laughter and voices echoed in their wake.

God, Travis loved this time of day. That in-between when darkness was about to fall. It was always quiet—even with the laughter and voices. It was hard to explain, more of the stillness that accompanied nightfall.

The three of them had a fire going in no time, the well-worn pit a center for the semicircle of chairs. Travis leaned back in his chair, sank his feet in the sand, and closed his eyes. He should be content. He should be relaxed after a long day of hard work and a belly full of pizza and wings. Tired, even.

But he wasn't.

His mind was racing, and every time he closed his eyes, he saw her. Ruby. He'd managed to get her cell number from Coach Hoder, but she'd not returned any of the calls or text messages he'd sent her. How in hell was he going to get her to fall back in love with him if he couldn't even get her to answer a damn phone call? What was it going to take?

"You okay over there?"

Travis lifted up his head, opened his eyes, and spied his brother Hudson staring at him.

"You look like you want to hit something."

Travis glanced down at his hands. Both of them were fisted. He stared at them so long, his vision blurred, and then, with a curse, he unclenched them.

"You want to talk about it?" Hudson asked.

"You guys aren't going to hold hands and sing Kumbaya are you?" Nash popped open another can and slid farther back in his chair. Both Blackwells ignored him.

"How'd you and Rebecca get back together?" Travis asked, watching his brother closely.

Hudson was silent for a few moments as if contemplating his

words. "It took a lot. You were too young to remember or know anything, but I ended things badly, and she pretty much hated me when I left town."

"Something we have in common," Travis mumbled. He wasn't sure his brother heard him.

"I came back because Dad was sick." He shook his head. "No, I came back because he was dying. I had no desire to stay here. I had a job and a life that was good. But then I saw her, and things changed."

"She still hated you."

"Damn right she did." Hudson was quiet for a few moments. "It's true what they say about love and hate. They're two sides of the same coin. You can toss that sucker in the air and pray it lands the way you want it to. But it's still a fifty-fifty shot."

He stirred the fire with a long stick. "I convinced myself that she and I were never going to be together again. For a lot of reasons. The main one being I didn't think I deserved her. She'd been through a lot. Shitty marriage. Moving back here. She was raising a young son on her own, and I was a complication she didn't need. In my mind, she should have been with someone who existed on a level I couldn't even aspire to. But then I realized I something. None of us are saints. We're all human and we all make mistakes. But more importantly, we all deserve to be happy."

"It doesn't always happen," Travis muttered.

"No." Hudson agreed. "It doesn't. But you've got to at least try."

"Hudsy," Nash groaned, straightening up in his chair. "Should I just call you Doctor Phil?"

Hudson tossed his empty can at his friend with a chuckle. "Do that and I'm going to start charging for all these words of wisdom."

Nash looked at Travis. "Why don't you just come out and tell us what the hell it is that's bugging you?" He leaned forward.

"Nope. Wait." He shot a look toward Hudson. "You're not the only Doctor Phil in the house." He focused on Travis again. "I bet she's about five foot six with blonde hair that almost touches her ass, a temper like no other woman in town, and the kind of eyes that can see right through a man."

Busted.

Travis sighed. "She won't take my calls or answer my text messages, even though I can see she's read them. I've driven to the spa and she's never there, which is bull. Her car is in the parking lot. Hell, I even dropped in to see Ryder."

"What'd he say?" Hudson asked.

"He told me to go fuck myself."

"What did you expect? He has his problems, but him and Ruby are family. They've always been tight. And he's going to have her back even if she doesn't want him to. If Ryder thinks you're going to screw his sister over again, he'll do whatever it takes to keep you away from her."

Travis had nothing to say. He got it. He'd do the same if it were his sister. And that fact was a sobering thought.

"What is it exactly you expected to happen? Do you want to apologize to her? Is that what this is about?"

"Already done that."

"So it's something more." Hudson's eyebrow shot up. "She's seeing the golf pro. You know that, right?"

"Not anymore."

Hudson exchanged a look with Nash, who was now grinning.

Silence fell between the men. It stretched long and thin and became a kind of roaring in Travis's ears. His chest was tight and his hands fisted once more. The emotion in him was like a big balloon that had filled and was about to burst.

"I don't know what I want. Not exactly. But there's still something between us. I know it. She knows it."

"What are you saying?"

"I'm saying I want to spend time with her. I'm saying I miss her. I'm saying maybe I should never have let her go."

"You're saying you want to have sex with her," Nash said dryly.

"No." The denial was instant. "I mean, yes, I want her, but it's more than just sex."

"What the hell does that mean?" Hudson asked. "Do you want her back, or is this a summer thing?"

Travis spied an eagle soaring over the water. It skimmed low across the lake, rising into the air and then dipping back, dragging its claws across the surface as it headed toward the forest that rose from the far shore. He thought back to the other night. To the expression in Ruby's eyes. To the sound of her voice. The tremble as she spoke.

"I don't know," he sighed. "It's not about wanting her back. It's about making it work."

"You have to be sure," Hudson said, shaking his head. "You don't want to open up old wounds for nothing. You could end up pushing her farther away."

Irritated, Travis looked at his brother. "If I could just track her down, I can make her see that we should at least try. Five minutes. That's all I need."

"Christ, you've got an inflated ego." Hudson snorted. "Only five minutes?"

"I can give you at least fifty."

Both men looked at Nash. "What do you mean?" Travis asked.

"At the charity golf dinner, I managed to snag the winning bid for a full-body massage at Ruby's spa." He paused, grinning wickedly. "It was offered up by the owner, which would be your ex."

"I'll double whatever you paid." Travis shot up.

"Triple it," Nash retorted.

"Done."

"Don't you want to know how much I paid?"

Travis shook his head. "Nope. Don't care. When's your appointment?"

"Tomorrow at four."

Travis's grin faded as he stared at the man across from him, and something dark curled in his gut. "You were going to get a massage from my Ruby?"

"First off, that woman doesn't belong to anyone but herself. And secondly, hell no," Nash said with a chuckle. "It was for my mother, but now I can get her an entire year's worth of fancy treatments at that spa with what you're going to give me."

Nash scratched his chin and grabbed a cold beer from the bucket. "Just don't screw it up, because if you piss her off, she'll kick both of our asses. And while you'd enjoy it, it's not something I look forward to. I've got enough complications in my life right now without adding Ruby Montgomery into the mix."

"Complications." Hudson looked at his friend. "What's that all about?"

Nash scowled. "You don't want to know."

"I kinda do," Hudson replied with a chuckle.

Travis however, wasn't paying attention because his mind was already on tomorrow. He had a plan, or at least the beginning of one. It wasn't perfect. Hell, it wasn't even thought out, which meant there was lots of room for error. He sat back in his chair and closed his eyes. All he needed was five minutes.

At least, he hoped so.

CHAPTER 12

*R*uby didn't look up when Jaylene walked into her office, because she'd been expecting her assistant. It was nearly five o'clock and had been hours since she'd grabbed a muffin and a coffee. When Jaylene offered to get her a bowl of butternut squash soup from The Blue Elephant, she'd happily agreed. Of course, she could have had someone from the restaurant run the soup up, but Jaylene had been flirting with Steven, one of the kitchen staff, for weeks now, and who was Ruby to stand in the way of that?

Besides, she had other things to worry about. She was nose-deep in catalogs and samples, trying to decide on a color scheme and "look" for the new bungalows being built adjacent to the main building. The painter needed her decision ASAP, and how could she offer the right choice when she was still unsure if she wanted a fresh Nantucket beach feel, or sultry Caribbean? She'd been finding it hard to concentrate all week. The reason was obvious. All six feet three inches of him.

Trying to block Travis Blackwell from her mind was exhausting.

On top of that, she had exactly twenty minutes until she was expected downstairs for Lisa Booker's massage.

Her nostrils flared as the aroma of sweet butternut filled the air, and she tossed her reading glasses onto her desk when Jaylene set down a generous bowl, along with a spoon and two large biscuits.

"Your brother's here," Jaylene said and stepped back.

Great. Another distraction.

She was trying to decide between a blue-based gray and a green-based gray. Then there was the clay color she liked. Or maybe she should stick with an earthier tone. She bit her lip, concentrating, and reached for the bowl. Right now, she didn't have time for Ryder and his problems. Lord knows she had enough of that stuff in her own life.

"Tell Ry I'm busy. Tell him to grab some dinner in the restaurant, and I'll stop in after I'm done with the massage."

"Why don't you tell him yourself?" Ryder slid into the leather chair in front of her desk and grinned.

Shit, was Ruby's first reaction. Her second? Surprise. Her brother looked—she blinked, just in case there was lint or something in her eyes. But when her vision cleared, her first impression was the same. Ryder looked damn good.

"Thanks, Jaylene," she murmured, pushing the catalogs aside. She opened her drawer, searching for the aspirin bottle she kept handy. Stress and lack of sleep had finally caught up to her. The headache that had been threatening all day was knocking on her door, and she just needed to get through a few more hours until she could kick back with a glass of wine and try to forget it all. She grabbed two small white pills, popped them in her mouth, and swallowed them down with a big gulp of water.

"You look like shit," Ryder said, leaning back and threading his hands behind his head. He was dressed casually. Plain white T-shirt, beige khakis, and tan deck shoes. His hair was clean, the russet waves thick and curling around his ears. His blue eyes were bright, and his handsome face looked rested. He was still on the thin side, the sharp cheekbones and jawline attested to that, but there was definitely something different about him.

"Thanks," she replied. "For once, you don't."

He laughed. And for one moment, Ruby's heart melted because it was a genuine, full-bodied laugh—a sound she hadn't heard in a very, very long time. She found herself smiling as she watched him, her hectic, stressful week fading away as she caught a glimpse of the brother she used to know. The one she missed so much, it hurt to think about. She couldn't help it. The hope she kept buried deep inside burst to life and warmed her from the inside out. It made her smile wider, her eyes misty and her throat tight.

But Ruby wasn't stupid. They'd been down this road before. Many times, in fact. Such was the cycle of an addict. They got clean. They got better. They went to work. Had relationships. Good relationships. Some that even lasted a significant amount of time. But then something gave way. A small crack no one noticed until it was too late. The crack split open, swallowing everything good and whole until there was nothing left but a shell. They were back using, and all the they'd accomplished slid into the gutter.

"What's up?" she asked lightly, watching her brother closely. The siblings stared at each other in silence until finally Ryder shrugged, that small smile still tugging on the corners of his mouth.

"I got a job."

Again, that small fire inside Ruby flared. He'd been without work for over a year. Ever since he'd been fired from his last job —working for her. She tried not to be too gushy—her brother didn't like that. She leaned forward. "Ryder, that's amazing. Where? What? Give me the details."

"It's not a big deal."

"It is, and you know it." When was the last time he'd done

something without her pushing him into it? Without her making the phone calls and scheduling the appointments? She'd been carrying his load for so long, she forgot what it felt like to have him take the initiative.

Something flickered in the depths of his eyes, and she could tell he was nervous. Who wouldn't be? He had a checkered past. There was no getting around that. A lot of ups and downs. In and out of rehab. Booze, pills, weed, and who knows what else. Her brother had had so much potential. So much to give this world, and it hurt her heart when she thought of all he'd lost. Especially the things he didn't *even know* he'd lost.

He held her gaze and then looked away, clearing his throat a bit, and brushing imaginary lint from his shirt.

"It's in the city."

"Traverse?"

He nodded. "I've been fooling around with my portfolio."

She was surprised. "You're taking pictures again?"

"I, ah…" He rolled his shoulders and settled back in the chair as if biding time, searching for the right words. "I was organizing the back room and came across some of my stuff. It got me thinking about how much I loved photography. I don't know. Maybe it's fate or something like that, but I saw an ad for the tourism board in Traverse City. I spent the last few days taking shots around here and emailed them in. They called this morning with the offer. I didn't even have to interview, which I guess is a good thing. They must have been desperate."

Ruby was up and out of her chair before Ryder had a chance to say anything else. She wrapped her arms around her brother. "They're not desperate," she whispered fiercely. "Your talent, your eye behind the lens is incredible. You've always seen things no one else does."

Blinking tears from her eyes, she exhaled and then slowly untangled her arms from around Ryder.

"There's just…"

"What?" She frowned, her heart sinking. There was always something, wasn't there?

"It's Traverse City. There's no bus, and I don't...well, the old Civic is on its last legs, so I was kind of hoping we could work something out. I thought maybe you could cosign so I could get new wheels. My credit's not so good." He looked away in embarrassment.

"Of course." She didn't need to think it over. Didn't need to ponder the pros and cons of signing her name on the dotted line for him. This was her brother. She would do whatever it took to make sure that this time, he made it. "Whatever you need, Ryder. We can go to the dealership tomorrow." She checked her watch. "Tonight, even. I have a massage—"

"Hey, slow down." He cracked a grin. "Tomorrow is good." Ryder frowned. "Since when do you give massages? I thought that part of your job was over and done with. You know, since you own the place."

"I offered a personal massage for the fundraiser last week, and Nash's mother is booked for five twenty." She glanced at her watch. "Shoot, I gotta run. Lisa must be here already, and I still have to change."

Ryder got to his feet, and she slipped her arms around him for one last hug. God, even the feel of him was different.

"I had lunch with Sid," he said slowly.

Ruby wasn't expecting that. She pulled away and looked up at him. "You still have the power to hurt her, Ry. You know that, right?"

He nodded. "She's a big girl, Ruby."

"Ryder." There was a warning in her voice, but she wasn't so sure Ryder heard it. He might see things not everyone did, but in other areas of his life, he was clueless.

"Relax. It was just lunch. And it was her that called me, just so you know." He paused, looking a bit sheepish. "Actually, it was

Sidney who showed the me the ad, and the lady who did the hiring knows her."

Ruby filed that information away. She'd been so busy trying not to think about her personal life that she'd closed herself off from everything. She hadn't talked to Sidney or Ryder. And she definitely hadn't talked to—

"Travis came to see me to."

"What?" Eyes wide, she took a step back. "Why? What did he want?"

Ryder watched her for a few seconds. "I didn't ask. I told him to go screw himself."

Good. That make her happy. Kind of.

"Are you two…"

"What?" She shook her head. "No. Never." Her denial sounded lame. So lame, in fact, that Ryder's eyebrows narrowed and he frowned.

"He drove me home a few weeks ago. From the Coach House. I'd had one too many, and he took my keys and drove me home. Put me to bed too."

"Oh." It was the only word Ruby managed to get out.

Ryder took a step toward the door and shrugged. "Maybe I should have asked what he wanted."

"No. I'm glad you didn't. Whatever it is, doesn't matter."

"You sure about that?"

"Positive." It was Ruby's turn to pick a piece of invisible lint from her skirt.

"If you were positive, you'd be looking me in the eye."

The door closed behind her brother, and she took a step after him—Ruby liked to have the last word—but then turned and headed to her private bathroom. She would get her last word in the next time she saw Ryder. She grabbed the bag she'd brought to work and changed into black yoga pants, a plain white V-neck T-shirt with the spa logo above her right breast, and pulled her hair back into a ponytail. It had been a long time since she'd given a massage, and she was looking forward to it. She would let the atmosphere; the soothing music, and scents take her to another place. One where she could forget all about the man who kept infiltrating her life.

She slipped her feet into comfortable flip-flops and grabbed a water bottle on the way out. It didn't take long to reach the spa area, and she spied Megan, the receptionist.

"Is my client in?" she asked, smiling at the lady paying for her services. Mrs. Avery was the local florist and a woman Ruby had known her entire life. She gave Ruby a sly smile and turned to Megan, who looked a bit uncomfortable, which made Ruby frown.

"Room three," Megan replied.

"Great."

"Ruby, um…"

She'd taken a few steps and looked back at Megan. "Yes?"

The phone rang, Mrs. Avery was still grinning, which should have set off a few alarm bells, and Ruby tapped her foot impatiently. Nash had paid a lot of money for his mother's massage.

"Can it wait?"

Her receptionist still looked uncomfortable or weird or…well, she definitely looked like *something*, but Ruby didn't have time to dig into the problem. "We'll talk about whatever it is tomorrow. I'll lock up since Lisa is the last client tonight." She winked at Mrs. Avery. "Have a great weekend."

"You too, dear." The woman's words echoed down the hall as Ruby made her way toward room three. She paused, realizing she didn't have the release form all clients were supposed to sign. Megan would have looked after this, and considering she knew the client and it was for the fundraiser, Ruby let herself in.

"Hey, Lisa."

The smell of peppermint and eucalyptus filled the air, while soft music and muted lighting set the tone. Ruby set her water bottle on the shelf just beside the door, noticing a large pair of flip-flops on the floor, and neatly folded clothing on the chair.

She smiled. Wow. Nash's mother had some big feet. She turned toward the table, and her grin slowly faded away. The naked back, muscled shoulders, tapered waist, and round ass definitely didn't belong to Lisa Booker. Hell, it didn't belong to any woman she knew. It was too masculine. Too damn perfect. It wasn't just any ass.

It was a hockey ass, and it was one she knew well.

Her eyes traveled back up until she spied the tattoo on the right shoulder. A vine with the initials R & T. She had the matching one on her lower back. To this day, it was an embarrassment Ruby was too chicken to have removed. What a cliché. The girl from the wrong side of town and the tramp stamp to show for it. Travis thought it was hot. He used to rub it when he was behind her and they were—

Cheeks warm, Ruby didn't know if she should yell or scream or turn around and leave. Like an idiot, she stared at Travis, silent, holding her breath, wondering if he'd fallen asleep and maybe didn't know she was there.

Maybe she could sneak out and get one of the other girls to come in. She took a step back, her mind racing. All the RMTs were busy with their last clients of the day, and that only left Megan, who wasn't certified to massage anything other than her own feet.

She clenched her hands together, her fingernails making crescent shapes in her palm as she inched toward the door. Travis was asleep. He had to be. If not, he would have hit her with something as soon as she'd opened the door.

She didn't know what game he was playing, but she had no desire to join in. She reached for the door, gently turned the handle, but then his voice cut through her body like a hot knife through butter.

"You're late."

Ruby froze, and every muscle in her body tensed. She took a moment, waiting for him to say something else. When he didn't, she relaxed a bit and slowly turned around.

"What are you doing here?"

"I came for a massage."

"I had Lisa Booker down as the fundraiser client."

"Nash sold me the bid."

"He did." *Mental note. Kill Nash next time you see him.*

"He did." Travis angled his head to the side.

"Why?"

"I tripled what he paid."

"No. I mean why would you think this is okay? Seriously. On what planet did you think I would be okay with this? What do you want, Travis? Just tell me, and let's get this over with."

"My back's a little tight from shoring up Dad's dock, and I pulled my quad lifting yesterday. My shoulders—"

"That's not what I meant," she snapped, moving toward the bed. He rolled over and nearly took the blanket with him. "Why are you here?"

He pushed himself up onto his elbows, and shadow caressed skin and bone and muscle. He looked like a god. *Of course he looks like a god.*

"I told you. I need a massage, and Nash was willing to take the cash for his winning bid."

Red-hot anger hit her. He looked so damn sure of himself, and she wanted to wipe the look off his face more than she cared to admit. A strange sort of exhilaration fell over her, and she found herself engaging him when she probably should have ignored him and marched her butt back out of the room.

"You want a massage," she repeated carefully.

He nodded.

"From me."

"You think you're up for it? I mean, I heard you're the best." He was playing her, and she was having none of it.

"Actually, Darnell is the best. He's not in today, so I would suggest you come back tomorrow or Monday, and he would be more than happy to work out your knots."

"I want you."

Her heart skipped a beat. "That's not a good idea."

"Why's that exactly?" A ghost of a smile touched his mouth and drew her gaze down. She realized her heart was nearly beating out of her chest, and it would be a miracle if he couldn't hear it.

His smile widened, and she tore her gaze from his mouth to settle back on his eyes. He'd just challenged her, and Ruby had actually considered leaving. Crawling out of this room and letting him win. In the words of one very wise and talented Tom Petty, no way was she backing down. A thought struck her then. A devious sort of thought that maybe, on another day when she was thinking clearly and not sleep deprived, would never have popped into her head. But it was there, taking hold and making her feel bold.

"I don't think you can handle me," she retorted softly, not bothering to hide the dangerous edge to her voice. "I've had clients leave, barely able to walk, depending on the type of massage they requested. What kind are you looking for?" Her words were light. Almost clinical.

"You know. The deep-tissue kind."

"I wouldn't want to hurt you."

Travis held her gaze, and she didn't back down. She watched him, breath held, anticipating...what? What the hell was she doing?

"Let's get started and see," he replied, voice so low, she barely heard him. "Do you want me on my stomach or back?"

Her heart lurched, and she swallowed thickly. She had to take a moment because she didn't trust herself to speak. Was she really going to do this?

"Stomach."

Yep. She was really going to do this.

Travis didn't hesitate. He turned over, and this time, the blanket slipped so low, his damn hockey ass was on full display. Hell, yeah, he was definitely naked. She yanked the blanket back in place and then reached for her oil. She could do this. She would rub the warmed liquid over every single inch of Travis Blackwell's body and get him so worked up, he wouldn't know what hit him. She would teach him a lesson. He thought he was seducing her, but she knew the score. She would bring him to the edge and then kick his butt out the door. She would make him regret ever coming back to Crystal Lake.

Ruby was in control here. Not him. Sex wasn't on the table. She could resist the pull.

Liar.

The word whispered through her brain, but it was so soft and low, she didn't hear it. Which was too bad, because as soon as Ruby's hand slid up Travis's back, she knew she was in trouble. But it was about three seconds too late to do anything about it.

CHAPTER 13

*T*wenty minutes of silence was all it took to get under Travis's skin. Well, twenty minutes of silence if you didn't count the heavy breathing (his) the music that was supposed to be relaxing but instead grated on every single nerve he owned, (hers) and the groaning of the bed as he kept moving around trying to find that elusive sweet spot. The one that allowed him a bit of relief and a whole lot more room for the hard package between his legs that was currently crushed against the massage bed.

Ruby's hands were now at the small of his back, and he stifled a groan as they crept a bit lower. If she got anywhere near his hips, he just might start humping the table like a damn animal. Maybe he hadn't thought his plan through. Maybe he was as crazy as Hudson thought he was. Or maybe he was just a glutton for punishment. He held his breath and clamped his teeth together as her hands worked their way back up his body.

He hadn't signed up for this torture.

"My goodness, you're tense," she said softly, her voice near his ear.

No shit, he thought.

His head was buried in the face pillow, and he grimaced, glad she couldn't see him. "Yeah," he managed to say without sounding too much like a candy ass. "The dock really did me in."

"Your father's, you said?" Again, her voice was close, throaty, sexy as hell. Her hands were insistent, and the smell of her was settled in his nostrils. God, she'd always smelled good. He kind of nodded, not trusting himself with words.

"Remember the first time we had sex?"

What the… His eyes flew open, and slowly, the floor beneath him materialized. His fingers dug into the face pillow and held on as if it were a life raft and he was drowning. He didn't answer because he couldn't.

"It was in your daddy's boathouse. The last night of the summer before senior year began. Do you remember?"

Images flashed before him. Naked limbs. Long blonde hair snaked around his body. Wide blue eyes filled with trust. His hand on her stomach.

Get. Your. Shit. Together.

With a hell of a lot of effort, Travis centered himself. He needed to get in the game before Ruby scored the first goal. And damned if she wasn't well on her way.

"You were a virgin."

Her hands stilled.

"You were scared."

She made a noise, like she'd unlocked something caught in her mind, and he kept going, not fighting the images anymore.

"It was raining, and we'd just come back from across the lake. Sunday barbecue at Bookers' cottage. You were wearing that baby blue bikini, the one that was my favorite, underneath a white dress."

"I remember that dress," she whispered. "It belonged to my mother."

"I knew I was in trouble the moment we tied up in the boathouse. You pulled that dress over your head and your hair got all tangled up in it. I had to help you. You were shaking. I think I told you we could wait, but you didn't want to."

"No." Ruby's hands lay on his skin, but they didn't move. "I wanted to know if everything I'd heard was true." She paused. "I wanted to know what it felt like to have you inside me."

Travis's heart was beating so loudly, it was a soundtrack inside his head. His dick was as hard as a rock, and he moved again, painfully aware that he was so close to the edge, he might not make it out of this room intact.

"What are you doing, Ruby?" he asked, voice rough and barely controlled.

He couldn't do this. He hadn't come to play games. He knew what she was up to. Ruby was trying to divert him from his mission. She was trying to use sex to get him off his game, and it had almost worked. But he hadn't come here to have sex with her.

He'd come here to make her see that this thing that still existed between them, it deserved another chance. *He* deserved another chance.

Travis pushed himself up and turned over in one smooth movement, catching Ruby by surprise. She took a step back and nearly tumbled onto her ass, but he grabbed her and pulled her to him. She was half on the bed with one of her legs braced on the floor, the other pretty much in his lap. Her hands splayed across his chest, the oil coating her fingers slick and warm. She looked down, and he followed her gaze, a tight smile in place because, *hello*, his dick was saluting them both as if it were the Fourth of July and he was the most patriotic man on the planet. The blanket she'd used barely covered him, not that it mattered.

She was breathing heavily but didn't turn away when he cradled the side of her head and, with a bit of pressure, slowly pulled her gaze back to his. God, she was so beautiful. He noticed her pulse beating at the base of her neck and the thin sheen of sweat on her forehead. Beneath the thin white T-shirt, her nipples pebbled—she was just as worked up as he was. He inhaled deeply, taking in the most basic scents known to man, the kind that couldn't be replicated. The kind that could drive a guy crazy.

It was primal. Want. Need. Desire.

It was all wrapped up in a heady mixture that circled them both like a hungry predator. Watching. Waiting to see who would break first.

"What do you think I'm doing?"

"I didn't come here for sex. I want you to know that." He measured his words carefully.

Her eyes widened, and she licked her bottom lip, but she held his gaze and didn't look away.

"I call bullshit, but whatever. I'll play along. What *did* you come here for?"

"You wouldn't take my phone calls or return my text messages."

"You've got to be kidding me." She blew out a long breath. "And coming here? Taking Lisa Booker's spot without my knowledge was the lightbulb going off in your brain? You thought this was the best place to have a conversation?"

He shrugged. "You didn't leave me much choice."

She pursed her lips, then opened her mouth. But then slammed it shut again without saying a word. The silence grew heavy and hot. It infiltrated his pores, and he shifted, still hard as a rock and more uncomfortable than he'd been in his entire life. This right here was his moment, and he needed to get it right.

"I miss you," he said after a while. "I miss everything about you."

"Travis. I miss my fifth-grade teacher, but that doesn't mean I want to have a relationship with her."

"I hope not. Mr. Rebuk might have a problem with that." He smiled, but she didn't return it, and then he decided to be completely honest. "Look, I still have feelings for you, and I'm pretty sure you do too."

"You still have feelings," she sputtered as she pulled away. Travis let her go, watching closely as she inched along the bed until there was some space between them. "When exactly did you figure that out? Two weeks ago when you realized that I'd moved on and had a life and was finally happy again? Did you see Chance and bang your damn chest like Tarzan and think you could walk back into my life and claim me like I'm some kind of animal?"

"Chance was an idiot. No way could he handle you."

"That's so not the point, Travis." Her eyes flashed. "But you'd like to think that, wouldn't you?" She smiled then, but it was the kind of smile that didn't reach her eyes. "For your information, he handled me just fine. Better than you, in fact."

Something dark and dangerous sparked inside him. His nostrils flared. His chest expanded. Truth be told, Tarzan was all wrong—at least he was evolved. Travis felt like a fucking Neanderthal. He wanted to grab hold of Ruby and make her forget she'd ever laid eyes on Chance McDougal.

"Ruby," he managed to get out before she shut him down.

"No. You don't get to talk right now."

Anger infused her skin. It filled her body and radiated heat. He saw it clear as day, and the Ruby he'd known, the one who used to drive him mad, was back. She was primed and ready to go, and nothing was going to stop whatever the hell was brewing inside her.

She slid from the bed and paced the small room, hands fisted at her side, head bowed. She paused in front of the door, and for a second, her hand rested on the handle. But then she pulled away and turned to him.

"I was happy, Travis. At least, as happy as I'm ever going to get. You might not like hearing that, but I was. You have no idea what it took to get to that place. A place where I didn't need you to make me happy. A place where I didn't think of you every day. Wonder about you. A place where I didn't hate you." Her voice shook. "Because I hated you." She fixed him with a pointed look. "God, I hated you." She exhaled a shaky breath. "I hated you as much as I loved you. And that was a lot."

She made no effort to hide her pain, and her words crushed Travis. He wanted to grab her up and hold her and make it all go away. All that pain. Pain that he'd caused.

She wrapped her arms around her body, and when she spoke, her voice was barely above a whisper.

"Those last few weeks before Nathan was born were so hard. You were on the road with the Red Wings, and I'd never felt so alone. I kept telling myself everything was going to be okay. That once the baby came, you'd forget about everything except us." She was silent for a few moments and met his gaze unflinchingly.

"You're right, you know. I stopped taking my pills. I wanted to get pregnant. I wanted to have a piece of you, a little human who was part of both of us, because I think even then I knew you were falling away from me. Falling away from us. And I was too young and too naïve to know that you didn't have to be my whole world. But back then? You were everything. I couldn't leave Crystal Lake because Dad was so sick and Ryder was mess. And you were in Chicago and on the road. You stopped coming home when you could and…"

Her voice caught, and it took everything in Travis to stay on the damn massage bed. He ached to hold her, but he knew if touched her right now, she would run. She might take a swipe at him. Maybe break his nose. But she'd run, and it would be over.

"Nathan was my miracle. My hope. He was this perfect little boy that I grew inside me, and he was everything." Tears slipped down her cheeks, but she made no move to wipe them away. "He had thick dark hair and blue eyes. He had ten perfect little toes and ten perfect little fingers. I kissed each and every one of them even as the doctors were telling me something was wrong. Even then." Her voice faded a bit, but only for a moment, and Travis got the feeling she was back there, in that hospital room, alone. With no one to lean on.

"How could a child that looked so perfect be damaged? How could he not survive? I remember thinking that I couldn't wait for you to meet him. For you to hold him and listen to him breathe. Because you would fall in love with him, and we would be a family. He was that perfect." She pounded her chest. "To me, he was that perfect. To me, he was exactly the way he was supposed to be.

"But it wasn't true. He wasn't perfect. He was broken. His heart…" She blew out a long breath, and when she spoke again, her voice was low and shaky. "When he died, something inside me broke, and I don't think it will ever be fixed. Sometimes I don't think I want it to, because it's the only link I have to Nathan. Our shared pain."

She swiped at her eyes. "I could have fallen completely apart. I could have withered and died, and then there would be no more pain. But I'm not wired that way. I couldn't let the darkness win. I learned to live with it."

Throat tight, Travis could only nod. She'd always been a fighter.

"I decided to remove the things from my life that hurt the most. The things I couldn't control. The things that made me want to curl up and hide." She pinned him with a look that made him go cold. "You were number one on that list, Travis. But unlike me, you didn't fight to save the marriage. You were relieved that it was over, and you didn't try to hide it. You could go on with your life and live your dream without us dragging you down. You signed those papers, gave me a lot of money, and that was it. Done."

"It wasn't that cut and dry." Not to his recollection, anyway. "You're making me out to be a coldhearted bastard."

"Weren't you?"

He was silent, not wanting to touch all the shit in their past.

But would there be a better time? Wasn't this what he'd come here for?

"You're wrong. I was a scared kid who was in deep, and I didn't have the tools to dig myself out. It was easier for me to let it ride. To convince myself that I was better off on my own. That I wouldn't be any good for you. And you know what? You made that easy. You didn't tell me you were in the hospital, Ruby. I had no clue you'd gone into early labor. No clue that you'd had Nathan." Pain hit him in the gut, and it clogged his throat so badly, he had to take a moment. "I would have been there for you. I know you don't believe it's true, but I know I would have been there."

"I don't believe that. You hadn't been home in weeks."

Travis drew in a ragged breath and ran his hand through the hair at his nape. "I didn't know anything until you called and told me the baby died." He looked her straight in the eye. "You didn't give me the chance to do the right thing. You took that away from me, and for a long time, I lived with that anger. I resented the hell out of you. And yeah, I backed away. It was how I dealt with it all. When you served those divorce papers, I thought the easiest way to make the pain stop was to sign them."

She scrubbed at her eyes again. "There's no point going over all this, Travis. Our connection is gone. It's severed. And it can't be fixed."

"It can."

She stared at him in silence, shoulders hunched forward, eyes filled with tears and pain and…regret?

This was not going the way he wanted it to. But then what had he expected? For Ruby to fall into his arms and forget the past?

"Let me prove it to you."

He got up from the massage bed, uncaring that he was fully nude, and crossed the room in three steps. She didn't move, but then she didn't really have anywhere to go. The door was at her back.

Travis stood in front of her, his heart aching, his body trembling with emotion. He reached for, breath held, sure that she was going to turn from him. When she didn't, that small sliver of hope burst into flame, and he sank his hands into the hair on either side of her head.

"Sex won't solve anything, Travis." Her words sounded small.

"This isn't about sex," he said, watching her closely. "That would be too easy. You know it. I know it. We both still want each other. There's no getting around that." He leaned forward, his warm breath caressing the side of her neck. He felt her tremble, and his body answered with a shudder.

He paused, and when he couldn't stand it anymore, when he felt like was going to break apart, he pressed his mouth to that spot just below her ear. The one where her pulse pounded crazily. Where her skin was silky soft. Where her scent was killer.

"Let me prove to you that there's still a chance to..."

"To what?" She made a sound of disgust. "What is it you see happening? What are we doing here?"

"I don't know," he answered truthfully. "But there's something here. Can't we at least see what it is?"

"Why?" she whispered.

"Why?" he answered roughly, pulling her closer. "Because this is me fighting, Ruby."

"Fighting for what? You've already lost, Travis. We've already lost."

"I'm not giving up."

She offered a small, sad smile. "You should. What you're feeling is guilt. And maybe I had a hand in that. But it's time to put this all behind us. We're no good for each other anymore. Maybe we never were."

Long seconds ticked by. Seconds when Travis felt his world tilt crazily. Seconds where his body tightened and his mind raced. This was it. The game was in overtime, and the clock was about to run out.

"Can we at least be friends?"

She turned her head. "I don't know." Ruby extricated herself from his grip and pushed him away. Truthfully? She could have pushed him onto his ass with one finger. She grabbed her water bottle from the table and left the room without another word.

He wanted to follow her and make her see that he was right. But he knew she needed some space, and he couldn't screw this up. He would give her space. All the space she needed.

For now.

CHAPTER 14

"*A*re you going to tell me what's going on?"

Ruby had just dropped off her brother and was about to back out of his driveway. Leave it to Ryder to let her get through the entire morning without asking the question he'd been dying to ask.

They'd spent an hour or so looking at cars, and he'd settled on a used Civic. It was a newer model than the one currently in the garage, with low mileage and a price that made it a no-brainer. They'd been lucky enough to have the credit people push his application through, and with Ruby cosigning, he would be able to pick up his new wheels in a few days. All in all, the exercise had taken less than two hours.

"Nothing is going on."

"That's not what I heard."

Wary, she watched her brother closely. "What did you hear exactly?"

Ryder leaned into her car, his eyes too penetrating, his mind too savvy. "I heard Blackwell showed at the spa last night, and you guys were locked in a room for almost an hour."

She yanked her head back and glared up at her brother. "Where in hell did you hear that?"

"You know what Crystal Lake is like. It's a well-oiled machine, and gossip is the fuel that makes the motor run." He stood up and shrugged. "I went for coffee first thing this morning. Mrs. Avery was in getting her triple cream and sugar with a bit of coffee on the side. She couldn't wait to tell me. And Ed Helms. And Joanne McBride."

Ruby gripped the steering wheel. She was cranky, tired, and more confused than she could ever remember feeling. And that was saying something. She couldn't do this with Ryder right now.

"It's not what you think," she managed to say.

"What is it, then?"

She drummed her fingers along the steering wheel, feeling defeated. "I don't know, Ry. I spent half the night asking myself that same question."

"Blackwell's always been your kryptonite." He was silent for a few moments. "You need to be careful with him. He might say he's changed, but it's hard to get your shit together when you reach a certain age. Too many battle scars. The idea sounds good, but the reality is different. On the other hand, sometimes a guy doesn't know what he had until he's lost it. If he's smart, that can be motivation enough for someone."

She looked up at her brother sharply. "Are you talking about Travis or yourself?"

"Maybe both." He sighed. "Look, I'm not normally the guy to give out advice."

"Then don't."

Ryder backed away. "Don't let him in again. Some of us are born to disappoint. It's in the blood." With a small wave, her brother disappeared inside the house. Ruby didn't want to dwell on Ryder's warning. She wanted to go home and forget about everything.

Crystal Lake was hopping, which wasn't surprising considering it was mid-July. It was still early, just past ten o'clock, and Ruby breezed through downtown, passing the coffee shop, which was conveniently located next to Mrs. Avery's flower shop. The woman in question stood on the sidewalk, a bunch of daisies in one hand and tulips in the other. She was chatting with Mrs. McGrath, whose husband owned the local art gallery, and both of them turned as she drove by. Ruby fought the urge to make a face, and instead offered a small wave. She was pretty sure Mrs. Avery had filled in Mrs. McGrath on the juicy Ruby/Travis gossip. At least, judging from the expression on their faces.

With a sigh, she sped out of town, heading toward River Road. She'd been gone since early this morning so they could be at the dealership for opening, and was looking forward to kicking back on her deck, with a good book and a bottle of wine.

She glanced down at her phone. There were no new messages, voice mail or text. And maybe she should have felt some sort of relief, but what she felt was deeper. Darker. And more intense. Why hadn't he made an effort to contact her? Was he rethinking all the things he'd said to her?

"Stop it," she muttered. She wasn't going to think about it.

Ruby followed the road as it curved around the large lake and eventually took an exit that led to an exclusive gated development filled with large, expensive homes that overlooked the lake. Hers was the last one, a large ultra-modern design of stone and glass. It featured an impressive wall of windows that brought nature right into her space, a large treed side lot, and a two-tier deck at the back that overlooked Crystal Lake.

The enclave was much sought after, and when she'd been approved to build, it had meant everything. That Ruby, the cliché born on the wrong side of town, had moved on up in this world. Of course, that feeling had lasted only a few months, and then she'd quickly realized money and prestige didn't buy happiness.

"God, stop thinking of that stuff," she muttered as she pulled into her driveway. Only then did she see a smart silver convertible parked near her door, and a man sitting on her front steps. *Travis.* He wore a ball cap, an old, worn-looking thing, and he hadn't shaved, which should make him look unkempt, but instead made him look sexy as hell and incredibly male. Aviators hid his eyes, but she felt his gaze as surely as if his hands were on her. A plain white T-shirt, beige deck shoes, and stone-colored khakis gave him a casual look.

Ruby felt her cheeks go hot, and the palms of her hands were slick with sweat. She parked and made a show out of gathering up her purse, but in reality, she was wiping her hands across her lap and desperately hoping her complexion faded by the time she managed to get herself out of the car. She caught sight of herself in the rearview mirror and winced. Several nights with hardly any sleep was catching up with her.

She heard a bark and spied Tasha peering through the side window by the front door. Her tail was wagging like crazy, and she was looking back and forth between Travis and Ruby.

With a silent prayer, she got out of her car and approached him.

"What are you doing here?"

"Nice day." Travis flashed a smile and ignored her question. He got to his feet and shoved his hands into the front pockets of his shorts.

"How do you know where I live?"

"Supposed to be low eighties."

She swore under her breath and glared at him. "Travis. Why are you here?" she asked again.

"Thought it was a good day for a drive," he said, stepping aside as she joined him on the steps.

"Really."

"Yeah." He rubbed at the whiskers on his chin. "You going to grab that dog or what?"

Ruby looked at her fur baby, but the little dog was staring up at Travis, head cocked to the side inquisitively. "Why would I grab the dog?"

Travis nodded. "I've got plans for us, and I'm guessing you don't come solo."

She looked at the convertible, a top-of-the-line Mercedes. "I don't think that's a good idea."

"You don't like convertibles?"

"I like convertibles just fine. It's the driver I have a problem with."

"You want to know what I think?"

"Not particularly."

"I think you don't want to spend the day with me because you're afraid."

"What am I afraid of?"

"That's the big question, isn't it?" He was challenging her. Getting under her skin. "Come with me, Ruby."

"Why should I?"

"What else have you got to do?" He took a step down and waited.

Tasha barked and jumped at the window. "Are we really going to do this? Pretend that we're friends? That everything is perfectly fine between us?"

"Yeah," he answered after a few seconds. "We are."

She was tired, and it just seemed easier to give in. At least, that was what she told herself when she found herself actually considering the idea. She thought ahead to the afternoon she'd planned. Hours of alone time with no company but her dog. It had sounded like heaven, but now...

"What do I need?"

"Nothing."

"Seriously?" She looked up. He'd taken off his aviators, and when her eyes slammed into his, she felt the pull from the top of her head to the bottoms of her toes. It left a trail of warmth that burned in her gut and made her feel jittery.

"Seriously," he murmured, a slow grin touching his face. "I've got everything covered. Just get the damn dog."

This was the moment when Ruby could have put a stop to this nonsense. That would have been the smart thing to do. Instead, she grabbed her dog and followed Travis to the car.

A few hours later, they cruised into Port Hagan, a beautiful town on the shores of Lake Michigan. Travis pulled into a marina and cut the engine. He got out of the car, walked around to the passenger side, and deftly lifted Tasha from her lap. The dog was way too eager to jump into Travis's arms, and she watched them as he walked to the back of the car and grabbed a large bag.

"You can change here."

"Change?" Surprised, she looked at him, but he only nodded and smiled. It was a killer smile, and he knew it. He'd always been so damn confident.

"Come on." He stood back and waited while she got out of the car. They walked side by side until Travis stopped in front a large cabin cruiser. The boat was big and expensive, and she looked at him questioningly. "It belongs to a friend."

Ruby didn't ask, and Travis didn't volunteer information, though the name of the boat was telling. *Black Note*. She figured it belonged to Crystal Lake's resident rocker, Cain Black. Though what his boat was doing docked in Port Hagan was anyone's guess. His own place in Crystal Lake was on the water and not far from where Ruby lived.

They jumped aboard, and she headed for the cabin. "I'll just... go inside and change."

"I'll be waiting." He winked. "You might need this."

She headed below with the bag he'd handed her and took a few moments to appreciate the luxurious furnishings. A guitar hung over the bar along with signed photos of Cain with various celebrities, including a few Oscar winners and the late Johnny Cash. She peered a bit closer at that one, noting how young Cain looked, and she concluded it had to have been taken when he'd first left Crystal Lake to live his dream.

She yanked open the bag, her hand brushing the contents as she slowly sank back onto the sofa and looked inside.

Carefully, she pulled out a white dress and held it up. The fabric was soft, the design simple—a halter with an A line that fell in soft ripples to just below the knee. There was also a sky-blue bikini, a pair of white flip-flops with the cutest applique, white sunglasses, and a floppy sun hat.

He'd thought of everything.

Ruby sat on the sofa for all of ten seconds, staring at the clothing until her eyes blurred. Was she making the biggest mistake of her life? Could she handle an entire day with her ex-husband?

"I guess there's only one way to find out," she whispered, gathering up the clothes. She quickly changed and took a few extra moments to freshen up in the bathroom. Toiletries were on hand as well as sunscreen, and once she brushed her hair and let it fall in long waves down her back, she was ready to go. She dabbed some glass on her lips and headed for the stairs.

The July heat felt amazing, though the humidity was high. There was a breeze coming off the water, and for that, she was grateful as she made her way over to Travis. He was chatting with a couple of guys near another boat, and he looked ridiculous holding Tasha in his arms, her glistening white fur offset by her pink rhinestone collar and two bow ties near her ears. A guy like Travis should have a shepherd or retriever, not some dainty little fur ball with dewy eyes and an excited bark that never stopped.

Travis turned her way. "There she is."

The tallest of the two whistled, running his hands over his shiny bald head. He was powerfully built with wide shoulders and legs that looked like tree trunks. The guy could have been Tiny's brother.

"Ruby, this is Dalton"—he pointed to the big bald guy—"and

Tim." The second man took off his sunglasses and slowly looked her up and down. He was smaller, with a full head of perfectly coifed hair and delicate features—eyes soft and brown, pillow-perfect lips. His clothes were expensive and expertly tailored, his teeth whiter than anyone she'd ever met, and his smile disarming. She instantly liked him.

"Why, aren't you a pretty thing?" Tim drawled with a wink. "I love that dress, and the shoes are divine." He frowned as he studied her feet. "Ferragamo? Versace?"

"No," she replied with a laugh. "Target, I think."

He chuckled. "Well, fry me in a skillet, but those are the best knock-offs I've ever seen."

"You're from the South," she said warmly.

"What gave me away? My accent and eccentric way of speaking? Or my obvious love of clothes and design."

"Definitely the accent."

"Well, darlin', you are correct. I'm from the state of Louisiana. I love mint julep and my mama—in that order, if you want to know the truth. I despise shrimp, and I absolutely abhor grits. They are hands down *the* worst food invention in the history of food inventions." He shot a look at Dalton. "Who in the hell invented grits anyway?"

"That I don't know. I can always google it, if in fact you really give a turd about who invented grits."

"Never mind," Tim replied, throwing his hands in the air dramatically. "I really don't care."

Dalton chuckled. "That's what I thought."

Ruby took Tasha off Travis's hands. "I don't think you need to worry about grits this far north. What brings you to Michigan?"

"He does." Tim gave Dalton a look that was hot enough to make Ruby blush. Now why couldn't her sweet Raj meet someone like Tim? "Dalton is from these parts, and he's been telling me about this raft picnic business for days and days. I finally just said, let's get on up to your neck of the woods and have a look see."

"Raft float?" Ruby felt Travis's eyes on her.

The River Float had been their first official date. Port Hagan was a coastal town located on the shores of Lake Michigan, but like a lot of small towns in the area, a tributary had long ago cut through the earth and carved its way down from the Huron Mountains until it reached the lake. Every summer, Port Hagan hosted a River Float, and couples, families, and all sorts of folk spent the day floating along the river that ran through town, picnicking, lounging, and having fun.

Just then, a shuttle pulled up. It would take them all to the starting point of the River Raft Floats, some eight or so miles away. Tim and Dalton started toward forward.

"Remember our first River Float?" Travis whispered, his warm breath sending small butterflies skittering across her skin and making her shiver.

"Vaguely," she managed to say.

"You two lovebirds coming or what?" Tim shouted from the shuttle. "I might need more than big D here to rescue my cute little butt if I wind up falling overboard."

Ruby looked at Travis. The river in question was less than four feet deep, so Tim should be fine. Ruby should know. She'd fallen in the last time they'd floated down it, and all she'd needed was Travis.

CHAPTER 15

he River Float lasted about three hours. And it was
perfect. The sun was shining, but the breeze was
enough to take the edge off the heat. When Ruby stripped down
to her bikini, Travis barely managed to keep his shit together
long enough to slap some suntan lotion on her back. He'd
arranged for a deluxe raft rental at the starting point, as well as a
picnic basket full of Ruby's favorites, grapes (green), kielbasa, old
cheese (the kind that smelled, but hey, she liked it), and the pita
biscuits she used to eat like nobody's business. Cold wine and
beer, as well as water and iced tea were also in the mix, and
Travis made a mental note to thank Regan, Wyatt's lady, who'd
helped him get it all organized.

As in past years, there were literally hundreds of rafts clog-
ging the river, including Dalton and Tim's, and by the time they
reached the downtown area where the float ended, they'd
become friendly with several couples.

Kate and Marcus were new to the area and considering a
permanent move to start their family.

Blake and Shayla were locals, celebrating their twenty-fifth
wedding anniversary.

Kimmy and Johnny were teenagers who could barely keep their hands off each other long enough to contribute to the conversation.

And of course, Dalton and Tim proved to be as entertaining as Travis's first impression suggested.

It was early afternoon by the time their rafts approached the end of the float. Tasha had pretty much slept the entire way and was full of spunk. She shook with the effort it took to keep still, and could hardly contain herself as their raft pulled up alongside the bank. Travis hopped overboard and reached for Tasha, trying not to let his gaze linger on Ruby as she shimmied back into her dress.

"Your little dog is an absolute cutie pie." Tim scratched the animal under her chin, and Tasha happily angled her head so the man could keep going and find that elusive sweet spot. "So tell me," Tim said once they were on solid land. "What's your story?" He nodded to Ruby, who was laughing at something Dalton was saying to the teenagers.

Her hair was still loose, hanging down her back, and he ached to sink his hands into it. The dress fit her like a glove, the soft material caressing curves he knew by heart. It had been so long. Years. And she still had the power to make him weak.

"We were married," he said. "And now we're not."

"Well, isn't that the most scandalous thing I've heard today." Tim's eyes were wide. "Details, please."

Travis looked down at Tim. He couldn't believe he was sharing this stuff with someone who was a virtual stranger. Hell, he hadn't even told Zach where he was headed today or with whom. The only thing he'd told his current roommate was that he might not to be home for a few days. Zach hadn't asked any questions. He shrugged, told him he was going to chill for a while longer if that was okay, and that they'd hook up when Travis got back to town. God, men were easy. It was the women who complicated things.

"It's a long story," Travis said.

Tim was nodding. "The good ones usually are."

"And kind of complicated."

"Ah-ha. Sounds about right."

They both turned toward the water. Dalton must have said something funny, because Ruby erupted in the kind of laughter that made people look her way. It was unbridled. Honest. Full bodied and real. Travis couldn't help but smile watching her. He was saved from his conversation when Dalton and Ruby made their way over. The two men were meeting Dalton's family for happy hour and said their goodbyes.

"What's on the schedule now?" Ruby asked when they were alone.

"Art in the park?"

Her face lit up. "They still have it?"

"That's what I hear."

They walked up from the river and followed the path until it opened up into a large area filled with vendors of all kinds. Food. Art. Crafts. Junk. It wasn't his usual thing, but it was Ruby's and therefore, today, his.

They meandered through the crowds and eventually stopped at a tent filled with hand-sketched, framed artwork. He took the dog and let Ruby wander the aisles, content to just watch her. He loved how her eyes moved over the displays. How her fingers gently caressed the frames and she cocked her head to the side to study them.

Travis stood there patiently, holding on to a dog with a pink collar and bows in its hair and not giving a crap that people were staring. It wasn't until a small boy approached him that he realized maybe it wasn't the dog garnering the attention. Maybe it was Travis himself.

The kid looked to be about nine or ten and was sporting a Red Wings T-shirt. Travis recognized the look on his face. Heck, it was one he'd worn more times than he cared to court when he was younger. It was a big deal for a young kid to meet someone in the pros. Hell, he'd had the same look even after he'd been drafted.

"You a Red Wings fan?" he asked casually, looking down at the boy, who was now joined by a girl about the same age.

"We both are," she answered for them. "Caleb told me you're Travis Blackwell, but I don't think you are."

"No?" Travis smiled and let Tasha down. "Why's that?"

"Because Travis Blackwell doesn't have a dog?" She looked at him with a *duh* expression on her face.

"Where'd you hear that?" Surprised, he took a step closer.

"I saw it on ESPN. They were interviewing Travis, and it was when the president was picking out his dog, and they asked Travis if he had one, and he said he didn't have time for a dog." She pointed to Tasha. "And if I'm not mistaken, that's a dog."

Christ, this kid has spunk. Reminded him of another female he knew.

"You're right about that. This is Tasha. And she's not my dog." He winked. "Because during regular season, I don't have a lot of time to look after a pet."

"See?" The boy poked the girl in the side. "I told you it was him." He shoved her out of the way. "I want to be just like you when I grow up."

"Well, if that's true," Travis said, "first thing you have to learn is you shouldn't shove a lady."

The kid shrugged. "She's not a lady. She's just my sister."

He chuckled at that. "Fair enough."

"Oh my goodness. Have my kids been bugging you? I'm so sorry." A harried-looking woman holding a baby on her hip stopped beside the kids.

"Mom," the little guy exclaimed. "It *is* Travis Blackwell."

"Oh...I..." The woman seemed confused.

"The goalie for the Detroit Red Wings?" The boy was

disgusted with his mother and tugged on his T-shirt, emphasizing his words.

"I'm sorry," she said again, glancing at Travis. "I don't really follow sports. That's my husband's thing, and he's down with a nasty summer cold, and the kids have been looking forward to the rides and stuff all week and—"

Her cell phone rang at the same time the baby on her hip began to cry. She fumbled in her pocket and scooped out the phone, but it fell through her fingers and landed on the grass.

"Shit," she muttered.

"Mom, that's the S word!" The look of horror on the little girl's face was comical.

"Here, let me." Travis meant to bend down and grab the phone, but the woman handed him the baby instead.

Travis didn't do babies. Not little ones. Or big ones. Hell, not even ones that could balance on a hip and look you right in the eye. But what was a guy to do? He looked at the baby and realized she (pink was a dead giveaway because there wasn't enough hair for him to decide otherwise) wasn't crying anymore. She was studying him with curious eyes, and before he knew what was happening, the little thing grabbed for his aviators and pulled them off.

"Hey, you," he said, eyeing the baby. "Those are mine." He tried to snatch them back, but the baby giggled. He stopped his hand midway, and she stopped giggling. Until he tried to grab them again, and the giggling started. Before he knew what was what, he was playing a game with a little human, and the two other kids joined in.

He finally managed to snag the glasses from the little girl's chubby hands, which set off a new round of giggles, when he glanced up and felt his world melt away.

Ruby was watching him from a few feet away. A small piece of artwork was clutched against her chest, and the expression on her face made his heart ache. It was a mixture of pain, sadness, and something else.

Aware that people had gathered a few feet away, some with their phones out, trying discreetly to get his picture, he turned back to the woman, who was thankfully done with her phone call. She took the baby from him, murmuring her thanks, and when the older kids asked to get their picture taken with Travis, it was Ruby who was there, taking Tasha from him. Offering to take the photo.

She accepted the mother's phone and took several pictures, obliging a few more folks brave enough to ask for a photo. The entire exercise took less than ten minutes, and when the folks got what they wanted, Travis and Ruby were left alone with each other.

"I see you bought something." Travis had never been good at small talk, but he needed to say something, because right now, the game had changed. Again. He couldn't read Ruby, and that bothered him more than he cared to admit.

She showed him a black-and-white photo of an old barn with white-washed walls and a muted red door. It was old Americana, both poignant and wistful. An ode to a simpler time that was fast disappearing.

"I thought maybe for my back porch." Her eyes slid away, and he took a step closer, pretending to study the photo closely.

"I like it. I'm sure it will look great for wherever you have in mind." He was stumbling over his words, but like an idiot, he couldn't seem to stop himself. "I haven't seen your back porch, but…"

Her head shot up. Shit. He'd done something wrong, and now he'd ruined their afternoon.

"No," she said eventually. "You haven't been to my home because we haven't been friends in years."

As if sensing discourse between the humans, Tasha chose that moment to jump to her feet and start barking like a maniac. The little animal ran full circles around Travis and Ruby, dragging her leash before they could grab it. By the time she was done, her sides were heaving and her tongue lolled out of her mouth.

"Did you make dinner plans?" Ruby asked, bending down to scratch between Tasha's ears.

"I did. But if you'd rather head home, I can take you." Had the day gone down in flames when he wasn't looking?

Ruby grabbed Tasha's leash. "I'm hungry."

Travis had been so sure she was about to end their day together that it took a few seconds for him mind to process what his ears had just heard.

"Okay, let's go." He held out his hand.

Four or five of the longest seconds of his life passed. Sweat pooled at the back of his neck. This was worse than the conference finals when his team was up by one, the clock was ticking, and he faced three forwards from the opposing team streaking down the ice.

One hundred times worse.

He held his breath, never in his life as unsure as he was in this moment.

And then she took his hand.

CHAPTER 16

*R*uby Montgomery hadn't gotten to where she was in life by hiding behind someone else. By being a coward or avoiding complicated situations. She reveled in confrontation and loved being right. When her mother left, she learned to stand up for herself because no one else would. It was in her blood to fight, and she came by it honestly, her handy right hook included. Good old Irish blood, she'd been told by her pugilist grandfather before he died. She thought of her mother, something she hadn't done in years, and just as quickly shook the memory of that weak, selfish woman from her mind.

It must have skipped a generation.

Which was why she wasn't used to feeling like this. She was being a coward. She was hiding behind the men sitting across from her.

But for the moment, she was okay with that. For the moment, she needed to regroup and get her head screwed on right. Seeing Travis holding that child had been like a knife to the chest. It was an open wound that had never healed, and she hadn't realized until now just how painful it still was.

Maybe she should have just kept her butt in Crystal Lake

where it belonged, because coming here had to be a mistake. She didn't want to remember the pain, because along with the pain was the other stuff. The love.

God, was it too late to save herself?

"Darlin', you look way too serious for a gal whose had at least half a bottle of that lovely Pinot Grigio. Everything okay?" Tim's slow Southern drawl shook her from her thoughts, and she sat up with a smile.

"Yes. I'm good. Just taking it all in."

They'd come back to the marina, and like the coward Ruby now acknowledged she was, she'd pretty much hogtied Dalton and Tim and convinced them they needed to come aboard the *Black Note* for dinner.

Of course, Travis most likely had something else in mind, but he graciously agreed and insisted the men join them. He'd taken the boat onto the lake, and they anchored in a spot that afforded them a beautiful view of the surrounding area. Thick, lush forests as far as the eye could see, covering hills and valleys and blanketing them in a deep green. They'd had a lovely meal of grilled steaks, fresh summer salad with strawberries, caramelized pecans, and goat cheese, as well as baked potatoes and jumbo shrimp to start. The wine was expertly paired, and the dessert, chocolate mousse with cinnamon and nuts, was to die for.

Well, Ruby was going to assume it was to die for, because truthfully, she'd spent most of the time monopolizing the conversation and pushing her food around her plate. The wine-to-food ratio wasn't in her favor, and that probably explained why she was feeling a bit light-headed.

"The view sure is something," Tim said, winking and then nodded toward Travis and Dalton. The two men were on the other side of the boat discussing motors and horsepower and something about a rotor.

"How long have you and Dalton been together?" she asked, curious about the pair, deftly changing the subject.

Tim wasn't fooled—she could tell—but he played along, and for that, she was grateful.

"Well, we have officially been a couple for coming up to three years. Unofficially? We've been together for almost fifteen. Next week is our anniversary of the uh, first time we...danced the dance, so to speak. It's partly why we're up here. Early anniversary trip for a memory only the two of us acknowledge."

"Unofficially?" Ruby asked. Tim made no effort to hide who he was, and as far as she could tell, neither did Dalton. Both men seemed very secure and happy.

"Unofficially, Dalton was married to his high school sweetheart for seven years. I met him and his wife when he was transferred to Springfield for work, and they moved into the house beside my mama's bed and breakfast."

"Oh."

"Uh-huh. Yep." Tim shrugged. "It was all quite scandalous when the truth came out. My mama didn't talk to me until last year, when she came down with breast cancer. I guess being sick was enough to erase the embarrassment of her only son having an affair with a married man. Either that, or she didn't want the hired help getting all up in the more delicate matters and such. She's a real Southern woman and doesn't like anyone to see her unless she's made up to the nines."

"I'm sorry," Ruby said softly.

"Oh, don't be. We're all fine now. In fact. Miranda, Dalton's ex-wife, is one of our closest allies. I mean it is the South. We love eccentricity. We practically kneel at its altar. But some things are still coming slow. Some folks still believe that there is only one kind of love, and anyone who isn't checked off in that narrow box is an abomination. They think that we're sex fiends or something, like that's all we have time for. Good Lord, if I had as much sex as some folks think people of my type do, I'd never get anything done. Hell, I wouldn't even be able to drag this cute little butt out of bed, I'd be so exhausted from all the sex. I mean, really. I'd like to ask those folks how someone like Ellen gets around to taping her show every day with all the non-hetero sex going on."

Ruby smiled at that, her eyes drawn once more to Travis.

"I know you and your man have had some difficulties." Tim stared at her.

She yanked her head back.

"Your husband told me told me it's complicated."

"Ex-husband," she corrected. "And yes, it kind of is."

"So are the two of you…"

"No. We're just…I don't know what we're doing but whatever it is isn't permanent."

"Why's that?"

"Because, like you said, it's complicated."

"Complicated is just a word people use when they don't know what damn word *to* use."

"But it covers a lot of bases."

"It does." Tim paused. "But it's also a word to hide behind. What is it you want, Ruby?"

"To be happy." She didn't hesitate. "To not struggle every day trying to find it."

"Darlin, there is no clean, easy road on this planet that will lead you to true happiness. That's the God's truth. But there is a path carved out of the earth, out of the dirt and stone. That path is full of potholes. Deep, malicious craters filled with all sorts of nasty things." He shook his head. "We all hit 'em. Try as we do not to. It's inevitable. But the real winners in life and love are the ones who get out of those potholes. The people who move forward no matter what. The trick, though?" He winked at her. "The trick is to get to your final destination with someone you love at your side. Someone who was in those potholes with you. Someone who helped dig you out. And maybe that someone was responsible for some of those holes. That can happen. Maybe they were even responsible for the big ones. But that's life, isn't?

It's messy and confusing and, yes, *complicated.* If it weren't, we'd all be bored to tears. Am I right?"

She didn't know what to say, so she stayed quiet.

"We all have the power to make change just as much as we have the power *to* change. Life has a funny way of bringing us all full circle. You just have to make sure that when you hit your next pothole, that someone beside deserves to be there. 'Cause he's the one who'll lend a hand and help get you out."

Tim's words brought tears to her eyes. And, feeling silly, she sniffled and leaned over to hug the man.

"I'm so glad we met," she whispered.

"Me too, darlin'," Tim said with grin. "I plan on visiting your spa soon. Travis says it's real nice."

"Anytime. I mean it."

Dalton cleared his throat, and Ruby and Tim got to their feet. "Travis is going to bring the boat back in. We should get going."

The sunset painted the dark horizon with streaks of red and gold as they pulled back into the marina. The stars were just coming out, and the water was calm. There were several boats moored nearby with lights on, including the boat that Dalton and Tim were renting. The four of them exchanged numbers and said their goodbyes...

And then there was just Ruby and Travis.

The look in his eyes made her body shudder. She was hot. And cold. And so damn jittery, she had to put down her wine-glass. The air between them was thick, full of the past and more than a few potholes.

"It's not too late. Barely gone nine. We can pack up and head back to Crystal Lake, or I can make us some coffee and we can enjoy the night." She felt the power of his dark eyes on her. It was a tangible, real thing. So real, it felt as if he was touching her. So real, it made her knees go weak.

A month ago, she would have pushed back. She would have told Travis to pack the car and take her home. Who was she kidding? A month ago, she wouldn't have been here. But maybe a month ago, she was stuck in one of the potholes Tim had talked about. A deep one. Maybe Travis had just pulled her out. Because truthfully, she hadn't felt as alive as she did right now, in this moment, here with him. Not for a long, long time. And for once, she was going to set aside the past. For once, she was just going to be.

"I'm going to have some more wine, if you don't mind." Ruby moved past Travis and grabbed the open bottle. She poured the rest of it into her glass and then took a seat on the back of the boat so that she could look out at the water. The breeze had picked up, but she wasn't cold anymore. In fact, she was hot, and more than a little bothered.

Decision made for him, Travis grabbed a cold beer from the cooler and joined her. He didn't sit too close. But then he didn't sit far enough away for her to be able to ignore the pull either. She wondered if he felt it as strongly as she did. He grabbed a remote, and music filled the air, making her smile as she relaxed against the seat.

"The Eagles," she murmured. "Good call." It was her favorite band ever. "You really did think of everything."

"It's all in the details."

She nodded. "It is." She took a sip of wine. "Where do you live when you're not here? When you're not playing hockey?"

He didn't seem surprised by the question and shrugged. "I have a condo near the arena. Had a place in LA that I bought on a whim, but I sold it last year. I think I slept in that house maybe two weeks out of the entire five years I owned it."

She knew the whim because Google was her friend. The whim's name was Ursula, and she was a Swedish model who'd made the cover of *Sport's Illustrated* three times. The swimsuit edition.

"I'm surprised," she said after a while. "About the condo."

"Yeah?" He leaned back. "Why?"

"You never seemed the type to settle in the city. At least not in a condo. I guess I pictured some fancy estate out in the suburbs."

He was quiet for a few moments. "It's just a place to put my head at night. I guess I don't really think of it as home. I've always thought of buying something else when I was ready."

"Ready? For what?"

His eyes were unreadable. The hairs on the back of Ruby's head stood on end, and her heart started racing.

"For a family."

He seemed surprised at his own words and looked away, his gaze drawn to something on the water.

"When will you be ready?" Sweet Jesus. Had she really spoken the words aloud? It was the sight of him earlier, holding that baby, that had her insides all knotted up.

Travis looked back, and she swallowed thickly. Yep. Her mouth had somehow acted on its own accord, and now everything was on the table. Could he see the yearning in her heart? Hear the want that colored the air between them? Feel the ache in her soul? The one that had never gone away?

"Oh God. That was a stupid thing to say," she said quickly, holding up her wineglass. "Too much of this."

Travis set his beer down and moved toward her. God help Ruby, but she was frozen in place. Not that she wanted to move. That was a thought she didn't want to analyze, because it would force her to think, and right now, she didn't want to think. She wanted to close her eyes and lose herself in this night. In this moment. In this man.

She slammed her eyes shut because she didn't want him to see what was there. She wanted him. Badly.

His hand slid into the tangle of hair at her nape, and his long fingers cupped her gently. She felt his breath on her cheek and inhaled as sharp, hot need swept through her body. It had been so long since she'd felt such a reaction. There'd been other men. Of course there had. Some had even been great lovers, and some had been just okay. But when want and need and desire intersected with love, it made the physical reach an entirely different level.

Love. God. That word. Was it possible she was still in love with Travis? After all this time? After all the pain and hurt?

"I feel like right now, I'm home." His voice was rough. Heavy with emotion. "Ruby, you've always been home to me. Even when I was too stupid to know it."

His mouth trailed a line of fire along her jawline and then made its way up until he swept the sweetest kiss across her lips. She opened beneath him, wanting more, but he pulled away and rested his forehead against hers.

"I want you," he whispered fiercely. "I want every single fucking inch of you. But, Ruby, we gotta be sure. I don't want to screw this up. So if you're not sure, I'm cool with that. You can sleep below, and I'll—"

"Stop talking."

She shook her head and got up before blowing out the candle on the table. Their boat was in darkness, save for the muted lights thrown from the few moored boats with people aboard.

"Ruby."

"Stop. Talking. Travis."

She pulled the white dress over her head and tossed it to the ground. She was doing this. She was jumping the hell out of a pothole, and she was going to enjoy every damn minute of it.

"Are you sure?" he asked hoarsely.

She tossed her bikini top in the vicinity of her dress and hooked her fingers into the top of her bottoms. A heartbeat passed.

"Ruby."

"No, Travis. I'm not even close to being sure."

And then her bottoms joined the top.

CHAPTER 17

*T*ravis thought he was going to lose his mind. Ruby stood in front him, naked, her skin awash in moonbeams and starlight. Every single exquisite inch of her was within his reach. All he had to do was touch her, and she'd be his. The fantasies that had crowded his brain for the last month would be silenced. So why was he hesitating? Why was he pulling back when he should be moving full steam ahead?

His dick was screaming at him. His mind was on overload. His senses were on fire. And yet...

"Ruby, maybe we should—"

"I told you to stop talking."

He opened his mouth but didn't get a chance to reply. On account of Ruby leaning over and sliding her lips across his. She straddled him, pushing his head back onto the seat as she planted her hands on either side of his shoulders. Her hair was all around him, her scent deep in his nostrils and her mouth claimed his with a hunger that left him breathless.

Travis wanted to do the right thing and slow down. That was what someone like Chance McDougal would do. But Travis wasn't a good man. He wasn't even close.

With a groan, he surrendered to the passion between them. To the heat and the fire that curled inside his gut. Her hot mouth was open, her tongue freely taking from him, and he kissed her back savagely. His hands gripped her hips to hold her in place, even as her hands sank into his hair so that he couldn't move. The kiss was long and hard, their bodies strained against each other, and Travis never wanted to let her go. When she yanked back and looked down at him, he inhaled deeply, jaw clenched as he tried to get his emotions in check.

Never had he been this close to the edge in so short a time. They'd barely started, and he was ready to blow.

He couldn't see her features, the shadows hid them from the moonlight, but her breasts hung in front of him, the dusky nipples taut, begging for his touch. Slowly, his hands worked their way upward, and she arched her back slightly, giving him the advantage he needed. He ran his finger over the tips, smiling when he heard her groan, and then followed with his lips and tongue.

"Trav," she whispered when his mouth closed over her. He smiled against her skin, cupping her breasts, suckling, teasing, until her hips began to move harder against him. Each time he thrust his tongue against her nipple, she answered with a grind to his cock. And that was something he couldn't do right now. Not yet anyway. He wanted this to last.

With a guttural sound, he yanked her off him and with one deft movement, sat her down on the seat and reversed positions. Except he wasn't straddling her. Hell no. He was on his knees, eyes on a prize that had eluded him for years.

Ruby made a throaty sound, the kind that would drive any sane man crazy. She gazed down at him, tongue between her teeth, and slowly let her legs fall apart.

His hands rested on her knees, and Travis took a moment because Ruby was more beautiful than he remembered. Every. Damn. Inch. She was still gyrating slowly, and he slid his palms up the inside of each thigh, gently spreading her until she was entirely open to him.

To his greedy gaze.

To his wandering hands.

To his hungry mouth.

He bent forward, inhaled that scent that was all hers...and smiled wickedly when he parted her folds. She was slick and wet. Her clitoris was engorged, and he looked up at her as his fingers slid along her wetness. Her chest heaved, and she groaned softly when he caressed her clit gently, then, as her breathing quickened, harder. He rubbed with his thumb and sank two fingers deep inside, at an angle, curved just the way she liked it.

"Oh my God," she whispered, "that feels so good."

"Babe, I'm just getting started." He replaced his thumb with his mouth. He used his teeth and his tongue. He sucked and licked and applied just the right amount of pressure to bring her to the edge. He got her there...and then pulled back, smiling to himself when she began to cuss.

There were many things he missed about Ruby. This was one of them. She was always vocal in their lovemaking. Never afraid to use the dirty words. To tell him exactly what she wanted.

"I cant take it," she moaned.

He brought her to the brink once more and then eased back.

"I'm going to kick your ass, Travis," she said roughly, her hands now in his hair as she pushed him deeper into her.

"I might like that." he growled against her skin.

"I'm sure you would." His tongue flicked against her, and she shuddered.

"I want you to make me come right now. Do you think you can do that for me?" She stopped moving for a second, and their eyes met.

"Pretty sure I can."

"That's not the answer I'm looking for."

His fingers were still inside her, and he moved them just so, hitting that honey spot. "Shit." She moved her hips, but he held her steady. Travis was in control, and he damn well liked it.

"Now we're talking. How many times?" she asked.

"More than once."

"That's my boy."

Travis got to work, and not more than a minute passed before she shuddered against his mouth, her groans rough as she bucked against him. Slowly, he got to his feet, uncaring that they were on the back of the boat and if anyone happened to glance their way, they'd see two shadowy figures doing things they should be doing inside.

Travis ripped off his T-shirt and stepped out of his shorts. His cock was rock hard, his body tense.

Ruby's head rested on the seat, her eyes half-open, her body still reeling from his mouth and his hands. Travis bent over her and pressed his lips to the base of her neck. Her pulse beat rapidly, and he made his way up to her mouth, claiming it in a kiss that made his gut clench. The need to possess and to worship was overwhelming, and when her hand wrapped around his dick, he almost lost it.

She made mewing sounds and her throat constricted rapidly as she tried to vocalize what was going on inside her head and her body.

"Slow down, Ruby. We've got all night."

"I don't want to slow down." She looked at him, chest heaving, a sheen of sweat making her skin glow. "I want it fast and hard, and I want it now."

He grinned wickedly. "You haven't changed at all."

"No." She spread her legs again. "I haven't."

Travis was only human. And a man at that. So he wasn't prepared for this. He'd thought their first time would be slow. Two bodies getting to know each other again while candlelight flickered across skin and music caressed their ears. Not this feverish, hungry need that was making him crazy.

But Travis was, if anything, a pleaser, and he wasn't about to disappoint his lady. A feral groan fell from his lips as he reached for her. He claimed her mouth once more, his hands between her legs, working her over until she was clawing at him like a cat. He flipped her over and grabbed her hips, lifting her ass in the air and shoving her knees forward for support. She grabbed the edge of the seat and glanced back at him. The look on her face was something he'd take to his grave. Happily.

Ruby Montgomery was the hottest thing he'd ever laid eyes on. And he'd been around the block a time or two.

He pressed down on the small of her back with one hand while the other gripped her hip. With his eyes on the tattoo that bore their initials, he sank sank into her. Deeply.

"Oh God, Travis."

She tried to force the play and move her hips, but he wasn't having any of it. Travis withdrew completely. He grinned when she swore at him and then sank into her again. And again. And again.

He kept his hold on her hip tight, because even though he wanted to accommodate her need, he also knew the end result would be that much more satisfying if he could just hold on a little longer.

"Travis," she said hoarsely. "I can't…"

"You can," he replied, bending over her, his thrusts measured and long. His eyes were closed. He wanted to this feeling to last forever. He wanted to punch his chest like he was Tarzan. Because the need to claim Ruby and possess her was older than time. It was basic. Raw. Primal.

And he'd never felt this way with any other woman.

In that moment, Travis knew he was wrecked. No way could he let her go again. A wave of emotion washed over him—it clogged his throat and made it hard to breathe. He gripped her hips tightly as he began to thrust harder, faster. She was so damn wet and tight. His gut clenched, her body rolled back into his, and they both came so hard, he nearly collapsed. It took all his strength to keep them from falling, and long seconds went by as they struggled to catch their breath.

Gently, he pulled her against him, and they lay down on the narrow seat, her body on top of his, his arms wrapped around her tight. Overhead, the night sky was blanketed with a million stars that shone like diamonds.

"That was…"

"Yeah," she replied, snuggling against his chest. "Do you think anyone heard us?"

He was pretty sure at least half the marina heard some of the business going on. "Do you care?"

"Not really."

He smiled and kissed the top of her head. "That's my girl. It's like that time at the hockey awards banquet, and we were back-stage because I was supposed to hand out an award."

"Oh my God." She wiggled and pulled herself up until they were face-to-face. "We thought we were good because we had at least fifteen minutes before intermission was over."

He shook his head wryly. Someone had left behind a live mic, and their backstage activities were inadvertently heard by the entire banquet room.

"Those fifteen minutes were well documented. Trust me, the guys didn't let me live that down for a good long while."

"Ten."

"What?"

"You were done in less than ten minutes."

"Was I now?" His fingers splayed across her butt, and he rocked her a bit. "I was young."

"You were." Her hips were moving to his rocking.

"I've got more staying power these days."

She arched her eyebrow, a slow smile curving her lips, and he chuckled.

"What just happened doesn't count. And for the record, I

lasted longer than fifteen minutes." He nipped at the base of her neck. "Had to have been at least seventeen."

"You ready for round two?" Her hands were between their bodies.

"I'm always ready." God, she had him. His stomach clenched as she began to massage his cock. Slowly. Methodically.

"Good," she whispered. "Think you can last at least twenty?"

She used her thumb and rubbed along the ridge beneath the head of his dick. With a guttural sound, he nodded. "Let's go for twenty-five."

She thrust her hips up, and he felt how warm and wet she was. "Maybe we should take this below." Ruby arched a wicked eyebrow.

Travis didn't answer. He scooped Ruby into his arms and decided he was going to go for at least half an hour before he made her come.

And that was just to start.

CHAPTER 18

*T*wenty-four hours.

One thousand, four hundred and forty minutes.

Eighty-six thousand, four hundred seconds.

All that equaled one full rotation of the earth since she'd been with Travis.

And she still felt his touch on her skin. God, if she closed her eyes right now and concentrated, Ruby was pretty sure she'd be able to feel him *inside* her. She pushed her chair back and rested her head on the seatback and did just that. What the hell. It wasn't as if she was getting any work done. She gripped the armrest, pictured Travis in her mind, and felt that familiar tingle between her legs. Her breasts swelled. Her heart sped up.

And then the door to her office flew open and Ruby damn near fell off her chair. "What the—"

Sidney Templeton walked into her office and, after closing the door, tossed her purse onto the sideboard. She poured herself a glass of water, sat down facing Ruby, and nailed her with a look that spoke volumes. The girl didn't miss a thing, and her direct gaze made Ruby uncomfortable. There were things she wasn't ready to discuss yet, because she had no idea what the consequences were. Not yet, anyway.

Sidney was relentless. She'd be all over it like a dirty shirt.

Ruby slowly uncrossed her legs and straightened her skirt. "Hey, I like your new bag. Is that Gucci?"

"Since when can I afford Gucci?" Sid's eyes narrowed. "Don't try to change the subject. I know what that look is all about, sister."

"Excuse me?" Ruby tried her hardest to act chill and calm and *devoid of all emotion.*

Sidney leaved forward and smiled. "That look. The one you can't hide."

"I don't know what you're talking about."

Sidney chuckled and shook her head. "You've been thinking about all the sex."

"I was thinking about work, Sid. I have a meeting later this week and—"

"You were thinking about all the sex you had this weekend. All the sex you had with Travis. And this?" She held up her water glass. "This right here is going to cool me down."

"And why would you need cooling down?"

Sidney smiled and sank deeper into the chair. "Because you're going to tell me about all the sex you had this weekend." She paused. "After you tell me how in hell Travis Blackwell managed to worm his way back into your life." She frowned. "No. Wait. I want to hear about the sex first."

Ruby sighed and shook her head. There was no point in denial. Sidney knew her better than anyone. She uncrossed her legs and winced.

"I knew it!" Sidney chuckled. "You had so much sex, you're sore."

"Okay, that's a little too much."

"I don't care. Spill. I want details."

"It just happened."

"Where?"

"On a boat."

Sidney leaned forward. "How many times?"

"Four. No, wait." A slow smile curved Ruby's lips. "Five."

"Wow. No wonder you're sore. Have you ever gone more than one round with Chance?"

Ruby sat in the chair. "No." Sex with Chance had been good. He was attractive. He knew his way around a woman. He scratched an itch that needed scratching. But it had never been all-consuming. She'd never felt as if she lost a piece of herself when they were together. What she had with Travis was different. The connection was deeper. The sex wasn't just good. It was off-the-charts good.

"Sid." She closed her eyes. "It's like we've never been apart. I can't explain it. That insane physical attraction is still there. Even after all the crap we've been through. It's like our bodies are meant to be together. Like we only come alive when we're…"

"Having sex?"

That, in a nutshell, was what Ruby was afraid of. Had their entire relationship been built on the physical? On the fact that Travis barely had to look at her and she orgasmed? Was that why they'd failed so horribly at all the real stuff? The emotional stuff? The relationship stuff?

She nodded and buried her face in her hands. "What have I done?" she muttered.

"This is going to sound weird coming from me, but do you want some advice?" Sidney asked.

Ruby blew out a hot breath. "Sure."

"Sometimes we need to take chances on the things we know are going to kick us in the butt. Because sometimes it's the only way to know we're alive. Even if being alive means getting hurt." Sid downed her glass of water in one long gulp. She wiped at the corner of her mouth, set the empty glass on her desk, and shrugged.

"Do you regret what happened this weekend?"

Regret? Ruby thought about it and slowly shook her head. "No. At least I don't think so." She cracked a small smile. "I mean, it was really hot sex, and it's been so long since I've felt that kind of connection. Maybe Travis is the only man I'll feel that way with, but I don't know what happens next. I don't know if I *want* what happens next."

"What happens next?"

"That's something I'm not real clear on."

"What does Travis want?" Sidney asked.

"Does it matter what he wants?" she pondered the question out loud.

"Not really," Sidney replied. "You're in control here. I just don't want you getting in over your head with him. Travis couldn't commit before. What makes you think he will now?"

She looked at her friend. "Who said I was looking for commitment?"

Sidney's mouth fell open. "Oh my God. You're my new hero. You're going to use Travis Blackwell before kicking him to the curb, aren't you?"

"What? No. That sounds cold-blooded. I mean, there would be rules if we did this but…" She threw up her hands. "I don't want to talk about it right now." Ruby eyed her friend as the thing that had been bothering her for a few days buzzed around her brain. Was she just changing the subject to take the heat off herself? Probably. But she was okay with that.

"What?" Sidney was guarded.

"When were you going to tell me you and Ryder were hanging out again?"

"He told you?"

"He's my brother. He tells me everything. Even the shit I don't want to know." She paused, considering her words carefully. "Sid—"

Her friend held up her hand. "Ruby, he's changed. I think this time for real. He looks so good. So healthy and...he's like the old Ryder."

God, how Ruby wanted to believe that. But she'd done this with her brother before. Many times, in fact. And so had Sidney. She should know better.

"A month ago, he looked like shit, Sid. A month ago, he was with Fiona Winters. Before that, Candace Seaton. A normal person might think that Ryder has commitment issues because he only screws married women. But we both know that's only part of it. He screws married women who like opioids and weed and booze as much as he does. He's an addict, Sidney. They don't change overnight or in a month or even a year. Most of them can't change at all. Not even in a lifetime. Just look at my father. His early grave was almost a blessing."

Sidney's face flushed, and she thrust out her chin. "If you think he's such a loser, why did you help him out with the car? Why did you pump him full of confidence when you think he's going to fail?"

"Because that's my job." Ruby swallowed the lump in her throat. "Because he's my brother, and I love him. Because he's an addict, and he needs to believe in himself before he can even begin to walk that road back to recovery. But do I think he's turned over a new leaf? Do I think he's no longer an addict? That he won't blow this job when the stress gets to be too much and he goes on a bender of booze and pills to cope? I can hope that. I can pray that none of that will happen. But the reality is a lot different, and you know it. You can't save him, Sid. Ryder needs to want to save himself first. And I hope he gets there. I really do. Just like I hope you know what you're getting yourself into again, because I can pretty much guarantee that things aren't going to end well. And I don't know if I have enough energy to fix you and Ryder. Not this time. I've got my own stuff to deal with."

Sidney got to her feet, obviously pissed. "It's good to know he has you in his corner."

"I've always had his back." Ruby was angry too. "You know that. I'm just…" She threw her hands into the air, frustrated and upset. "I want so many things. I want Ryder healthy. I want him focused and productive. I want you not to be hurt. I want you to be happy. I want…"

I want to be happy. The thought startled her. She was happy…wasn't she?

"Life is messy, Ruby. It's imperfect. And bad things happen to good people. Maybe Ryder's a bad thing for me. But I might be the good thing he needs to help him get to where he has to be. I might be the good thing that doesn't give up on him. I know he has to want to get healthy for himself. But maybe he needs a good thing beside him to get there." Sidney walked around the desk and hugged Ruby. "Sometimes, we need to take a chance on the things we know are going to kick us in the ass. Sometimes, it's the only way to really know we're alive. Even if being alive means getting hurt."

Sidney kissed her cheek and stepped back. "Look. Maybe we should just agree to stay out of each other's business unless asked."

"Okay." Ruby smiled. "I'm sorry, I—"

"Don't apologize. You know I'm there for you, Ruby, because I love you and you're my best friend. Just like I know I can count on you if things go sideways. It's what we do. I know you think I'm setting myself up to be hurt, but I have to believe this time, things will be different. I'm tired of waiting for the rest of my life to start. Tired of waiting for the man that I love to get his shit together. Tired of watching everyone else move on and I'm standing still because Ryder is the only person I want to move on with. So, I'm not going to dwell on the many ways this can end badly. I'm just going to try like hell to make the ending I want." She smiled. "Maybe you should too."

"Once I figure it out."

"Yes." Sidney's smile widened. "Once you figure it out." Her girlfriend grabbed her purse. "I came here for a reason, you know."

"What's up?"

"The Metaphors are playing the Coach House tonight."

"Get out." The Metaphors were an Irish Celtic/rock band that featured two burly bald men in kilts who played the bagpipes. The Coach House would be packed.

"Right? I just found out. I told Nash to save us four tickets at the door. You in? Or do you have plans with Travis?"

"I haven't talked to him since he dropped me off last night."

"He hasn't called you?"

"I told him I would call him in a couple of days. Said I was going to be busy at work and needed to focus."

"Well, that sounds like a line of bull if I ever heard it."

"He told to take all the time I need."

"Maybe there's hope for him yet." Sidney winked. "But we're not going to talk about the men in our lives. Let's dance our butts off and have fun."

Ruby frowned. "Who are the other tickets for?"

"Regan Thorne and her friend Gwen. Regan volunteered to drive,, so she'll pick us up around eight."

Regan Thorne. The girl Wyatt Blackwell was head over heels for.

"It's just us girls?" she asked.

Sidney nodded. "Regan said it was just girls."

"I don't know," she murmured. The Coach House wasn't really her thing anymore.

"Ruby, you need to forget about everything and come out with us and have some fun. You're way too uptight, and, honestly, you need to let your hair down and embrace the woman you used to be. The girl who could dance all night and go to work with no sleep."

"We did used to get crazy, didn't we?"

"Yeah." Sidney leaned forward. "So you're in?"

She found herself nodding. "Why not."

Okay. This was good. Travis could wait until she had her head screwed on and her stuff figured out. Until she knew for sure he wasn't the pothole but the helping hand. If she saw him tonight, it would only muddy the waters, because things would happen. Dark and sinful things. The kind of things that led to more complications. It wasn't as if she needed another night of hot, passionate sex. Not really.

But she sure as hell wanted it.

CHAPTER 19

*A*s the youngest of three boys growing up in a home with only a token mother figure for most of his teenage years, Travis Blackwell had been fed a steady diet of testosterone. It was in the milk he used to wrangle from Wyatt's death grip or the last piece of steak he'd wrestle Hudson for. It was his father looking the other way when one of his brothers gave him a wedgie or pantsed him as he was about to get on the school bus.

His hockey brothers were no different. They took pleasure in making their fellow teammates do questionable things only men would do, because women were a hell of a lot smarter. No woman Travis knew would attempt to walk across a parking lot buck naked, with Oreo cookies clenched between her butt cheeks. Or use a razor blade in places no razor blade had any business being near. Sure, it was dumb, but it was all part of a brotherhood, and it was a brotherhood he called family. He's was a guy's guy, and that was that.

In the off-season, he loved nothing more than hunting and fishing with his pals. Golf vacations in Scotland. Weekends in Vegas or diving in Belize. He could afford all the toys and hung with an elite crowd of men who had a lot of disposable income and no family ties. They were single, rich athletes, and the world was theirs for the taking. Women were the icing on the proverbial cake, and unless you had a real sweet tooth, there was no issue. Women were background noise. You could hit mute and make them go away.

So why was it on a beautiful night in July, five men in a boat didn't cut it? Hell, even Zach hadn't brought his game. They weren't laughing and telling off-color jokes. In fact, Hudson, Wyatt, and Brad spent most of the time discussing the finer points of microbreweries. Travis didn't give a flying crap about microbreweries. Beer was beer. At least in his books. That wasn't the worst of it. They'd even discussed going on a wine tour along the Niagara escarpment. What guy did wine tours on a Sunday afternoon? On a bus?

This night wasn't what he'd envisioned. He'd wanted to forget about a certain dilemma waiting for him back in Crystal Lake. A five-foot-six dilemma that wasn't going away no matter how hard he tried not to think about it.

The plan was to night fish for trout. The spot was a beauty, and the temperature was perfect. It wasn't stinking hot, but it wasn't cool either. There were no bugs, and the water was calm. It was the kind of summertime in Michigan he missed. And yet...

All he could think about was Ruby. She'd asked him to give her some space, and he was willing to do that. She deserved some time to think about what had happened between. Lord knows it had kept him up the last few nights. And, like a dummy, he thought it would be easy. Like a dummy, he'd thought the guys would take his mind off things. Travis scowled as he watched Brad and Hudson. His crew had failed miserably.

He reached for his phone and stopped himself. How many times had he checked his cell phone today? Looking for a simple text. Maybe a voice mail. A small crumb to tide him over until he could lick her fingers and enjoy the whole cake. If Ruby didn't call him tomorrow, he was going to lose his shit. In the meantime, he was stuck on the water with these knuckleheads.

Christ, now they were discussing couples massages. He groaned. What. The. Hell. Travis decided to zone out. He didn't care whether Brad and Gwen got pedicures together either. He sat back, his thoughts jumbled, and was just getting comfortable when his brother kneed him.

"Anyone want to head back early?" Hudson asked the question, and Travis looked at him in surprise.

"It's not even midnight." Travis glanced at his brother Wyatt, who shrugged. What the hell?

"Sounds good to me." Zach was already packing up his gear. "You mind dropping me off at the Coach House?"

Travis could only think of one reason Zach would want to go to the Coach House tonight. Too bad his buddy couldn't see that Honey had no interest at all. She was too busy giving Nash the stink-eye to even look at another man. That woman was prickly as hell, and the chip on her shoulders was bigger than the damn lake.

Hudson nodded. "Sure."

"I'm down for that," Wyatt said. "Regan's there."

"So is Gwen. I'll tag along if you don't mind." The three men looked at Travis expectantly. "You coming?"

He found himself shaking his head. "Nah. If we're done fishing, then I'm done for the night. I'll head home."

"Don't wait up for me." Zach chuckled.

"What's her story anyway?" Hudson asked as he waited for everyone to reel in. At Travis's questionable look, he said, "Honey."

Travis shrugged. "You'd have to ask Nash that one."

"I have."

"And?"

Hudson started the motor. "All he says is that she's a pain in the ass."

Zach slapped Hudson on the shoulder. "She can be a pain in my ass any day."

"Good luck with that," Travis said wryly. "I have a feeling any man she lays claim to will have his hands full."

Wyatt sat down beside him as the boat headed toward shore. "Kind of like Ruby."

"Kind of like Ruby," Travis muttered to himself.

It was after midnight when Hudson pulled up to the cabin. The moon was partially hidden, and deep shadows fell across the small structure. They'd dropped off the boys at the Coach House, and Travis was the last stop.

"Looks like you got company."

Travis followed his brother's gaze, and his eyes widened in surprise. A woman sat on the front steps, or rather was slumped against the railing. It was dark, but the fact she was a blonde was unmistakeable. She didn't move when he got out of the truck, or when he slammed the door shut behind him.

Travis gave his brother a wave and made his way over to the small porch Ruby Montgomery was currently using as a bed. She was asleep—that much was obvious—and once he got close enough to see her properly, he noticed a few things.

1. She was snoring softly, which meant she'd been drinking.
2. Her clothes were not the usual garb for the lady she'd become. They were more of a throwback. Formfitting jeans. Black heels. Tight black tank top. Visible pink bra underneath.
3. She still liked her lips deep red. Ruby red. God, those lips.

He didn't take the time to wonder why she was here. He bent forward, his intent to taste and touch, but her eyes flew open and he froze. A lazy smile curved her lips, and she made a sound, that sound that got a guy thinking of things he maybe shouldn't be.

"Trav," she said, struggling to sit up. "Where were you?"

"Fishing."

She gave him a peculiar look. "At night?"

"Yeah."

"Oh." Silence fell between them. "Did you catch anything?"

"No."

She licked her lips again—a nervous gesture—and slowly blinked. "I went dancing." She hiccupped, and he tried to keep a straight face. She'd definitely had a few.

"You did?"

"With the girls. It got kind of crazy."

"I bet."

"Chance was there."

That wiped the smile from his face. "Was he now."

She nodded. "Yep. He was there. He told me he loved me and says I should forgive him for what he did at the tournament. Says it was a dumb move." She leaned back and sighed. "And it was. It really was. I mean, who would set up his girlfriend with her ex-husband?" Her eyebrows rose, and she blew out a long breath.

Travis didn't say a word, in part because he wanted to put his fist through the wall. But mostly because he didn't know what to say. She looked up at him, eyes big and misty.

"He asked me to dance." She waited, but again, he had nothing. "And I was going to…"

A muscle worked its way along his jaw, and he managed to unclamp his teeth long enough to speak. "Why didn't you?"

Ruby grabbed at the railing, swatting his hands away when he would have helped her. She stood over him, and he slowly straightened. She stood on the second step, so she was at eye level. That damn mouth of hers was slick and red, and he could see the tip of her tongue. A tongue that had nearly brought him to his knees only a few days earlier.

She held his gaze for so long, his neck tightened, and he slowly unclenched his hands. Her chest rose and fell, and that subtle flowery scent that was all hers drifted over him, covering him in a fine mist of Ruby.

"I came here instead," she said, swaying slightly and grabbing on to his T-shirt. Her mouth was now so close, he didn't have to move in order to claim it. "I wanted to dance with you instead." She made a face. "But you weren't here."

"Sorry about that."

"You should be." Her eyes were on his mouth. "The cab didn't wait for me."

"We can launch a complaint against the company."

"We can't." She shook her head and stumbled a bit. He didn't mind; she was practically in his arms.

"Why's that?"

"It's old Mr. Stewart. He does it for extra money, and I got him out of bed when I called." She looked over his shoulder. "I hope he made it home okay."

"I'm sure he did."

"You think so?"

"Yes."

"I suppose you're right. He's been driving for like, one hundred years or something." Her forehead furrowed, as if she were thinking hard. "They played this song. I want to dance," she said abruptly, walking ahead of him and waiting at his door. Her eyes were half-closed. "I just want to dance."

"Okay. We can do that." Travis unlocked the cabin door and led her inside. The air was thick. He was hot as hell. And he wasn't entirely sure what was happening. The only thing he was sure about was that Ruby had had too much to drink.

YOU ROCK MY WORLD

He would have turned on a light, but she stopped him. "No. I like it like this."

She fumbled in the back pockets of her jeans and pulled out her cell phone. He watched as she chewed on her bottom lip and swayed a bit, her fingers scrolling through the device until she found what she wanted. She set the phone down on the small table next to sofa, and a bluesy song about Tennessee whiskey filled the room.

She slid up against him, and his arms automatically went around her. Ruby fit against Travis as if she were made for his body. Hips just where they were supposed to be. Soft breasts swelling against his chest. Head on his shoulder. Heart beating next to his.

Travis held on, and the two of them swayed to the song, which repeated at least three times before her phone died. And still they moved, Ruby melted into Travis, his chest so damn tight, it was a miracle he could breathe.

He wasn't sure how long they were like that. How long her body breathed into his. How long his arms wrapped themselves around her possessively. It could have been ten minutes or twenty. An hour or two. All that Travis knew was that he didn't want it to end. He would have stayed that way forever, except Ruby sniffled and her body shuddered slightly.

Travis's eyes flew open, and he realized she'd stopped moving. Something was wrong. He could feel it.

"Hey," he whispered, moving slightly so he could see her face. Her eyes shimmered with unshed tears, and as he slid his hand along her jawline, a big fat one rolled down and slid across his thumb. "Babe, what's wrong?" Had he done something inappropriate?

"I loved you, Travis. So much." She sniffled again. "Too much."

His heart tumbled over, and his stomach dropped. Travis felt sick and ashamed that he was responsible for her pain.

"Remember how we danced at our wedding?" She blinked,

and another tear fell. "In the parking lot of the courthouse. Remember that?" Her voice was barely above a whisper.

He nodded. She'd worn a simple white dress, and it had rained. Her long hair was plastered to her skin, and mud splattered along the hemline, but she didn't care. She smiled at him, and his world was complete.

Until it wasn't. Until he screwed it up.

"There was this young couple at the bar tonight." She smiled and looked away, but it was a small, sad smile, and it made his heart ache. "They reminded me of us. They looked so in love and sure of themselves. So confident that nothing will tear them apart and they'll get their forever. We looked like that once." Her eyes met his again. "We thought we were forever, but it only lasted two years." Her bottom lip trembled. "This won't work. Whatever this is between us. You know that, right?"

Travis finally managed to find his voice. "Ruby, you've had a lot to drink."

She nodded. "I have."

"So maybe we shouldn't be having this conversation right now."

"I think right now is the perfect time."

He opened his mouth to respond, but she pressed her fingers over his mouth and shook her head.

"We won't work, Travis, but that doesn't mean we don't have options."

"Ruby—"

"No. I want you to listen to me." She swayed against him, clutching at his chest. "I've thought a lot about this. When are you leaving Crystal Lake?"

He stared down at her, not really sure where she was headed. "Beginning of September, I guess."

She hiccupped. "Okay. So we've got a month or so to enjoy ourselves. But on my terms."

"When you say enjoy…" Travis wasn't so sure he liked what he was hearing. This sounded calculated. He didn't do calculated. He was more of an organic kind of guy.

"You're going to take me inside, and we're going to have sex." She paused. "And then we're going to have it again, and if you're real lucky, maybe one more time." She thumped him in the chest. "And that's just tonight."

He studied her carefully. "This is about sex."

"Pretty much."

"You want to use me for sex."

"I think we're using each other, don't you?"

Nope. No way. He started to shake his head because this was all wrong. What the hell was she saying?

But Ruby reached for him. She kissed away his confusion and, despite his conviction, felt himself respond. He *was* only human. Travis groaned and sank his hands into her hair, pulling her closer, hungry for more. Hungry for all of her. He poured his heart and soul into the kiss, and eventually, they broke apart, each breathing hard. He looked down at her, unsure and out of his element.

"We need to talk about this," he managed to say.

Her hand slowly made its way down his chest. Past his abdomen and lower until it settled over the hard bulge in his shorts. Wickedly, seductively, she rubbed him, and he nearly lost it when she ground against him.

"I want to go on record and say this is a bad idea." Jesus, he sounded like a twelve-year-old whose voice was changing.

"Travis?"

"What?" Shit. She licked her lips and smiled up at him.

"Shut the hell up."

If Travis Blackwell was a stronger man, he would have walked away. It was the right thing to do. For a lot of reasons. But Travis wasn't a strong man—not when it came to Ruby Montgomery. When she reached for him and opened her hot mouth against his, he was pretty much done. And when she whispered dirty things into his ear, his reluctance disappeared like water down the drain.

There was a nibbling of something. A whisper that said, *this won't end well for you*. But like a fool, he ignored it.

He scooped her into his arms and headed for the bedroom.

CHAPTER 20

"*Y*ou're in a good mood."

Ruby tucked her laptop into her bag. "Is it that obvious?" She glanced up at Jaylene as she reached for her keys. Her assistant chuckled.

"You've been singing Taylor Swift songs all day. And not the breakup ones."

"So that's how we're measuring happiness these days, is it?"

"It's all in the songs." Jaylene smiled. "Seriously, though. I don't know what flavor Kool-Aid you're drinking, but can I have some?"

Ruby hoped the blush in her cheeks wouldn't give her away. The simple truth was that the flavor of Kool-Aid she'd been enjoying for the last few weeks wasn't one she was willing to share. She glanced at her watch.

"Are you leaving early?" Jaylene asked.

"I am. Everything that was in my calendar has been dealt with. If you're caught up, you can take off as well."

Jaylene's smiled widened. "Thank you. What are you up to this weekend?"

Ruby grabbed her laptop and purse and headed for the door.

"I'm thirsty."

"For what?"

She winked at her assistant. "A tall, cold glass of Kool-Aid."

Jaylene's giggles followed her out of the office. Her steps were light as she waved goodbye to her staff and headed out into the sunshine. It was three o'clock, and Travis was at her place working on some landscaping—something she hadn't gotten around to finessing after she'd moved in. He'd insisted, and who was she to say no to a half-naked man working up a sweat in her backyard?

The last three weeks had been a bit of a blur. There'd been lots of Kool-Aid. Kool-Aid in the morning on her back porch. Kool-Aid in the evening on the dock. Heck, she'd even had Kool-Aid on her desk the afternoon before when he'd snuck into her office. But they'd been careful. Ruby had made it clear she didn't want folks in town knowing what they were up to. She could tell Travis hadn't been thrilled with the idea of sneaking around, but he'd been good about keeping things on the down low. Sure, he grumbled about being a glorified cabana boy and nothing else, but he kept coming back.

She smiled. She was glad of it.

The fact that she'd thought of nothing else but knocking off early to surprise Travis should have set off all kinds of alarm bells, and the fact that it didn't said something. What that something was, she didn't dwell on. No way was Ruby going to think about things that would crash the wave she was riding.

She'd do it...eventually.

Twenty minutes later, she pulled into her driveway and frowned when she spied a Ranger Rover beside Travis's truck. Ruby parked her car and sat there for a few moments. She was early, and Travis wasn't expecting her for a few hours, but still, she didn't think he'd take it upon himself to invite someone to her home.

Or would he?

She slid from her car and headed inside. There were no frantic nails clicking on the hardwood floors, or excited barking to greet her, but she assumed Tasha was in the backyard with Travis. Ruby slipped out of her heels, untucked her cream-colored blouse from her pale pink skirt, and loosened her hair from its clip. She padded through the foyer into the large open space that occupied the entire width of the home. There was half an acre in her backyard, and beyond that, the lake.

She spied Tasha running like mad along the beachfront, barking and yipping at the wind, it seemed, and then the small dog stopped and raced back toward the boathouse. Back to Travis and his brother Wyatt. The two men were moving a large piece of stone, black granite from the looks of it. From what Ruby could tell, it was the finishing touch to a beautiful retaining wall that he'd readied for shrubs and plants.

Both of the men were shirtless—both tall and handsome—but it was Travis who drew her eye. He'd tied a bandana around his head, and his eyes were covered by mirrored aviators. He was unshaven (which was hot as hell), his muscles slick with sweat, and his shorts hung so damn low, it didn't take a rocket scientist to know the man was commando.

Watching him made blood rush to every part of her body and had her heart beating so fast and hard, she felt dizzy. Travis Blackwell was a drug. A potent, intoxicating, addictive drug. The withdrawal was going to kill her when he left. And he would leave, that was a given.

But she wasn't going to think about that. At least not yet.

Annoyed that his brother was here, Ruby hesitated, but the need to see Travis trumped her discomfort, and she opened the garden doors and headed for the beach. Over the past week, Travis had designed beautiful gardens that wrapped around her deck and followed the new flagstone path he'd laid down to the beach. The retaining wall he was currently working on sheltered a fire pit and seating area.

He looked up in surprise as she approached and then checked his watch. "You're early." His eyes slid from hers. "I needed help to finish the wall, and Wyatt was available."

Ruby nodded, eyes on his brother, wondering how this was going to go. She and Wyatt weren't exactly friends. The guy hadn't been around much when she and Travis were together. That being said, he'd never been anything other than nice when they'd met up in the past. She didn't *not* like him, but she wasn't exactly jumping for joy to see him in her backyard. There would be questions. Questions she didn't want to answer. He shouldn't be here.

"Hey, Wyatt."

Wyatt offered a smile. "Your place is great, Ruby. Amazing view."

"Thank you."

"Been here long?" he asked.

"About a year."

"Did you build, or was the place—"

"I built it." She cut him off, not meaning to, but wanting the conversation over. She wasn't in the mood to make small talk with Travis's brother. At the moment, she wasn't sure what she was in the mood for. Her earlier lustful thoughts seemed a long way away.

Tasha ran past them chasing after a butterfly, her antics a bit of an ice-breaker, and Wyatt reached down to pet the little animal as she rushed past. "*Okay.*" He glanced up at his brother. "I should get going. Let me know if you're coming for dinner." He smiled at Ruby. "Regan and I hope to see you guys later. And bring Tasha. Our little mutt, Bella, would love the company.

"Oh, I'm not sure what… I mean, I think I have plans." Her voice petered off into silence, and inside, she fumed. How dare Travis put her in this position?

Ruby shot a look toward Travis, but he turned slightly, avoiding her gaze. What the hell? He knew the rules, and now she looked like an idiot. The two men said their goodbyes while Ruby made a fuss over Tasha.

"That was awkward." Travis threw some tools into a bin.

"You think?" Ruby wanted to hit him over the head. He was acting like she was at fault.

"You didn't have to be rude to Wyatt."

"I wasn't rude." But even Ruby winced at her lie. "I might have been a bit...cold. But he shouldn't have been here."

Travis whipped his head around. He was angry and not making any attempt to hide it.

"Are you kidding me? I needed help, and he was available."

"I didn't ask you to build this, Travis. You insisted."

He made a strangled sound and took a step back. His jaw was clenched, his hands were fisted, and he was about as close to losing his cool as she'd ever seen him.

This was so not how she'd envisioned her afternoon. The two of them should have been naked—making out like the horny teenagers they'd become—not arguing over his brother and a damn retaining wall.

Her anger left as quick as it had come, leaving her knees weak and her skin clammy. God, normally, she loved to fight because the making up was so damn good. But today it wasn't in her. "Look, Travis, we had an understanding. Wyatt being here kind of punched a hole in it."

His anger, however, was still front and center. "Understanding." He made the word sound distasteful. He grabbed the bin of tools and began walking toward her boathouse. His strides were long, purposeful, and Ruby had to jog to keep up.

"Why are you so pissed off?" she asked, out of breath by the time she caught up to him. "Seriously. If anyone has the right to be angry it's me, not you."

Travis set down the bin. He stood for a few moments, his back to her, before slowly turning around.

"What exactly are you angry about?" he asked, his voice

183

dangerous and low. "The fact that I asked Wyatt to help me? Or the fact that my brother knows we're banging?"

She winced at his crudeness. "Can you not use that word? It's juvenile."

"Well, this," he motioned in the air with his hands, "Is juvenile."

She ignored his comment. "You've had that conversation with your family? Did you tell all of them? Jesus, Travis. Why didn't you rent out a billboard?"

"You're being unreasonable."

"No." She shook her head. "I'm not." Why did he insist on making her the bad guy?

"Wyatt's my brother. We talk about shit."

"You never used to. Your brothers were too focused on their own problems, and your dad acted like you didn't exist."

That scored a point or two. He looked ready to explode.

"Something we have in common," he replied, eyes dark and flashing. "The whole crap-father thing. What else do you want to throw at me?"

"That's about it," she retorted. "Isn't it enough?" Her anger sizzled like a hot poker in the fire. "Look, neither one of us belongs on a *family of the year* poster. They suck, and we're damaged. You know it, and so do I. They might come off as prettier or more polished, but nothing's changed. Not really."

He stared at her for several long moments. "If you really think that, then I feel sorry for you."

He feels sorry for me? She opened her mouth, a hot retort on her lips, but he didn't give her the chance to respond.

"I've changed. I've grown, and so has my family. Some, like my dad, expect a little too much, but I can't fault him for trying. Some things can't be forgotten, but we do move on and we try." He paused and ran his hand over his hair, tugging off the bandana. "You know he told me he admired you, the other day. Said you had a lot of strength. Who wouldn't think that? Look at all you've accomplished. But I'm not so sure anymore. I see a woman who's still living in the past. A woman who wants me to stay there with her, and I don't know if I can." He shrugged. "This sneaking around? I don't think I can do it anymore. I don't think I want to. I'm not going to live in your bubble, Ruby. The one you've created because you're too afraid to face reality."

She wanted to punch him. Hard. Annihilate the words coming out of his mouth because she didn't want to hear him. Travis was wrong. She had changed. There would have been a time when she would have done whatever it took to shut him up. Guess, she'd done some growing after all.

She took a moment and centered her chaotic thoughts. But most of them boiled down to one thing. He was pulling away and she wasn't ready for that.

"What happened to the no strings? Why are you ruining the last few weeks? Why can't we just…" She didn't know how to articulate the feelings inside. Didn't know how to express her need for him, as well as the need to protect herself.

A muscle worked its way across Travis's jaw. He was still angry. "Why am I… Christ, are you listening to yourself? This isn't about strings. Which, I'm going to point out, is your thing, not mine. This is about the fact that we're adults now. We're not the kids we were the first time around. I'm ready to own my actions. I'm not afraid to admit to the mistakes I made when I was younger. I'm not afraid to be held accountable. And I sure as hell am not afraid of what people might say if they find out we're back together."

"We're not back together, Travis." She spoke quietly, but the effect was powerful. She saw it. His expression changed. His eyes hardened. "We're hanging out. We're enjoying a physical relationship without the emotional component. Most men would think they'd died and gone to heaven."

"I'm not most men." His mouth tightened.

This whole thing was spiraling, and Ruby didn't know how to stop it.

Travis swore. He said something unintelligible and then looked her square in the eye. "Regan and Wyatt are having a barbecue. They've invited us, and I plan on going. It's up to you if you want to join us. They live at the end of Ridge Road."

He walked past Ruby and didn't bother to look back. Not even when Tasha ran circles behind him and barked like a banshee. Ruby followed him out of the boathouse and watched until he disappeared from view. She heard the rumble when his truck roared to life, and winced at the squeal of tires as he left.

He was more than just a little angry. Thing was? Ruby thought *she'd* be more than just a little angry. But instead of anger, she was anxious, confused, and more afraid than she cared to admit to. The scary thing was that she was afraid to figure out what it was she was afraid of.

How screwed up was that?

Was she afraid of losing a man she'd convinced herself she didn't want anymore? Or was she afraid of exploring what she felt for him? Was this more than just sex? If so, was she smart not to let him in, or a damn fool?

"Ruby, you've gotten yourself into a pickle," she whispered as she slowly headed to the house. Once inside, she stood in the great room that she took such pride in, and glanced around at all the nice things she'd accumulated over the last few years. Expensive furniture. Artwork. Décor. Her closets were filled with clothes, some she'd never worn and still sporting their price tags. She had jewelry and name-brand bags she barely used. When had she become that girl? When had she decided those things equated happiness?

Of course, the nagging question, the one she refused to acknowledge or think about, was the one she needed to ask the most.

What would it take for Ruby Montgomery to be happy again?

CHAPTER 21

The crap mood Travis had been in since he left Ruby's followed him to his brother's place. He tried to shake it, Lord knows he'd tried, but alcohol and the darkness he felt didn't mix, and he was smart enough to know it. Neither did people for that matter, but he was here now and couldn't leave. Zach was back at the cottage with some girl he'd met on the golf course, and unless he left town, there wasn't anywhere else he could go and be alone. Travis was stuck here and would make the best of it.

Regan's bungalow was beautiful, and though the yard was not nearly as impressive as Ruby's, there was more than enough space to host a get-together. The two-tier deck was something out of *Better Homes & Garden*, and Travis watched from inside as Wyatt barbecued up a storm, while Regan kicked back with Gwen and Brad. Their son, Patrick, was at a sleepover, leaving Travis the odd man out.

He frowned and reached for the garden door, his hands full of the condiments he'd been asked to grab, when the doorbell went off. No one could hear it outside, and with a halfhearted curse, he set down the condiment tray and headed for the foyer. The place was open concept, bright and sunny from an abundance of windows, but Travis noticed none of this as he walked to the door. It must be Hudson and his wife, Becca. The oldest Blackwell had called earlier to say he'd be late—something about a dirty diaper.

He yanked open the door and froze. Ruby stood in front of him, a bottle of wine in one hand, a mixed bunch of summer flowers in the other. She wore a baby-blue sun dress that left her shoulders bare, and white slip-ons. Her hair was left loose, the soft, silky waves spilling down her back, and the only makeup she sported was light pink gloss on her lips. She looked so damn beautiful, and if he was feeling in a generous mood, he'd have planted a kiss on her so fast, her head would spin.

But he wasn't in a generous mood. In fact, he was still mad as hell. He arched an eyebrow questioningly. "You lost?"

She was surprised, that he could see, but like always, she recovered quickly. "No, Travis, I'm not lost."

At that moment, a car door slammed shut, and they both had a look over Ruby's shoulder. Hudson and Rebecca made their way up the steps, the baby and all the necessary paraphilia associated with said baby in tow. Rebecca had that flustered *I hope I remembered everything* look, and might have said something more, but one look at Travis and she offered a quick hello before heading inside.

"Hudsy," Travis said, offering his hand for a shake and settling on a diaper bag in return. His brother grinned and nodded to Ruby before following his wife.

"You sure you're not lost?" he asked.

"I didn't realize it was a dinner party." She looked like a deer caught in the headlights.

"Brad Bergen and Gwen are here too."

"Oh."

"That all you got?" He watched her closely, his anger held in check—barely. She looked uncomfortable, which made him feel pretty damn good. Childish, he knew, but there you had it. His tone must have set something off, because her eyes fired up and her chin jutted out.

"Are you going to let me in?"

"Not sure. Depends."

She looked like she wanted to throw a punch. "On what?"

"On how effectively you convince me to move out of the way."

She said something unintelligible, and her eyes narrowed. "I could move you if I wanted to."

"I'm sure you could. A well-placed jab with your fist...and knee to the groin. But I'm looking for words."

Travis was starting to enjoy himself. He leaned on the door and waited. He knew he'd won at least a small victory—she was standing in front of him. But a part of him needed to hear the words, and damn if he was going to feel bad about it.

Ruby's chest rose and fell rapidly. Her cheeks were flush and her eyes flashed bloody murder.

"What do you want me to say, Travis? That I acted like an idiot before?"

"Sounds about right."

"That I'm sorry?"

"I'll take that too."

"That you drive me freaking crazy, and I lose my mind when I'm around you?"

He waited a heartbeat. "Why?"

"Why what?" she snapped.

"Why do I make you lose your mind?'

It was Ruby's turn to pause. For a moment, he thought she might throw the flowers and toss the wine, but then she sighed. "Travis, I'm here. And that's a big step for me. I didn't want to do this. I didn't want to do the family thing because we're not family anymore. But then I realized I don't know what the hell we are, so I'm here. Let me in."

Travis leaned forward. "What's the password?"

"What?"

Okay, now he was being a dick. "Password?"

She studied him for a few seconds and then reached up, pressing her lips against his in the sweetest kiss he could remember. She was soft and pliant, and his heart pounded so heavily, he was sure she heard it. He opened his mouth, and it was all she needed. Her tongue slipped inside, and she nipped at him, deepening the kiss until both of them were breathing hard. Slowly, she extracted herself.

"Will that do?" she asked, voice throaty with that hint of rasp that drove him crazy.

Travis nodded. "That will do." He stepped aside, and she walked by, her scent surrounded him seductively. It wasn't fair, really, the arsenal of weapons this woman possessed. And all of them warheads with his name emblazoned on them. The thing was, he'd take every single one of them because she was here.

She's here.

Travis followed her into the house and plopped the diaper bag onto the island. He scrounged around in the kitchen, found a vase and handed it to her, and then waited until she'd added the flowers and water. Once that was done, he grabbed the tray of condiments and pointed to the sliding door.

"Are you sure about this?" he asked, giving her one last out.

"No." Ruby opened the door and headed outside.

* * *

Hours later, after Hudson and Rebecca had excused themselves and Brad and Gwen had left, Travis and Ruby found themselves alone in the backyard with his brother and Regan. They'd had a great meal—his brother grilled up a mean steak—and a lot of laughs. There'd been no awkward moments, no questions asked that were intrusive, and the evening seemed to be a success. He settled back in his seat, his hand loose on the chair behind Ruby's head, though a part of him was tense. The part that was waiting for something to happen.

"When do you leave for training camp?" Regan asked, settling back against Wyatt.

Yeah. Here is was. That something waiting to happen.

"A couple of weeks. I have to get back to the gym, and then we're on the ice for training camp mid-September."

"Gosh, summer has flown by," Regan said with a smile. "And so much has happened. I think it's wonderful the two of you found your way back to each other. It's like a movie or something." She laughed. "True love always wins."

Ruby moved and hunched her shoulders. She didn't reply, and Travis didn't know what the hell to say. But Regan was unaware and, still smiling, looked at Ruby. "I suppose you guys are going to do the long-distance thing? Or are you headed to the city with Travis?"

Silence met her words, and Regan looked at Travis. "You guys have talked about this, right?"

Wyatt cleared his throat. "I think we should mind our own business, don't you?"

"I can't move to the city," Ruby replied coolly, pulling at the edge of her dress. "The spa takes up a lot of time, and my brother lives here, so......"

"Oh, right. I've been meaning to book a treatment. I've heard it's an amazing place to visit. I just don't have a lot of time between the hospital and my practice."

"That's okay, baby." Wyatt nuzzled her neck. "I've got magical hands." His brother's hand was under Regan's top, and that was enough for Travis. He jumped to his feet.

"I think it's time for us to head out."

"You sure?" Wyatt didn't look their way, even when Regan slapped his hand.

"We'll see ourselves out."

Travis and Ruby walked through the house and paused on the

street. Fog curled along the path, glowing from the moon's reflection. It was eerie and somehow fit the mood. Gone was the ease of the evening just passed. There was something between them now, something thick and dark, and it made his gut clench. He hated not knowing where he stood with this woman.

"My truck's parked down the way," he said, eyes on Ruby.

"I see that." Her voice was barely above a whisper. She started walking toward her car. "Are you coming to my place?" She turned to look at him.

"Do you want me to?"

She didn't answer right away, but then nodded. "Yes. I think we need to talk."

He watched her for a few seconds, hating the distance between them. A distance that hadn't existed twenty minutes ago.

"Okay."

She nodded, got into her car, and he walked to his truck. They could have been strangers on the street, the divide between them was that big. By the time he revved up his engine, she was gone, her taillights small embers of red in the dark. He sat in the truck for a good long while, listening to the engine rumble, listening to the doubt that crowded his mind.

Today had been wrong pretty much from the get-go. Something had shifted, and it wasn't anything good. Ruby was right. It was time for a talk. He took his time on the drive over, thinking of the things he wanted to say. Things that had been on his mind for a while now. Things she didn't want to hear.

It was then he realized a big one. Something life changing. Something that was probably going to kick him in the ass.

Travis Blackwell loved Ruby Montgomery. This wasn't just about making things right or exploring an intense physical attraction. He'd given his heart to her over ten years ago. A heart that still belonged to her. There was a reason he'd never found someone else. Hell, he hadn't even looked.

Because there was no one else.

He pulled into her driveway and was up her steps before the last rattle of the engine was heard. He didn't bother to knock. He strode inside, absently patted Tasha on the head, and called for Ruby. She didn't answer, and then he spied her sandals in the middle of the foyer. A few feet farther, her dress.

Travis followed the trail like Hansel after breadcrumbs, picking up the items as he headed to the great room at the back. Her bra was tossed onto one of the wing chairs near the garden doors. Pink and delicate. He glanced up. Her silky, barely there underwear hung from the door handle.

The door was cracked open.

Like a bloodhound, Travis headed outside. The moon hung low over the lake, spilling soft light over the entire yard. She was there, in the shadows near the edge of her deck. He saw the curve of her cheek, the soft swell of her breast.

"Come here." Her words were spoken slowly, a hint of seduction coating them like candy.

Travis swallowed hard. His body responded immediately, and it took some effort to override the desire coursing through his blood. They needed to talk. He couldn't do this anymore. Not until they cleared the air.

"You come here," he commanded, hands fisted at his side, jaw clamped so tight that pain radiated up the side of his face.

She didn't hesitate. Ruby walked like a cat, long, lithe limbs and soft, padded feet. Her body was slowly revealed to him, the shadows receding as she moved into the moonlight. A breeze lifted her hair, and it billowed around her, a moonbeam halo that made her look like a goddess. Was she aware of the effect?

She stopped in front of him and licked her lips, her eyes on the bulge between his legs. He was so damn hard and filled with an urge to possess. It made it difficult to concentrate. To organize his thoughts and get the words out. The ones he needed to say. The ones she needed to hear.

"Ruby, we need to talk before we…"

But her hands were at his waist and she went for the zipper. "We'll talk tomorrow," she whispered.

"I really think…"

She was on her knees, her soft, warm hands on his cock. She looked up at him, her eyes in shadow, her mouth glistening as her tongue slowly swept across her lips. She was killing him. And she knew it.

His hands found their way to her head, his intention to push back—to take a second and clear his head—but she closed her warm mouth over him.

And he was done.

CHAPTER 22

*R*uby was dreaming the kind of dream you didn't want to let go of. She was floating. Weightless. Riding the midnight sky. Languishing under a tropical sun. Awash in warm sensations and hedonistic thoughts. The dream was so real. The colors vibrant and alive. The images incredibly erotic.

She shifted slightly and gasped. A slow smile curved her mouth, even as her sleep-heavy eyelids struggled to open. That sweet ache, the one that started deep within and pulled hard, made her moan. It had a rhythm. A cadence that was older than time. Her hips began to move, and slowly she became aware. Mr. Sandman let go, and she realized a few things.

First off, she wasn't dreaming.

Secondly, Travis was inside her.

His hard, warm body was pressed against her back, while his hands cupped her breasts, his fingers making music, his touch driving her crazy.

She said nothing at first, just let her body rock with his, fighting not to whimper when he withdrew and then slowly eased himself back inside. He stretched and filled her completely, his body so in tune that words weren't needed. This was sensory overload.

This was all a woman could ask for.

Ruby bit back a groan when his hand left her breast and settled on her hip, pulling her back into him. He nipped her shoulder, a love bite that hurt—the good kind of hurt—and then he stopped.

Her eyes flew open. It took a bit to focus. Then even more time for her brain to unravel what her eyes saw in the mirror that hung over her dresser.

Blankets tangled around their legs.

His tanned body a contrast to her honey gold.

A possessive hand on her hip.

Muscles that strained.

Bruised lips and flushed cheeks.

Skin on skin.

"Good morning." Travis nipped her shoulder again, eyes on hers in the mirror. His jaw was dark and unshaven, his sensual mouth curved into a grin. He flexed his hips slightly, and she gasped at the sensation.

"Morning," she managed to say, watching him, anticipating his next move.

"Lift your leg."

"What? I…"

His hand left her hip and grabbed her knee, gently moving her leg up and open. Sweet Jesus. She saw herself. Saw him inside her. He held her knee and pressed his mouth against the side of her neck as he began to move. In and out. In and out. Slowly. Methodically. And then he picked up the pace.

She'd never seen anything as hot and sexy as this. Their bodies intertwined intimately, taking and receiving. The pleasure was intense. It was a miracle, really. How the human body worked. How desire and want and need shaped the dance. How one man's body could make her feel as if she were coming undone.

He growled into her neck, his whiskers scratching along skin already raw from the previous night. "You like that?" he asked roughly, angling his body a bit and hitting that sweet spot deep inside.

She couldn't speak. Hell, she was barely able to manage a nod. Her head fell back against him. His tempo increased. Their bodies were slick with sweat, and she arched her back slightly, a guttural, animalistic sound escaping as she felt her muscles tighten.

"That's it," he whispered. His long, measured strokes elicited whimpers, and when he increased the rhythm, the fire inside Ruby erupted tenfold. She was coming apart. Her orgasm was building. It swelled and pressed against her. It clawed at her, and she squeezed hard, smiling when he grunted.

"Open your eyes," he said roughly. "Look at us."

Ruby watched them in the mirror. The muscles on Travis's neck strained with his effort to control himself. To draw out the pleasure for as long as he could. She placed her hand on him. Felt his strength as he stroked in and out. When she began to rub herself, to increase the pressure, the look on his face was something she knew she would never forget. It was feral. Possessive.

He was as lost in their coupling as she was.

"Now, Trav," she said, her voice catching. "I can't wait."

Travis thrust harder and faster, his hand holding her in place, his eyes capturing hers in the mirror and not letting go. Her mouth opened, and she began to buck as her orgasm ripped through her body. They watched each other climb as high as they could go, before crashing back together.

For a long while, they stayed like that, joined in the most intimate way a man and woman could be. When their breathing slowed and their heartbeats lessened, he rolled onto his back, taking Ruby with him.

There were no words. Just his arms around her, and his head resting against hers. Her body still tingled from the aftershocks of her orgasm, and though she was warm and languid, a part of her was not. A part of her was remembering the day before. It was burrowed deep, held captive at the back of her mind, and it wouldn't let go.

It was that part of her that wouldn't let her fall back asleep. When Travis's breathing was even and she knew he'd given in, Ruby slipped from his embrace. She slid off the bed and, without looking back, headed to the shower. She needed to think, and she needed to be alone.

She wasn't long in the shower, just enough time to let the water run over her, and to lather up and wash her hair. She used a clip and pinned the wet length loosely on top of her head. Then dressed quickly in an old pair of white cotton shorts and a plain blue tank top, and shoved her feet into a pair of fluffy slippers.

Travis was still sleeping, laid out on his back, one hand flung over his head, the other across his abdomen. He looked darkly handsome, incredibly male, and just taking those few seconds to study him had her body responding in a way she couldn't deal with. It only reinforced to Ruby how close she'd come to letting go. To opening herself up to the kind of hurt only Travis could rain down on her.

Quietly, she slipped from the room and headed to the kitchen. The sun was up, spilling an early morning glow over the black stainless-steel appliances and shiny white granite countertops. The smell of coffee hit her at about the same time she spied someone hunched over the island.

Ryder.

He glanced up, sporting rumpled hair, five-o'clock shadow, and a lopsided grin. There were circles under his eyes, and his features were pinched. She didn't want to think about what that meant. At the moment, Ruby didn't have the mental energy to deal with anyone's problems but her own.

"You look tired, Ryder."

He ignored her comment. "You ever going to change your code?"

She breezed past him and grabbed a mug for herself. "What's the point?"

"So people like me can't let themselves into your home?"

"Other than Sidney, you're the only one with my code. So unless you're planning on stealing everything that I own, it will stay the same."

"I'm just saying you can't be too careful."

"I have Tasha."

"That thing?" They both looked at the dog. Ryder had obviously fed her, and she sat like a queen, ignoring her humans completely. "She never barked once when I walked in from the garage."

"How long have you been here?" she asked lightly, thinking that only twenty minutes ago, she and Travis had made enough noise to wake the neighborhood.

"Ten minutes? I heard the shower, so I thought I'd make a pot of coffee." He nodded toward her bedroom. "I take it Blackwell's still in there?"

"He's asleep." She threaded her fingers through the handle on her mug and sipped the hot brew. "Do you remember when Mom left?" The question came from nowhere, and she saw the surprise on her brother's face.

He set down his mug. "It was raining."

Ruby thought hard and slowly nodded. "Yes. Thanksgiving weekend. I got up early that morning to help make the pies." Her throat tightened, and she slowly exhaled. "I loved making pies with her."

"Remember she'd roll out the leftover dough and sprinkle it with brown sugar and bake it? Damn, I loved that stuff better than the pie."

"We made three that morning. One pumpkin. One apple. And

one strawberry because that's what Daddy liked." *Daddy.* She'd never outgrown the endearment. Not even when he was piss drunk and passed out on the front porch.

They'd had a traditional meal with all the fixings. Just the four of them. Both sets of grandparents had passed.

"She smelled like pumpkin spice. I remember when she hugged me." Ruby's eyes closed as the memory washed over her. "She held me tight. Really tight. And there were tears in her eyes. I should have known something was wrong. But she hugged me, and I ran into the living room to watch football with you and Daddy."

"When it was over, she was gone."

"And she took Daddy with her. She broke his heart, and he never recovered." She looked at her brother. "Do you ever wonder about her? Like, is she still alive, and if she is, where does she live?"

"Nope." Ryder finished his coffee. It was a lie, and they both knew it. "What's this all about? Why are you bringing Mom up?" His eyes narrowed. "This has to do with him, doesn't it? Travis?"

"No. I mean, probably not." She sighed. "I don't know." Her bottom lip trembled, and she pushed her cup away. Suddenly, the smell of it made her nauseous. She knew what she had to do to protect herself, but didn't know if she had the strength to go through with it.

She cleared her throat, aware that Ryder was watching her closely.

"What's going on with you and Sidney anyway?" Her attempt to change the subject was greeted with a raised eyebrow and a quick shake of the head.

"Not gonna work, kiddo. What's up with you? Why are you looking so stressed?"

Her brother knew her better than anyone. Maybe it was a twin thing, or maybe it was just good intuition. She couldn't lie to him any more than he could with her. It was why he'd avoided her observation earlier. He knew he looked like shit. He knew the why of it, and he didn't want to share.

"I can't do this anymore," she whispered, more to herself than anything. Which was why she jumped when her brother spoke.

"This thing with Travis?"

She nodded, pushing back the lump at the back of her throat. "I have to end it. He's not going to be happy, and I should have done it last night. I meant to." The misery in her heart spilled over, and she felt her eyes water. She swiped at the corners and looked away.

"Why?" Ryder's question was simple. Straightforward. But, man, the answer was complicated. "And don't tell me it's complicated, because that's bull. Relationships are not complicated. They're either good or bad. They either make sense or they don't. They're either worth fighting for or they're not."

"That's a pretty simplistic way to look at things."

"You muddy the waters when you start adding noise. Do you love him?"

"I…" Ruby looked down at her hands. At a ring finger that had been bare for so long, she couldn't remember what it looked like wearing gold. "I don't think that's a relevant question."

"It's probably the most important question, don't you think?"

"No." She shook her head. "It's not. Because love doesn't always mean happy ever after."

"Okay, but humor me. Do you love him?"

Images crowded her brain. Travis smiling up at her. His eyes flashing when he laughed. The way he held her tenderly while they made love. The wicked smile before he threw her in the lake. The glint in his eye when he was up to something.

"There are things he doesn't know, Ryder."

"Do you love him?"

"Things I didn't think mattered until last night."

"Do you love him?"

"Then there's my trust issues. My daddy issues. Hell, I have so many issues, a man would have to be insane to want me."

"But do you love him?" Ryder wasn't giving up.

Did she?

Yes. The word was a whisper in her head. But it was a secret she needed to hold tight. Love was a complication she couldn't afford, because she knew there was no future for her and Travis.

She looked her brother in the eye. Could she carry this off? Would he believe her? "No, Ryder. I don't love Travis. I loved the sex. I loved having someone in my bed. Someone to do the damn gardening."

Travis cleared his throat, and she froze. Her blood turned to ice, and for a moment, she thought she was going to be sick. She heard the jingle of keys. The slow, steady slap of his shoes against the tile floor. Tasha barked once and then settled back in her bed when Travis walked by her without a word. He opened the front door, and then he was gone.

She was numb. Or maybe paralyzed.

Ryder sat back in his chair. "You are hands down the worst liar. Ever."

"Do you think he believed me?" she whispered.

A long silence fell, and then Ryder spoke.

"Yeah, Rubes. He believed you." Another pause. "You going after him?"

I want to.

"No," she whispered. "It's probably for the best if I stay put."

Ryder gave her a look. And if that look was to speak, it would say, bullshit. He got up and hugged her. He kissed the top of her head. "I hope you know what you're doing."

The sad thing was, Ruby had no clue. She was floundering, and if she wasn't careful she would drown.

CHAPTER 23

*T*hroughout his life, Travis Blackwell had had his ass handed to him many times. Which wasn't to say he was unlike most people he knew. Everyone had stuff to deal with. Tragedies. Setbacks. Disappointments. The past shaped a person's future, there was no getting around that. It bled into your psyche and affected how you looked at life. Even if you didn't know it.

Some people survived multiple attacks, while others withered and died. He supposed it was how a person learned to cope. Travis had always been a fighter. From a young age, he'd learned to rally. To compartmentalize the negative and focus on the positive. It was what allowed him the mental strength to make it to the NHL, and to keep his job between the pipes. It was what allowed him to go on after his marriage to Ruby imploded. After Nathan. He'd tucked that shit away and deemed it a waste of his time to wallow or think about. What was the point? The marriage was dead in the water, crushed beneath a boatload of hurt, lies, and immaturity.

He'd gone on with his life, foolishly convinced that Ruby Montgomery was in the past. That she was his first love, which implied there would be a second. Maybe a third. Wasn't that what growing up meant? Finding yourself and your path and the person you were meant to spend your life with?

It was a bitter disappointment for him to realize there was no one else. Ruby was it. The love of his life. The yin to his yang. The calm to his storm.

What was even worse, she didn't love him anymore. Maybe she never did.

He carried his bags out of his room and set them by the front door before taking a look around to make sure he hadn't missed anything. He spied an old white picture frame near the table under the front window, and slowly walked over. It was the picture he'd taken from Ruby's bedroom all those weeks ago. He'd forgotten about it.

His hands gripped the frame, and he gazed down at a guy he barely recognized, and a girl who'd haunted his dreams forever, it seemed. It was candid shot taken at a bonfire. Ruby was gazing up at him, smiling at something he was saying to her.

God, they were just kids and already so in love. Carefully, he set the picture down and took a step back.

"What's all this?" Zach asked, walking into the cabin and nearly tripping over Travis's things. It was Saturday afternoon, and Travis had thought his buddy was gone for the day. He'd left a note on the kitchen table because he didn't want to deal with the questions.

From the look on Zach's face, there would be questions.

"Are you leaving?"

"Yep." He moved toward the door.

Zach didn't bother to hide his surprise. "Are you coming back?"

"Nope."

"You wanna talk about it?"

"Not really."

Zach headed for the fridge and grabbed the milk carton.

"Okay." He took a good long chug and then turned, leaning against the counter as he wiped milk from the corner of his mouth. "When you say leaving…"

"I'm headed back to Detroit."

"Huh." Zach rubbed the impressive beard he'd accumulated over the last week or so. "Training camp doesn't start for four weeks.

"Four and a half weeks." At Zach's look, Travis shrugged. "I counted."

"There's the charity game for your foundation. So, if you want to get technical, we have two weeks until we hit the ice."

Crap. Travis had forgotten all about fundraiser for the foundation he'd help organize with a few other guys on the team, including Zach. It was geared toward sport for inner-city kids. Helping underprivileged children with funding so their families could afford to enroll them in sports like hockey, something they wouldn't otherwise be able to do.

"Right." Travis rooted around the mess of things on the counter, looking for his keys. "Make sure you're back by then." He tossed a few magazines out of the way, but they slid to the floor and scattered. With a curse, he grabbed them and shoved them in the garbage.

"You sure you're okay?"

"I never said I was okay." Travis glanced at Zach, his anger barely in check. He was so far from okay, he wouldn't recognize okay if it tapped him on the shoulder and said hello.

Zach was quiet for a few moments. "Sorry it didn't work out with Ruby."

Travis found his keys and shoved them in his pocket. "Yeah, me too." He grabbed his bags. "Stay as long as you like. I'll see you back in Detroit."

"You sure you don't have time for a beer?"

"No." Travis opened the door. "I'm headed to my dad's place and then I'm gone." He didn't wait for a response. Travis walked outside and climbed into his truck. The engine roared to life. He put the machine in gear. And just like that, his summer was over.

The sky was overcast, and big fat drops of rain splashed against his windshield. Not many, but it was a promise of what was to come. The wind had picked up, and a storm was definitely moving in, brought on by the billowing dark clouds overhead. He scowled as he accelerated down the road. It was as if the universe was throwing down a big *fuck you*.

"Right back atcha," he muttered. Twenty minutes later, he pulled into the driveway of the house he'd grown up in. Wyatt's Range Rover was there, so he parked beside it and hopped out. No sense in putting this off. He'd say his goodbyes and be in his condo by nightfall.

He strode inside the house and spied Darlene at the kitchen table, leopard-print reading glasses on her nose as she perused the weekly flyers. Dressed in a pale pink velvet track suit, silver hair perfectly coiffed, she looked like any other rich suburban housewife in Crystal Lake.

She didn't seem surprised to see him, and Travis was going to guess Wyatt had spilled the beans.

"Your father is in the boathouse with Wyatt. I think they're organizing the fishing gear," she said, setting her glasses down with a smile. It didn't quite reach her eyes, and he saw the disappointment. Another reason to feel like a shit.

"I came to say goodbye."

"I heard." Darlene got to her feet. She barely reached the top of his shoulders. Her arms wrapped around him, and Travis hugged her back fiercely. He'd not always been good to this woman. Lord knows she'd put up with a lot of attitude from him when he was younger. But she was the closest thing to a mother he had, and her genuine love for the Blackwell boys had never been questioned.

Slowly, she stood back. "I wish you would stay a bit longer. At least until Labor Day. You know how your father loves that weekend."

"I know. But I have a thing in the city. For the foundation..." He sighed. "And I need to get my head screwed on right before training camp. I'm not getting any younger, and I've got a hot rookie nipping at my heels."

"Bah," Darlene said. "Your goals against average is the best in the league. I don't see that changing anytime soon." Her eyes softened at the look of surprise on his face. "Just because we don't go to the games doesn't mean your father and I don't watch every single game here at home. It's why he bought that massive flat screen." She paused. "It's hard for him to admit to his mistakes. His pride is unparalleled. Something I think you boys share with him."

Pride? Hell, Travis seemed to have lost his over the last several weeks. "We'll see what this season brings."

"We will," she said, stepping back, her eyes serious as she studied him. "I just want you to be happy."

"I know."

"I wish..." She paused and then shook her head. "Never mind what I wish. I'm just a silly old woman with romantic ideals." She reached up onto her tiptoes and cupped his face between her hands. "You will be happy one day, Travis. It takes time is all." She kissed his cheek and let him go.

He headed for the boathouse and glanced up at the sky. The rain was still holding off, the skies teasing an occasional drop. He smiled to himself as the familiar strains of Hank Williams rolled across the deck. His father was sitting just inside the boathouse, his old fishing hat askew, dark socks pulled up to his knees, and a cigar dangling from his mouth. Wyatt sat on a toolbox, sporting a near identical look—save for the socks.

"Darlene thinks you boys are organizing your tackle boxes." Travis leaned against the doorframe and looked around. The tackle boxes were nowhere in sight.

"We could be," his father said with a chuckle. He held up his hand and pointed to the cigar. "You have time for one?"

"Nah. I've got to take off."

John slowly nodded. "Darlene and I might try to get up to the city depending on how good this old heart of mine is in the fall. Do you think you could get us some tickets to a game?"

Travis couldn't remember the last time his father had come to watch him play. There was always some excuse in the early days, and after a while, he'd stopped asking.

"Jesus, Dad. He's the starting goalie for the Red Wings. I think the man can get tickets whenever he wants."

Travis shrugged. "It won't be a problem. Just let me know when you're up to it."

John blew out a long plume of smoke. He sat back in his chair, unfazed by the loud creaking the movement created, and stared up at his son.

"That girl is going to regret letting you go a second time."

"Dad, I don't want to talk about it."

John Blackwell struggled to his feet, and in that moment, Travis was shocked at how small he appeared. He'd lost inches in height, and his longtime illness had left him frail. His collarbone looked sharp, his cheeks gaunt, and his eyes weren't nearly as bright as they used to be.

Travis held out his hand, but his father drew him into an embrace. It was short and abrupt in the way it was for some men, and his father's voice was thick as he sat back down.

"It was good to see you, son."

"You too, Dad."

"I'll walk you out to the truck." Wyatt got up and followed Travis down the path that led around the house.

"Tell Hudson I'll call him later this week."

"Will do." Wyatt kicked the tires on his truck. "This your last stop?"

"Yeah. I want to be back in the city before dark."

Wyatt nodded, an odd expression on his face. "What happened, Trav? You and Ruby seemed good last night. Real good."

Travis sighed and ran his hands along the back of his head. He was too proud to tell his brother what he'd overheard and too angry at the pain her words had caused to do anything other than shrug it off.

"Easy come, easy go, bro."

But Wyatt wasn't fooled. "That's lame." He shook Travis's hand and pulled him close to tap his shoulder. "Call me if you want to talk or have a beer."

Travis's eyebrow rose. "Detroit's a long way to come for a beer."

"I know," Wyatt said. "But you're my brother, so distance doesn't matter."

The two men stared at each other for several moments, and then Travis backed away. "I gotta go."

"Send me a text message when you get in. The old man wants to make sure you get there safe but didn't want to make a fuss."

"Will do."

Travis slid into his truck and before long was headed toward Crystal Lake. He needed to cross the bridge and catch the highway on the other side of town. Then he'd hop on the interstate, and Crystal Lake would be in his rearview.

He rolled down main street and caught a red at the downtown core. His palms drummed an aggressive rhythm on the steering wheel, and when the light turned green, his tires squealed as he accelerated. He passed familiar storefronts, the old movie house where he'd gone to second base with Melanie way back when, and the coffee shop he and Ruby would spend hours in.

He frowned darkly and hung a left, deviating from the path he should be taking and not really knowing why until he drove up a small hill and spotted the park. He pulled in behind a metallic blue Honda and stared out his windshield, face grim. He did have one more stop after all.

Travis slid from his truck and, shoulders hunched against the wind, headed for the cemetery. By the time he reached his destination, the skies opened up, and the rain that promised to fall all afternoon came down in a steady stream.

He didn't feel any of it. He stood in front of his son's gravestone, hands clenched at his sides, face dark and grim. He thought of everything he'd lost. Of everything he'd never have. He thought of Ruby's words.

"I don't love Travis. I loved the sex. I loved having someone in my bed. Someone to do the damn gardening."

And he nearly choked on the anger.

CHAPTER 24

*R*uby sat on the sofa, her legs curled underneath her body, a heavy blanket pulled up to her chin. A half-eaten carton of peanut-butter-chunk-chocolate ice cream was melting on the coffee table, which Tasha was asleep under. Gone was the summer sun. It had been replaced with dark, angry clouds threatening to spill rain at any moment.

Her eyes were swollen from crying. And the sad thing was, she was still trying to figure out what exactly she was crying about. There was the obvious. That she had, in fact, lied this morning. She loved Travis. She probably had never stopped. But it was more than that. It was more than A = B. That was actually the easy part to figure out. Love equates heartache. And she'd shed so many tears over that particular equation, it was a no-brainer.

She sniffled and picked at the corner of her blanket. She and Travis were over. No way were they coming back from what had happened this morning. She'd handled things badly and winced as she thought of him walking in on her conversation with her brother. He'd left without saying a word, and that made things worse. So much worse, because fighting was their thing. He'd slammed the door shut behind him, and that harsh sound spelled it out. There was nothing left for him to fight for.

One solitary tear seeped from the corner of her eye, and she wiped at it angrily. She never meant to hurt him. She never meant for things to go this far. God, this was supposed to have been strictly physical. Sex without the strings.

How dumb was that. As if she could turn off that part of her brain. She knew there was no way a future existed for them. Aside from the logistics, there was the other stuff, the history, her family ties, the things he didn't know. But that didn't mean she didn't want it. Didn't mean she didn't think about it or dream about it.

Her thoughts swirled faster and faster, and her head hurt because she was so confused. Was she crazy? Had she just thrown away the only relationship she was ever going to have? Because what she shared with Chance or the few who'd come before him had been biding time. She'd been waiting. *Waiting for Travis to come back, to her.*

"What does it matter," she whispered to the voice in her head. It was too late. She'd screwed things up. And Travis didn't even know why.

You should tell him.

Tell him what?

The truth.

Okay. She was going crazy. She was sitting on her sofa, having a conversation inside her head. Trying to convince herself to go and see Travis. He wouldn't want to see her. Not now. Not after the things she'd said this morning.

How do you know that?

Frustrated, she rolled off the sofa and staggered to her feet, taking the blanket with her. Shivering, she stood by the garden doors and looked out over the steel-gray lake. Whitecaps crashed against the beach as the wind picked up speed. It washed an air of desolation over the place, and the ache in her heart grew bigger.

She'd never felt so damn alone in her entire life. Not even after Nathan. She rested her cheek against the cool glass, drinking in the silence of her home, and jumped when Tasha barked. She ignored it. But the dog barked again, and she turned around to find the small animal sitting at the front door, tail wagging like a windmill. Tasha jumped up and scratched the front door, which was weird. The little thing went into the back-yard to do her duties.

"Hold on," Ruby said, shedding the blanket. She grabbed a small plastic bag from the kitchen and headed for the front door. She let Tasha out, but the dog didn't run onto the grass. The dog stood and waited.

Ruby knelt down and scratched behind her ears. "What do you want?" Of course, the dog couldn't answer. All Tasha could do was wag a tail and bark. Slowly, Ruby straightened and walked over to one of the large Adirondack chairs on her porch. She scooped up a faded Yankees ball cap. Travis must have tossed it there the day before and forgotten about it.

She fingered the frayed brim and turned the cap over. It was his favorite. Just the week before, she'd told him she would buy him a new one, but he'd given her that sexy, lopsided grin and shaken his head. The hat had sentimental value, and he'd wear it until it fell apart. A drop of rain hit her square in the forehead, and she swiped at it absently, still holding on to the ball cap. She glanced at her car and then over to Tasha, who still stood on the porch, wagging her tail crazily as if she were going somewhere.

Another drop of rain fell, and she turned, running back into the house for her purse. Maybe there was still time to at least make Travis understand. Time for her to apologize. He could accept it or not. But at least she could give back his hat.

Like that's not the lamest excuse ever.

She told off the voice inside her head, scooped her keys from the counter, and, with Tasha hot on her heels, headed for the car. Her cell phone was dead, though she doubted Travis would answer anyway. Ruby tossed it onto the seat and sped down River Road. It didn't take long to reach Travis's brother's resort, and she whipped around several tradesmen's vehicles and headed for the cabin. She spied Zach out front on his cell phone and skidded to a halt, her heart dropping because Travis's truck wasn't there.

Heart pounding, she gripped the steering wheel and tried to calm down. Shit. Where was he? Eyes on the porch, she reached for the gear shift. She should leave. This was a dumb idea. Zach pocket his cell and jumped off the small porch, his long legs eating up the distance to her car in no time.

Not really sure what she was going to say, she hit a button, and her window slid down. He leaned on her car and bent down so their faces were level. His eyes seemed curious, and she glanced down, embarrassed to realize she was still in the clothes she'd thrown on after her shower. The loose cotton shorts, the tight tank top that clearly showed anyone with an eyeball in their head, she wasn't wearing a bra.

Tasha growled and barked, and that jumpstarted Ruby's heart again. She exhaled and offered a wan smile, though she couldn't quite meet his gaze.

"Hi, Zach."

"Ruby."

"I don't suppose you know where Travis is?"

"I might."

She glanced up sharply, a spark of anger lighting a fire in her chest. "Might as in, I have no idea? Or might as in, I do, but I don't want to share the info?"

"He's not in a very good mood."

"I'm not surprised."

"Maybe you should give him some time to cool off. Go see him in Detroit."

Her eyes widened in alarm. She was too late. "He's left town?" She slammed her palms against the steering wheel and felt the hot prick of tears. She couldn't lose it here. She'd wait until she was alone.

Zach straightened and nodded toward the road. "He was swinging by his dad's first. You might be able to catch him there. He left maybe twenty minutes ago."

His dad's. She looked at the clock. She could do this. She put the car in Reverse and sped back the way she'd come. By the time she reached the Blackwell home, rain was pelting the windshield, but she ignored it as she hopped from her car and ran up the steps. She rang the doorbell, shivering as she waited, and was about to ring it one more time when the door opened.

Darlene didn't seem surprised to see her there, but the expression on her face wasn't reassuring. She looked sad.

"He's already gone."

"Oh. I…" Ruby whipped around. She'd been so focused on getting here. On ringing the damn doorbell and falling into Travis's arms to beg for his forgiveness that she'd not noticed his truck wasn't there.

"I'm sorry, Ruby."

Miserable, she could only nod and whisper. "Me too."

"Don't give up on him," Darlene said softly.

"I don't think that's the problem this time," she replied. She stepped out into the rain and walked back to her car. There was no reason to hurry considering this had been a fool's errand from the start.

"He's not here, Tash." The dog stared at her from her perch on the seat and whimpered, butting her head against Ruby's hand. With sluggish movements, she maneuvered the car out of the driveway and once more found herself driving along River Road.

She drove aimlessly. Not in any real hurry to go home. A home that, while exquisite and large, thoroughly new and modern, was empty. Who was she kidding? It wasn't a home. Not really. At least it didn't feel that way right now, if it ever did.

Ruby found herself driving through downtown Crystal Lake.

It was Saturday, so the place was busy, but the rain had put a damper on things. Families and couples ran down the sidewalks, seeking shelter. She watched a young couple, the male cradling a young child as they laughingly ran into the Ice Cream Shoppe. It broke her heart. Another time and place, a past that hadn't imploded, and that could have been her and Travis.

And Nathan.

She sat at the traffic light, lost in thought, staring at the doorway in which the young family had disappeared. She didn't move until a blaring horn sounded behind her. And by this time, her eyes were so blurred with tears, she couldn't see. Ruby drove to the next intersection and hung a right. She blinked to clear her eyes and pulled over when she realized where she was. When she realized Travis's truck was there as well.

By now, the rain was falling steady and, because of the wind, had some force behind it. Large drops slammed against her windshield. They splashed against the road, bouncing up an inch or so. Ruby let herself out of her car and ran down a path she'd traversed many times. Tasha ran beside her, and both of them were panting by the time she reached the gravesite.

The dog ran past her, barking madly when she spied Travis, and the small animal didn't stop until she sat beside him. He didn't acknowledge the dog. He didn't turn around to face Ruby. He just stared down at the small granite marker, hands fisted at his side.

She shoved long tendrils of hair from her face—she must have lost the hairclip at some point—and took a few steps closer.

"Travis." She barely whispered his name, but his body jerked at the sound of her voice.

"Why are you here, Ruby?" He angled his head to the side and listened.

She studied his profile. The strong jaw, a nose that had been broken more than once, and the ache inside her grew. His voice was cold. Devoid of emotion. She closed the distance between them and stood a few inches to his left.

"I wanted to apologize."

He looked at her then, and her insides quaked at the anger in his eyes. Hurt didn't begin to cover the host of things she saw.

"For this morning," she blurted. The rain let up a bit, and she wiped moisture from her eyes. "I didn't mean for you to hear that. It's not what I..." Her voice caught, and she had to work hard to push out the rest of the words. "I was going to tell you some things and try to explain."

He stepped toward her, so close now that she could see the drops of rain on his eyelashes. "Things? Go on. Tell me."

This wasn't the place. But then would there ever be the perfect time? Perfect place? Her teeth started to chatter, and she wrapped her arms around herself, looking for comfort. Looking for strength.

"I didn't use you for sex, Travis. You have to believe me."

His mouth tightened, and he didn't say a thing. Thoughts jumbled, she struggled for a way to make him see.

"You're like this pothole."

"What?" His frown darkened.

"A big pothole that I'm not sure I can climb out of."

"You're not making any sense."

"I know." Frustrated, she swore and shook her head, long wet strands of hair slapping her in the face as a reward. Why was this so hard for her?

"You've had me running in circles for weeks now, and I'm done, Ruby. I'm not doing this anymore. I can't take the hot and cold. The long silences when I don't know what the hell is going on inside that head or yours. I told you I'm sorry for the past. Told you I've changed. I want to be a family again. I want that with you."

Pain bloomed in her chest, and she forced herself to speak the words she'd been holding back for days. "I can't give that to you.

217

We had our chance, and…" Her gaze dropped to Nathan's headstone. "It's gone," she whispered.

He grabbed her. Put his hands on her shoulders and dragged her close. "You don't mean that. I know you feel the same, Ruby. I know it."

She blinked rapidly, trying to sweep the tears from her eyes. "Watching you last night, holding your nephew, broke my heart." She looked up at him. "And not for the reason you think. I saw how awkward you were at first. How you didn't want Hudson to hand over his son. But then you took him. And your heart was in your eyes, Travis. I saw what you lost. And I saw what you want. A family. And I can't give that to you." She was now crying, but unable to stop the deluge of tears. Throat tight, she whispered hoarsely. "I can't have any more children. Nathan was my miracle, and I'm all out."

"What the hell are you talking about?"

She shuddered. "After he was born, I found out I had endometriosis. The doctor said it was a one in a million shot that I'd conceived when I did." She could tell he had no idea what she was talking about.

"I have one ovary left, and it's not in good shape. If it was a miracle for me to get pregnant with Nathan, it would a hundred times more so if I tried again. It's not going to happen."

"I don't care about that."

She shook her head, eyes sad as she looked up at him. "But you do. I saw your face last night." She exhaled shakily. "You do."

He looked into her eyes for so long, Ruby's knees started to wobble. She was cold and wet and miserable. She wanted nothing more than for Travis to grab her close and tell her everything was going to be okay.

"This is just another one of your excuses. A reason to cover up the real problem."

"And what's that?" she asked, breath held.

"Your fear of commitment. Your fear of letting people in.

Letting yourself be loved." He let go, and she nearly fell when her knees buckled. Recovering, she staggered a bit, eyes never leaving his.

"I meant what I said earlier. I'm not doing this anymore. I love you. I never stopped loving you even when I'd convinced myself I had. I want us to be together. But you have to be all in. You need to own your shit and deal with it. You need to stop using your brother and the past to hide behind. I can't promise I won't let you down again. I'm human. But I'll do everything in my power not to. I know you think I won't be there for you if you need me, but I will. I promise I will. But you have to meet me halfway. I can't do this alone."

Her breath caught at the words. She wanted to run to him. To hold him tight and never let go. But something stopped her. Something always stopped her.

Fear of commitment.

When the silence grew so big it, pressed down on them, he broke it. His voice was resigned. His eyes shuttered.

"I'm going back to the city. I've got to start working with my trainer. I've got to get ready for the upcoming season. I've got a game in two weeks. Labor Day Saturday. A charity game for our inner-city foundation. There will be a ticket for you at the door. If you don't use it, then you won't hear from me again."

"Travis." But she couldn't speak. It was as if her throat was paralyzed.

"I'm being the good guy here. I'm letting you have this time to figure your shit out. If you do. If you decide that we have a future together, come to Detroit. If I don't see you, then I'll know.'

He walked past her, and she jumped when she heard his truck door slam shut. The engine roared to life, and she turned in time to see his taillights disappear down the street. Wet and shivering, Ruby walked back to her car and slid inside, turning up the heat and adjusting the blanket for Tasha to sit on.

The frayed brim of Travis's ball cap caught her eye. Shit. A keening noise erupted from inside her as she grabbed the hat and crushed it to her chest. Later, when she finally calmed down and made it through the doors of her home, she lay down on the bed that still smelled of Travis, pulled up the sheets, cradled the cap in her arms, and eventually went to sleep.

CHAPTER 25

*R*uby ran around her home like a chicken with its head cut off. She had less than an hour before the car service picked her up and so much to do. Her bedroom was a disaster, clothes strewn everywhere, two suitcases open near the door, but empty, and the shoes... She sighed when she saw the pile. When had she become a shoeaholic? Was that even a word? And did she really have time to worry about shoes?

No. No she did not.

She was nervous. Holy hell was she nervous. She just needed to find her list, and she'd be okay. She rooted around the top of her dresser and paused. Was that her cell phone? It had been pinging off and on all morning. Whatever. She had no time to chat. Excitement made her heart palpitate.

She was really doing this.

She checked her watch, looked at the pile, and got started. She tossed in enough outfits to last at least two weeks, as well as sexy nightwear, see-through bras, and underwear that was so skimpy, why bother? Which, of course made them mandatory.

Tasha watched from the corner of her bedroom. The dog wasn't dumb. She knew something was up, and she knew that something involved her master leaving. The dog sighed as she turned in a circle and then flopped down in the middle of her bed.

"You'll get spoiled, princess. Don't worry. Uncle Ryder will be here soon." Ruby bit her lip and held up a red dress with a plunging neckline. She'd never worn it, mostly because it was sexy as hell and she'd never had an occasion to. Until now. She tossed it into the suitcase and then headed to her bathroom to grab the toiletries she needed.

By the time she was packed and ready, she had less than ten minutes to spare. She placed her luggage near the front door and tapped her foot, eyes moving around the room. Ah. Her cell phone. She scooped it off the island and tossed it into her purse before deciding to take one last look in her closet.

She'd just pulled a sleek black dress off its hanger when the doorbell rang. Shoot. The driver was early. Ruby tossed the dress back inside the closet, where it landed in a pile on the floor next to all the other rejects. She'd deal with the mess later.

She was halfway to the front door when she remembered something and ran back to her bedroom, hopefully for the last time, and grabbed Travis's old ball cap from the night table beside the bed.

The doorbell rang out once more, and she reached down to kiss the top of Tasha's head, and gave the little girl a scratch under the chin. With one last look around, she headed back to the foyer and yanked open the door, an apology on her lips.

But it wasn't the driver who stood there, and her apology died.

Sidney's eyes were swollen and red-rimmed. Her expression was so inconsolable that Ruby's heart dropped.

"I tried calling, but…" Sid's voice caught, and she grimaced. "Ruby," she whispered. "It's Ry."

"What do you mean?"

Cold. She was so damn cold. Even though the sun beat down

and an August heatwave had rolled into the area, she shivered. Ruby felt the blood drain from her body. She sagged against the doorframe and struggled to speak.

Sidney struggled to speak but it didn't matter. Ruby cut her off.

"What are you trying to say?" She licked dry lips. "He's coming here to get Tasha." Her voice rose, her words almost a shriek. "He's babysitting her while I go and make things right with Travis."

Sidney shook her head slowly. "No," she whispered. "He's not."

"What do you mean he's not? Did he hurt himself?" Anger hit her square in the chest, and she pushed off from the door. "What did he do this time? Get drunk at the Coach House last night? Is he on a bender with one of the floozies he likes to screw? Is he still sleeping it off?"

Sidney just shook her head. She reached for Ruby, but Ruby backed away. She didn't want to be touched. She didn't want this connection. Not this one. Because she knew it was bad. It was going to rip her heart out.

She whirled around. "I need to call him."

"You can't." The words came out of Sidney in a rush. "He can't... You need to come with me."

Slowly, Ruby turned around. The car she'd hired to drive her to the airport had pulled in behind Sidney, and the driver stood a few paces away.

"I'm here for Miss Montgomery." He tipped his hat and looked at both women. Ruby was silent for a few seconds while she tried to gather her thoughts and the strength to speak.

"I'm so sorry," Sidney said to the man. "We have to cancel. We'll make sure you're looked after for your trouble."

"Of course." He looked at both women, nodded, and then drove off.

"Ruby."

Startled, Ruby looked at her friend. "I was supposed to go see Travis."

"I know. But you need to come with me."

"Ryder isn't at home is he?"

"No."

Her stomach turned over, and she thought she was going to puke. "Where?" she whispered.

A tear slid down Sidney's face. "The hospital."

CHAPTER 26

*L*abor Day came and went. Ruby never showed, and Travis Blackwell did his best to put the woman and their past behind him. He kept his word. He didn't pick up the phone and call. Didn't reach out to her brother or Sidney or anyone, for that matter. He put his head down, spent his days at the gym or on the ice and worked his ass off. He was in the best physical condition he'd ever been in. With the young rookie Hal Oberman looking sharp, he needed to be.

Because this was all he had.

He glanced around his condo, taking in the sparse modern furniture, the minimalist art on the wall, the black and chrome and utter lack of character. He'd thought it was cutting edge when he'd first seen it. The interior designer had said so.

The interior designer was full of crap. He missed the cabin. He missed the lake. He missed...

"Jesus, Trav. Stop whining and get your shit together." He straightened his tie, grabbed his keys, and headed to Little Caesars Arena. The home opener was tonight, and he needed to focus. They were playing the defending Stanley Cup champions, the Red Wings rivals, and it was a big game.

He got to the arena before anyone else. Like most athletes he knew, he had a routine that he followed before every game. His included running to loosen up then quiet time to focus and prepare. By this time, the rest of the guys would arrive, and he'd stretch and get limber.

It was what he did. Without question. Not unlike how he always wore black laces on his left skate, and white on the right.

The arena was new, and he enjoyed his run, ending with a twenty-minute workout session in the gym. By the time the rest of the guys showed up, he was ready to go and full of nervous energy. He grabbed a Gatorade and headed out of the dressing room, his intention to walk off some of the energy before he got into his gear.

Zach rounded the corner. "Hey, I been looking for you."

"What's up?"

"Your family is here."

Travis was surprised. He hadn't talked to anyone over the last few weeks. He'd been busy, and he'd been avoiding. He thought back to several messages left on his voice mail. Messages he'd yet to listen to.

"I took them up to the lounge, but if you get your ass in gear you've got time to see them."

"Thanks." Travis rolled his shoulders and sprinted up the stairs that led to the players' lounge. It was a luxurious suite, big enough to accommodate wives, girlfriends, and family. He strode inside, nodded to a few of the ladies he knew, and stopped when he spied his father, Darlene, and Wyatt.

"Hey," he said gruffly, walking over to them. His dad didn't look to great. His color was off, but he smiled and shook Travis's hand.

"I thought I'd better get a game in before this old ticker craps out."

"Hush," Darlene admonished. She kissed Travis's cheek. "Wyatt told us this game would be good, so we decided to come to the city. I hope you don't mind. Your friend brought us up here." She held up a wineglass and whispered, "I helped myself to wine."

He chuckled. "That's what it's there for."

Travis glanced at Wyatt. "Nice seeing you, bro. Where's Regan?"

"She's at the hospital." His brother had a weird look on his face. "I guess you don't know."

"Know what?" Travis's gut clenched. He knew that look was trouble.

"Ryder Montgomery. He's not good."

"What does that mean?" He glanced at Darlene, who was shaking her head slowly as she came up beside Travis.

"He OD'd Labor Day weekend. Apparently, it was accidental, but he's been on life support ever since." Wyatt's shook his head, face grim.

Shit. Travis and Ryder weren't close. Hell, the guy had probably jumped for joy when he left town, but still…

Darlene sighed. "Poor Ruby. She was supposed to leave for the weekend, from what I heard. Was all packed and ready to go, but then she had to rush to the hospital. He'd flatlined, but they managed to bring him back. Now he's in a coma." Darlene looked at Wyatt. "What did Regan tell you? What is the latest?"

"She has to make a decision this weekend."

Wait. "This happened Labor Day weekend?"

Wyatt nodded. "Sorry, bro. I thought you would know."

Darlene began to speak, and his father joined in. Travis had no idea what they were saying. He dropped his gaze as his mind raced. Was it possible she was coming to see him? He thought of her alone in a hospital room with her brother. A brother who was dying. A brother she had to… He glanced up sharply.

"Wyatt, what do you mean she has to make a decision?"

Wyatt shrugged. "Whether or not to pull the plug."

No. No way. Ryder was all the family she had. How in hell was Ruby going to come back from this?

Travis looked at his family. "It means a lot. You guys being here." His thoughts were dark and chaotic. "But I gotta go. I have to be somewhere else."

"What do you mean?" Wyatt looked confused, but Travis paid him no mind.

He ran out of the lounge and didn't stop until he stood in front of the coach's door. Travis didn't think. He didn't hesitate. He knocked, opened the door and walked in.

CHAPTER 27

"Can I get you anything?"

Ruby glanced up as Regan Thorne walked into the private hospital room. *Doctor* Regan Thorne. Ryder's doctor. How ironic.

"I'm fine. Sidney went to let out Tasha and is bringing back coffee."

Regan stopped at the monitors and checked each and every one of them carefully. All those machines and tubes and wires keeping a body alive that wouldn't be able to on its own. Ruby hated them. Hated the sounds they made. Hated the neon-colored blips, even though she needed to see them. Because if they weren't there...

She inhaled a big gulp of air and shuddered. She was so damn tired. Regan placed a hand on her shoulder, her voice kind and gentle and soft. "I'll check in later."

Ruby could only nod. She didn't trust herself to speak. She looked everywhere but at the body on the bed. At the shell that belonged to her brother. A brother who existed only through the grace of these damn machines.

She got to her feet and crossed to the window. It was dark,

but she had no idea what time it was. She was wearing the same clothes she'd put on the day before. Old track pants, a big baggy sweatshirt, and her UGGs. Her hand crept up to the hair piled loosely on top of her head. Had she even brushed it? God, she must look awful.

She giggled at that. A hysterical, harsh sound. Her brother was dying, and she was worried about whether she'd brushed her hair or not.

Ryder.

God. She turned abruptly and walked to the bed. She stared down at him. He was intubated and had lines going in his arms, tubes everywhere, it seemed. It was awful seeing him like this.

Awful and infuriating. She was so damn mad at him, her body shook. This roller coaster she'd been riding with him was almost over, and she didn't want it to end. How crazy was that? How many times in the past had she prayed for it all to end? Not for her brother's death. But for the emotional hurt he put her through. And now? Now she'd take it every single day if it meant he would open his eyes and look up at her.

She took his hand and gently clasped her fingers through his. He was cold. Or maybe it was Ruby. She listened to the machine that kept his lungs working. The slow hiss in and out. It was the worst sound in the world. He would hate it as much as she did.

"You have to come back to me, Ry." Her voice broke. "I'm sorry I wasn't there for you. I'm sorry that I was too wrapped up in my own crap to notice you were failing. It won't happen again. I promise. But you have to fight this. You have to try harder. You're all I have, and…" She shook her head and watched a tear splash onto his hand. "I can't do this again, Ry. I can't. I don't want to be alone."

"You're not."

Ruby wiped at her face and turned around. "Travis? What are you… How did you…"

He didn't give her a chance to say another word. He ate up the space between them in two long strides and enveloped her in his warm embrace. Ruby had tried so hard to be strong. For Ryder. For Sidney. For herself. But right now, in this moment, with Travis holding her close, she let everything out.

All the pain and heartache she'd accumulated over the years. Her mother. Her father. Their baby. Ryder. All of it came out, and when she was done, when her body was empty of tears and her throat raw from crying, he carried her to the sofa.

He held her close until her body stopped shuddering. Until the chills and chattering teeth ceased. Until she fell asleep, safe and warm in the arms of the only man she'd ever loved.

"You're not alone," he whispered. "I'm here for you as long as you need me to be."

She didn't hear the words, but it didn't matter. She felt them. She felt *him.* Travis had come back to her, and this time, she wasn't letting go.

EPILOGUE

*R*yder Montgomery was laid to rest a week later. In the end, Ruby didn't have to make the decision. His heart, weak from years of addiction, gave out. For that, she was grateful. He wasn't going to suffer anymore. His pain didn't exist where he was now.

His wake was held at the Coach House, and the many folks who'd come to share stories had warmed her heart. Her brother might have battled addiction most of his adult life, but he'd been kind and funny and talented. And no one was shy to let her know these things. These important things she would hold close.

It had been a difficult few weeks, and he would be missed. Ruby knew the hole in her heart would never go away. But the pain would lessen, and there would be room for joy and happiness. Until then, she took one day at a time, glad she had someone in her corner.

Travis had come back to her. He'd missed the first few games of the season to be with her, which meant more than she could express. He'd been her rock. Her shoulder to cry on. The one to listen as she raged against her brother's fate. He held her up when she was in public, and held her close when they were alone at night.

They'd fallen into a routine of sorts. He flew back to Crystal Lake when he could and for now it would be enough. She had things to take care of. Loose ends to tie. And then she could think of the future.

It was Thanksgiving weekend, and she was packing up the house she'd grown up in. Getting it ready to sell as soon as she could. She glanced around, taking in the worn linoleum, the tired wallpaper, and the well-used furniture. This house held her past. It held her history. But it was only part of the story. A small part.

"What about this?" Travis walked into the kitchen holding a small white box in his hands. He'd flown in after a game the night before and wasn't expected back in Detroit until the following evening. They were expected for turkey dinner at his dad's place, but had decided to work on this house for a few hours before they headed back out to the lake.

"What is it?" Curious, she walked over and peered inside the box. "Oh my God. Where'd you find this?"

"Your bedroom."

A sly smile touched her mouth. "My bedroom is off-limits. You know the rules."

Travis laughed and grabbed her close. "Those rules don't exist anymore. Hell, they didn't exist when they existed. How many times did I sneak in your window so we could get busy when your dad was out here drinking his beer, watching *Jeopardy?*"

She laughed. "Too many times to count." She reached into the box and retrieved a delicate gold ring. It was thin, barely enough gold to matter, with a small opal centered around diamond chips.

It was her promise ring.

"I gave you that after our first summer together."

"I remember," Ruby replied slowly, sliding the ring onto her finger, more than a little surprised it still fit. "We'd got into a fight because Marlene wouldn't stop flirting with you, and you seemed to like it."

"So you decided to get back at me by going to the drive-in with Pete McMillan."

"I did."

"To make me jealous."

She laughed. "It worked." But the laughter died at the look in his eyes. They were dark and intense, and suddenly, the air was charged with an electricity that had her hair standing on end.

"Why are you looking at me like that?"

He set down the box. "How am I looking at you?"

Mouth dry, she held her breath when he bent forward and planted a kiss at the base of her neck. Her pulse went crazy, and she saw the half smile. He trailed kisses along her jaw and teased the corners of her mouth. She tried to turn to him, but he wouldn't let her. He grabbed her arms and held them over her head, and then nuzzled between her breasts.

"Travis," she breathed, arching into him. He yanked her top down, exposing her bra, and she groaned as he opened his hot, wet mouth over her nipple.

"We've never had sex in the kitchen," he growled against her. He lifted her up and put her on the countertop.

His words penetrated the fog, and she shook her head. "Jesus, Trav. If Mrs. Davis is out back, she can see us from here."

"Don't worry about Mrs. Davis." He kissed her then. A deep, intense, sensual kiss that spread tingles along her limbs and had her body humming an erotic melody. He tugged on her jeans, and she lifted her hips to help him. And by the time he had them down to her ankles, they were both breathing hard.

"Let me see you," she whispered, tearing at his Henley. He lifted it over his head, and she sighed at the sight of all that muscle and definition. Her hands splayed across his chest, and she held on as he lifted her butt and positioned himself between her legs.

She looked into his eyes, and her heart jumped. She couldn't tear her gaze away. Not when he eased himself inside her. Or when he began to move. Slowly. Then faster. She held his gaze until his eyes darkened like coal, and he rocked into her. Until her own cries matched his, and he collapsed against her.

Long moment passed, filled with deep breaths and accelerated hearts.

"Shoot," he said, leaning close with a wicked grin.

"What?"

"Mrs. Davis."

Ruby nearly fell off the counter. "You're kidding? She's out there?"

Travis chuckled. "Yeah."

"Yes, you're kidding or yes, she's out there."

He dropped a kiss to her mouth. "I'm kidding."

He let her down, though his hand held hers tight. "What?" she asked, watching him closely. Travis didn't say anything. He pulled off her promise ring and reached into the front pocket of his jeans. Exactly one second later, he held out a small black box and offered it to her.

"Open it," he said, voice low and urgent.

Her heart beat so fast and hard, she could barely hear a thing. She opened the box, and nestled inside was a beautiful diamond solitaire. It was breathtaking. Simple and elegant and so perfect. She blinked back tears. They still had stuff to figure out. A lot of stuff. Logistics. Her business. Her baggage. Hell, his baggage. But they'd do it together.

"Yes," she said.

Travis smiled wickedly. "I didn't ask you anything."

"I know." He slid the ring onto her finger, and she smiled up at him. "But my answer is still yes."

Travis held her close and rested his chin on top of her head. "Good, because that's the only answer I'll accept."

She rested her head against Travis's chest and for a long while they were silent.

"What are you thinking about?" he asked, gently stroking her hair.

"Ryder. I was thinking that he would be happy for me. For us."

"He would."

Ruby blew out a shaky breath as she tried to clamp down on her emotions. "I wanted so much for him."

"He knew you loved him."

"Yes," she whispered. "He did."

She looked outside. Snow had started to fall. Great big fluffy flakes that fell lazily from the sky. It was like a new beginning. A new hope. The first snowfall of the season always felt the same. God willing, it would be the first of many, many more, and all of them shared with the man she loved.

With Travis at her side she could face anything.

The End

ABOUT THE AUTHOR

USA Today bestselling author and 2015 RITA® winner JULIANA STONE fell in love with books in the fifth grade when her teacher introduced her to Tom Sawyer. A tomboy at heart, she splits her time between baseball, books, and music. When she's not singing with her band, she's thrilled to be writing young adult as well as adult contemporary romance—books that have garnered starred reviews from *Publishers Weekly* & *Booklist*—from somewhere in the wilds of Canada.

Please visit me at the following places.

www.julianastone.com
juliana@julianastone.com

ALSO BY JULIANA STONE

The Blackwells of Crystal Lake
You Make Me Weak
You Drive Me Crazy
You Rock My World

The Family Simon series...
Tucker -Free
Jack
Maverick
Teague
Grace
Cooper

THE BARKER TRIPLETS TRILOGY
Offside - Free
Collide
Conceal
A Barker Family Christmas

56846086R00136

Made in the USA
Middletown, DE
24 July 2019